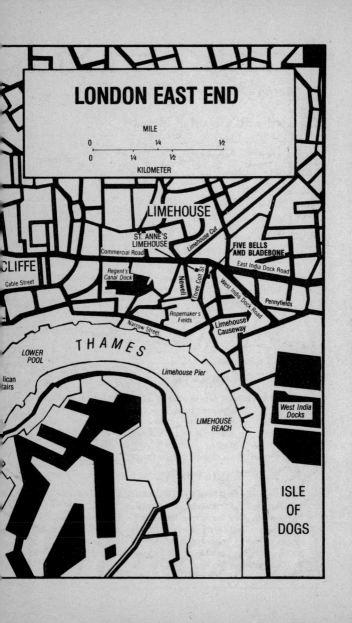

By Martha Grimes

The Man with a Load of Mischief
The Old Fox Deceiv'd
The Anodyne Necklace
The Dirty Duck
Jerusalem Inn
Help the Poor Struggler
The Deer Leap
I Am the Only Running Footman
The Five Bells and Bladebone

THE FIVE BELLS AND BLADEBONE

Martha Grimes

A DELL BOOK

To my editor, Ray Roberts,
who keeps Jury out of the gutter;

and to Kit Potter Ward,
who saved him from the slush

Published by
Dell Publishing
a division of
The Bantam Doubleday Dell Publishing Group, Inc.
666 Fifth Avenue
New York, New York 10103

ISBN: 0-440-20133-0

Reprinted by arrangement with Little, Brown and Company

Printed in the United States of America

Published simultaneously in Canada

September 1988

10 9 8 7 6 5 4 3 2 1

OPM

Oranges and lemons,
Say the bells of St. Clement's.
Brickbats and tiles,
Say the bells of St. Giles'.
Halfpence and farthings,
Say the bells of St. Martin's.
Two sticks and an apple,
Say the bells of Whitechapel.
You owe me ten shillings,
Say the bells of St. Helen's.
When will you pay me?
Say the bells of Old Bailey.
When I grow rich,
Say the bells of Shoreditch.
Pray, when will that be?
Say the bells of old Stepney.
I'm sure I don't know,
Say the sweet bells of Bow.

—Old nursery game

Contents

Acknowledgments

Contrary to Lady Ardry's conviction that she is wholly responsible for any invaluable information contained in this book, I would like especially to thank Alan Webb for the Limehouse–Wapping walks; Harry Webb for the Thames information; and Diane and Bill Grimes for the *secrétaire à abattant.*

PART ONE —

*Two sticks and
  an apple
Say the bells of
  Whitechapel.*

1

————————🔔 WHAT else could you think of but getting your throat slit?

Whitechapel, Shadwell, the Ratcliffe Highway: images of the bloody East End flashed like knives in and out of Sadie Diver's mind each time she heard the sound of footsteps behind her on the dark walk from Limehouse. She was still thinking of it as her heels clicked wetly on the fog-draped pavements of Wapping. Never caught him either, did they? So much for police.

The sickly yellow sign of the fish and eel shop ahead glowed through the drapery of fog. *LIVE EEL'S. COOKED EEL'S. JELLIED EEL'S.* In the last two months Sadie Diver had learned more writing and reading than she had in all her twenty-eight years. She knew the mark shouldn't have been between the *L* and the *S.* Probably the only one walking about Wapping that does, she thought.

It was a twenty-minute walk from the flat in Limehouse to the Town of Ramsgate, and she was irritated that he'd decided on what he called a "dress rehearsal." My God, but hadn't they been over it and over it? And she didn't dare tell him that Tommy was coming in tomorrow night. He'd have killed her.

When she was abreast of the eel shop, they simply walked up to her: there were three of them, but they managed to look like a wall of punks, coming out of the shadows of the alley by the shop, one spitting into the gutter, one smiling crazily, one stony-faced.

There were the usual *'ello, luv'* s, the usual salacious remarks, as they stood planted firmly in her path. Anything behind her made her nervous; anything in front of her she could handle. Sadie was used to it. She had got so used to it, in fact, that she simply slipped her hand in her shoulder bag and brought out the flick-knife. Seeing it there so unexpectedly, dimpled by the watery light of the sign, they disbursed quickly, calling back over their shoulders and then disappearing down the alleyway behind that curtain of fog.

She stopped to check her watch beneath a streetlamp that seemed to smoke in its nimbus of light. Stuffing her hands in the old raincoat, something she'd not be caught dead in ordinarily, she felt the handle of the knife as she kept walking. He'd wanted her to wear what she'd worn before at their meetings and what she'd be wearing on that last day. At least, she liked to think of it as the last day of her old life. In these clothes and no makeup, she was surprised the bunch back there were interested.

It had been a long time since she'd seen such a layering of fog. And here it was the first of May. Spring. Cold as a convent wall; cold as a nun's . . . She pulled her collar close around her chin and smiled, thinking of the Little Sisters of Charity. She considered herself a good Catholic, but she'd not had it in mind to be a better one. Her a nun. What a laugh.

She turned off to her left and then to her right, taking the narrow street that ran by the river. Why had he wanted to meet at Wapping Old Stairs, and why now, after the pub was closed? A wall of warehouses loomed through the darkness, shrouded in mist coming off the Thames. A person felt like brushing it away, like cobwebs. Still, it clung. As she passed Wapping headquarters, she smiled. The police station was all lit up, about the only sign of life after eleven.

When she reached the pub called the Town of Ramsgate, once again she heard footsteps behind her. They couldn't have been the same ones; she'd lost them back there at the eel shop. Nevertheless, she was almost glad to step off the road into the shadows of Wapping Old Stairs. There were two sets of stairs, the very old ones moss-covered; below was a small slipway and an old boat, tarpaulin-covered.

A dull tread of feet went by above her; she craned

her neck upward and saw nothing but the hazy light cast by a lamp hanging from a wagon. She went down a step or two and stopped suddenly when she heard wood scraping against stone, the creak of oars against metal. Her eyes widened at the sight of the figure in the little boat. The long coat against the black background of the Thames made it impossible to see clearly. It was a rowboat or wherry that someone must be working on; she couldn't make it out and wasn't about to stand there on the steps waiting to find out.

Sadie started walking backward up the steps, slipped on the wet stone, caught her heel, and nearly lost her balance. There was really no way to gain purchase. When she slipped her hands could grab only at the slick, cold mossy steps so beveled with age they had all but lost the outline of steps.

The person who had emerged from the boat was standing on the step below, facing her now.

Sadie couldn't believe her eyes.

An arm came out from the long black coat, holding what looked like a blade far more devilish than the one Sadie herself carried. If she tried to fly up the stairs, it would land in her back.

So she threw herself down, the figure reeling above her, and went sliding down the stair and halfway into the Thames. The long knife sliced through the thick, rancid air, missing her by so little, Sadie heard the swish as it streaked downward.

Snatching her own knife from her pocket, she clambered into the boat. She was good with boats, like Tommy. Out there was the black hulk of what was probably a sailing barge that would be making for the Essex brickfields. Still farther was a patchwork of lighters. In her shaking fright to get at the oars, and with that figure coming down after her, she dropped the flick-knife into the bilge water that had collected in the boat.

But she found it, and as her fingers curved round it, she looked up to see the white hands dragging at the boat's side.

* * *

Tommy Diver stood on the dock looking off toward the lighthouses of Gravesend and Galleon's Reach. Over the estuary a ragged stream of orange and red made the mist smoke like the aftermath of cannon-fire. Docks, wharves, and warehouses stretched for miles up the Thames to London Bridge and the Isle of Dogs. Not so long ago, as many as eight hundred ships might be on their way to London's dockland; now, nothing went much farther than Tilbury.

He could imagine what it had been like during the trading days of India and the East: varnished bowsprits and the rust-colored sails like bruises against a viscous sky. When he'd said to his friend Sid that all that river traffic must be like Venice, Sid had just laughed. *Don't be so romantic, lad.* Sid had been to Venice and everywhere else Tommy had only heard of. *Venice is all gilt and blue, like a jeweled dragon. But that ship there* (and he'd pointed to one lying at anchor) *ain't nothing but an old dog sleeping in a Gravesend doorway.*

Tommy felt a surge of guilt over lying to Aunt

Glad and Uncle John, but they'd never have let him go up to London, not even for the two days. He thought he deserved at least this chance to see Sadie, no matter what they thought of her. Sid would cover for him. He hunched even further into the black leather jacket he'd got at the Oxfam shop with some of the money his sister had sent. It was too big for him, but it was real leather, not that stiff cheap stuff that cracked when you moved. When he ran his hand over it, it felt like down.

Wapping wasn't more than thirty miles away, as the bird flew and the London river ran. He knew the course of the Thames like the palm of his hand —Tilbury, Greenhithe, Rotterhithe, Bermondsey, Deptford. Even for these two days, he knew he would miss it, working the tug with Sid.

She'd said that someday he could maybe come to Limehouse and live with her, when she got a bigger place. But she'd been saying that for a long time now—*school, after you finish school.* Tommy tried to shrug off the painful feeling he'd got when he felt she didn't really want him to come even now. Still, she'd sent the money. He'd never seen seventy-five quid all at once in his life.

From Galleon's Reach came the desolate warning of a bell-buoy. A tug sounded a note of gloom in its passage toward a black ship's hulk some distance out in the estuary. He had not left, yet he felt heartsick; felt the gloom of the passing tug, wondered how many mugs of strong tea he'd carried from the engine room to the deck.

He loved the river, but he loved Sadie, too, and one of his saddest days was when she'd left Gravesend for London. His memory of her shifted so much, was so dream-like, he sometimes thought he'd made it all up. But he was sure he recalled clearly many incidents in their childhood days. Well, *his* childhood. She was twelve years older, but he thought he had memories of her letting him tag along, buying him sweets at the newsagent's, chalking naughts and crosses on the pavement for him, playing in the Wendy-house.

Two more tugs spurted across the water, turning blood-brown in the last of the sunset, a stretch on which the bald sun seemed to float and then settle. Way out he could see the tiny black figures of the tug's crew scrambling onto the lighters to separate them, tie them to the boat, and drag them back to the wharf.

When the sun went down there was an air of desolation, of estrangement in the deserted buildings, the boarded windows of the warehouses. He watched as the tug chugged back toward the wharf, the string of lighters in tow.

How strange that tomorrow he should be climbing aboard a train to go to a place that lay only a few miles upriver, that would be infinitely simpler to reach by way of that river, where all he needed to do was step from a boat or climb down from a tug to Wapping Old Stairs or Pelican Stairs where he would like to think some sort of fortune awaited him.

But not, he was sure, like the one that awaited Marco Polo.

* * *

Its dish was empty; no one called.

The white cat padded round the drained pools and down the pebbled path through the formal gardens. It sat quite still for a moment and then twined through a border of viburnum. Again, it stopped beneath bushy roses, whose white petals sifted down as the white cat darted toward a flash of gray on the pebble walk. It was tracking a field mouse. The field mouse blended into the gray and brown of the pebble and stone just as the white cat blended into a border of pearl-drops, as if neither were substantial, shadow chasing shadow.

The white cat sat now in the enclosed garden by a stone figure, a young woman holding a broken bowl filled by rain. Finches and wrens sometimes lit there. The cat sat looking down the length of the rose-covered pergola, listening in the early light. It was as if it could pick, from the trills and warbles of birdsong, the tiny threshing of mouse through yew hedge and ground cover. Light filtered through the vines and lay in pearly stripes across the cat's fur.

Scarves of mist across the grass were dissolving in the sun, dew dripping from the vines and rose petals that covered the pergola. The white cat watched the progress of a drop gathering on the edge of a petal, a dot of blue in a crystal suspension, falling and dispersing before he could swipe it with his paw. The cat yawned, blinked, dozed where it sat.

A sound, a smell, it opened its eyes and perked its

ears. It gazed upward as a robin left its perch in a laurel and flew off. The cat walked out of the secluded garden and toward the bank of a stream farther on. Here it crouched and watched a wren having a dust bath. Before it could pounce, the wren was away, skimming across the water. Looking into the stream, as if the bird might have fallen there, the cat saw shadows deep inside darting, hanging suspended, darting forward again. The cat struck at the water, trying to fix the moving shadow with its paw.

It yawned again, washed at the paw, stopped when it saw something skittering across the footbridge, and followed. On the other side of the bridge, it looked around. Nothing moved. The sun was nearly over the horizon now, spreading a sudden crust of gold across the lake and a shimmering light on the windows of the summerhouse.

The cat liked the summerhouse; it was cool and shadowy. There were pleasant lumpy chairs, wool throws tossed over the one nearest the hearth, and here the white cat loved to lie. It would sleep there for a day, two days, making its movable feast of whatever small things lurked in the dark corners. It ignored whistles and cries from the outside; eventually, it would leave and cross the wide lawn and long gardens and inspect its dish on the patio.

For a while it sat as still as garden statuary itself, blinking and watching the floor by the french windows. It spied a bit of shadow in the corner, separating from the darkness and skittering along the baseboard.

The white cat quivered, crouched, and went slithering across the rug to squeeze itself into the narrow space between a large *secrétaire* and the floor.

In a minute it squeezed out again and sat washing the blood from its paw. Then it walked through the open french window, down a short path, and onto a small dock. Here it sat looking over the lake, yawning.

2

🔔 IN the Jack and Hammer, Dick Scroggs could barely be called from his toils long enough to set the pint of beer and ploughman's before his single customer.

"There's been more activity around here in the last month than I've seen in a lifetime," said Melrose Plant. "You're expecting a lot of tourist trade, are you?"

"Got to keep up with the times, m'lord," said Scroggs, around the nails in his mouth and over the pounding of the hammer in his hand.

Melrose imagined he was not so much keeping up with the times as with the Blue Parrot, a freshly named and painted pub off the Dorking Dean–Northampton Road. A derivative name, surely— one might say, nicked from Sydney Greenstreet, though it was unlikely that the clientele of a Moroccan saloon, imaginary at that, would go caravanning down the dirt road to the new Blue Parrot.

As he watched his pickled onion roll round his plate and tried to drink Dick's Thunderbolt, Melrose asked, "Where'd you get that snob screen?" He was looking down the bar at a row of beautifully etched, beveled-glass partitions.

"Trueblood, sir. He watches out for things for me." Dick, whose usual position in the Jack and Hammer was arms akimbo over his newspaper, wiped his heavy arm across his forehead. "Thought it might add a bit of interest. No one else hereabouts has one," he added, his tone heavy with significance.

"That's certainly true." Melrose adjusted his gold-rimmed spectacles and settled in for a session with the *Times* crossword. It was propped against his copy of Rimbaud, which in turn was positioned atop Polly Praed's latest thriller, *The Nine Barristers.* The crossword was a little like a lettuce leaf he used to clear the palate between poetry and Polly. He was livening things up by inventing other words to fit the spaces.

All of Dick's activity was mildly irritating. Melrose was used at this time of day to nothing but the ticking of the clock and the snoring of Mrs. Withersby. Now Scroggs had left off hammering to hurry past him with a paint bucket, on his way to touch up the turquoise trim of the Jack and Hammer's façade. Scroggs had even taken to trying to brew some manner of beer, without (Melrose was sure, tasting the Thunderbolt) much idea of the difficulty of the process.

This bustle might have made him feel like a sluggard had he not been a sensible man who had got his priorities straight some years ago. Having swept out his titles of Earl of Caverness, fifth Viscount Ardry, and all the rest, he could settle down in his well-aired family seat of Ardry End and enjoy his fortune.

Well, it *was* spring! he thought. Just smell that air—

Unfortunately the air that Scroggs had ushered in when he opened the door had also ushered in Melrose's aunt, being extremely ostentatious with her crutches, which she leaned first here, and then there, groping her way to the chintz-cushioned bench. That Melrose made only the smallest gesture toward assisting her was not because he wasn't a gentleman, but because he knew the bandaged ankle was pure trumpery, something she'd got the local doctor to do with many a painful and laborious sigh on both parts.

"I rang the house. You weren't there," she said, thumping herself down at his table with a practiced moan.

"That's very observant of you, Agatha," he said, filling in *D-O-L-T* where *T-O-L-D* was called for. This was fun.

"Thought you said he was coming today, Melrose."

"Jury? He is."

Never the one to kowtow to the needs of others, Lady Ardry wound out the little window behind her, sending down a shower of petals from the climbing roses, and called to Dick Scroggs to bring her her shooting sherry.

"Can't see why the man isn't in here tending to business rather than slapping on that bilious blue paint."

A three-letter word to use in place of *tin*. Melrose pondered. "Well, since the Blue Parrot is doing such a whale of a business, Scroggs is afraid it'll snap up all the tourist trade."

"What tourists? That's why we like it here. No strangers running amok tossing iced-lolly wrappers on the pavement, no screaming kiddies. What's happened to him, then?"

Melrose looked up quizzically.

"To Superintendent *Jury.*" You stupid nit, the sigh said.

Ah! That was it! thought Melrose, his pen poised over the crossword. "He's had a flat tire," lied Melrose while filling in *N-I-T.* Since she seemed to think he was equipped with radar for tracking Richard Jury's movements, it would only encourage her to guess at Jury's arrival time.

"I knew something would happen. Always does. This is the third, no, the fourth time he's been supposed to visit—" She broke off and demanded her glass of sherry as Dick came in with his paint tin. Dick kept on walking.

Melrose changed the subject. "What are you doing in here when you are supposed to be in your cottage resting your foot?"

"I'm making quite sure my witnesses will stick to their story. Miss Crisp is already wavering. And here comes Vivian, who certainly is no help at all."

Vivian Rivington, looking like the harbinger of spring in a pale pink frock, told Agatha that she was being ridiculous, that she should forgive and forget. Vivian added, "Actually, it's Mr. Jurvis who should forgive. You're the one causing the trouble, Agatha. Where's Superintendent Jury?" Any interest in Agatha's "case" was forgotten in the light of an event that came round less often than an eclipse of the sun.

"He's had a breakdown. No, not a nervous one. He's had a flat tire on the M-1. Called me from one of those Trusthouse Forte restaurants." Gleefully, Melrose found another four-letter word: *fool.* It ran through the *O* and *L* for *dolt.* Perhaps he had a talent in an unsuspected quarter, making up puzzles for the *Times.* Eagerly he filled it in and awaited the next challenge.

That might have been found in the appearance of Marshall Trueblood, looking like a maypole. Today a flame-red scarf was twisted in the neck of a tea-rose-yellow shirt in such a way that the ends hung like streamers.

Agatha, already in a fit of pique over Vivian's ignoring her plight, apparently found her archenemy's entrance a bit too much for human endurance. "Well, one knows who one's friends are when it comes to a legal battle." She reached, as if painfully, for her crutches.

"Old sweat," said Trueblood, "I couldn't agree more. If I hear the odious bookshop owner villify me again, I'll sue and have you beat him to death with your crutch. And where is Richard Jury? Thought he was supposed to be here by now."

Without looking up from his paper, Melrose said, "He's had a flat on the M-1 and called to say he might be late as he's waiting for the garage to fix it." (*Idiot* would just pick up that *T* in *nit*.) "Met an old chum there, he said, and he's having a nice long natter."

Vivian asked with suspicion, "Old chum? What sort?"

"Female sort. He's having tea with her in the Trusthouse Forte at the Woburn turn-off."

Melrose smiled round the table and went back to his puzzle.

3

🔔 IT was Jury, but he was not finishing tea in a Trusthouse Forte on the M-1. He was in his Islington flat, trying to finish his packing. His packing and his argument. Tossing socks and shirts into a duffel bag, he was trying to talk the tenant from upstairs out of her latest harebrained behavior.

The tenant from upstairs, Carole-anne Palutski, was paying precious little attention, for she was too busy making small adjustments to her exotic costume in front of Jury's mirror.

As she applied more Poppies-from-Heav'n lipstick, Jury said, "He wants a shop assistant, love, not a belly dancer." He held up a Shetland sweater, inspecting it for mothy bites. He frowned.

"That's what *you* know. Andrew'll *love* my outfit. Add a bit of sparkle and shine to the shop." She put her arms out straight and spun briefly like a top.

19

And some outfit it was: gold netting over cerise silk for the brief top; the same silk for the pantaloons; gold braiding round the bottom of the halter and the top of the pants, allowing an even stronger definition of the naked torso in between. Not completely naked, no: something filmy covered the skin there, serving the illusion that it was even more skinlike. And round her coppery hair, Carole-anne had affixed a band of crushed gold lamé, a fake sapphire embedded in the center.

Talk about gilding a lily. Carole-anne was too beautiful in a chenille bathrobe for her own good, much less in her new harem costume.

There was a tiny tinkle as she rose on her toes to get in one or two stretching exercises before going off to work. Jury looked over the top of the sweater where he had found a moth hole big enough to put three fingers through. "Do I hear bells?"

She was huffing a bit as she did her jumping jacks. "It's just these," she said, sticking out her foot. Tiny bells were strung round her ankle below the layers of pantaloon.

"I hope the camel train makes it," said Jury. "If the Riffs don't carry you away, you'll be able to get to your lessons." It was her missing her acting lesson that had caused the argument. She had whined and whined about Jury's arguing her out of that all-night job in a Leicester Square club because it interfered with her acting career. Now the reverse was true; she loved her daytime job at the little shop in Covent Garden so much, she wasn't finding time for her acting. And it hadn't taken long for Jury to believe that Carole-anne was an extraordinary actress. To say nothing of those knock-'em-in-the-aisle looks.

She flopped on the sofa, sprawling like a ten-year-old, musical ankles resting on the coffee table. "I've only got that little-bitty part in Camden-bloody-Town. It's not even *speaking.*"

She made such a meal of the word, and such a face with it, Jury wanted to laugh. "You don't need to speak. As Mrs. Wassermann says, 'She walks down the street, it's an entire conversation.' I thought you wanted to be another Shirley MacLaine. Or was it Julie Andrews? Although I can't see you running downhill in a dirndl. Besides, you can't sing."

"I don't want to be them. I wish to play Medea."

He looked up from his duffel bag. "You *wish* to play *who?*"

Having cadged one of Jury's cigarettes, she was now wrapping her toes round the telephone receiver, trying to lift it. "I saw it on the telly, Zoë Caldwell, you ever seen her?"

Sorting through mismatched socks, Jury said, "Take your acting lessons for maybe two millennia and you might get to understudy her understudy." He nodded at her costume. "If you take off those rags."

"Well, I agree, the costumes in *Medea* should be changed. I was thinking maybe updating it and wearing my red."

"Your 'red.' I can just see Medea in Chinatown red. And get your foot off my telephone."

It chose that moment to ring.

"Don't answer," said Carole-anne, in a stagey whisper. "It's probably only SB-stroke-H."

The telephone brred. "I hear seldom from Miss Bredon-Hunt. You took care of that. Who it is, is probably C-stroke-S Racer. Damn." Jury strangled his socks.

Carole-anne bounced up. "Let me answer, say you've gone. Oh, do, do, do."

It was hideously unprofessional, but then so was the chief superintendent's calling him on the first day of his holiday to delay him at best, or to keep him in London at worst. Jury nodded.

" 'El-*lo*," she fluted, reclining on the sofa in perfect harem position. "Sup-er-in-ten-dent Jury's flat." Silence. "Oh, it's *you*, love." She had the syllables pouring like syrup. "Just missed him, you did. Gone to Northants." Her sigh was long and sad, as if both she and the speaker knew how much Superintendent Jury would be missed. "No. . . . His friend's ex-directory." Pause. "Oh, love, I wouldn't, now, if I was you. It's Lord Caverness or something like that. Very sick, 'e is." Carole-anne's accent was surfacing. "Funeral? Well, he ain't—isn't—dead yet, dearie. Just dying is all. That's right. Lingering illness, yes."

Poor Melrose Plant. Ill, dying, dead. She was so convincing, he was almost hoping he'd make it to Northants in time.

Jury gave her a black look. But Carole-anne was deep into her role. Once she had told Racer she was Jury's char. Now she was charring it up by polishing his coffee table with his socks. "Ooooooohhh." She made a silly, kissing sound with her Poppies-from-Heav'n lips. "Now that *is* a shame, dear. . . ."

And Jury (to say nothing of Racer) was treated to an aching monologue on love, marriage, and mistresses, in which Carole-anne sat, legs crossed, painted fingers arched on knee, eyes raised to ceiling as if there she saw her script.

Jury was mesmerized; he couldn't help it. He just stood with two clean shirts he meant to put in his bag, listening. She became her role. For the time on the telephone, she *was* whatever the situation demanded. When she hung it up, she would immediately be Carole-anne again.

Plunk went the receiver. "These ones have holes," she said, holding up two socks that she had slipped over her hands.

"What the hell did he say?"

She was up now, trying to do some sort of a wiggle. "Him? Oh, just he hoped you'd have a good time. Is he kinky, or something? Do funerals always make him laugh? Listen, do you think I could do it?"

"Huh? Do what?"

"Belly-dance. I mean the real kind. Takes a lot of training, I expect."

"Carole-anne, you could be Prime Minister if you wanted to."

She stopped grinding away, stood arms akimbo and feet splayed, looking like a gorgeous clown. Her hands still wore Jury's socks. She was thinking. "I dunno. Maggie's costumes are so dowdy." Then she ran at Jury, hugged him, gave him a whopping kiss, and ran out.

23

It would never have occurred to her to tell him she'd miss him.

Just as it would never have occurred to her she couldn't be Prime Minister, if it hadn't been for the dowdy clothes.

* * *

He'd tried calling in at the basement flat but found it empty. When he went up the stone steps and out to his car, he saw Mrs. Wassermann chugging along the pavement with her shopping bag. Upwards from its rim stuck some celery, behind it a lettuce.

"Such prices he's asking, Mr. Jury." The greengrocer on Upper Street had come in for a good trouncing several times lately. "Oh, thank you."

Jury had taken the bag from her, and walked with her down the steps.

"Now, I know you must be going, but wait here, there's something for you." Inside she popped and was back again with a picnic basket. "Your evening meal. I know how men are, they don't stop. They're impatient."

"Well, thank you, Mrs. Wassermann." She always fixed him something if she found he was going farther away than Victoria Street. Last year, it had been Brighton, call for two sandwiches. This year, he was going much farther, and staying much longer. That meant a banquet. Half a cold chicken, salad, gâteau, two bottles of Carlsberg. He smiled. "This will last me my whole holiday."

"I certainly hope so." There was the strong suggestion that out there in the bush with strange people, Jury would never get a proper meal. "It is much nicer to have you here. But I've Carole-anne to keep me company. So sweet, that child is. She comes in most nights and tells my fortune. And yours." She was unpinning her small, black hat from her coil of gray hair.

"Mine? How can she tell my fortune if I'm not here?" He could hardly wait.

"But you know she's clairvoyant. A seventh sense she says she has."

Not even six were enough for Carole-anne. Since she'd started working for Andrew Starr she thought she could fly off roofs. "How does it look, my future?"

She rocked her hand back and forth. "Oh, so-so, Mr. Jury. Not bad," she was quick to add. "But . . . well, not much of anything."

"No exotic women on night-trains, that it?"

"For me, she sees a handsome stranger. Tell me," she held her arms out and looked up and down the street. "Here, there are handsome strangers?"

"And me?" Jury stuck his tongue in his cheek.

"For you, no one." Mrs. Wassermann sighed. "And I thought that Miss Bredon-Hunt . . . well, you know. I don't pry, Mr. Jury."

"Hmm. That doesn't seem to be working out very well—"

"Oh, it won't work out at all. What a pity. Such a handsome girl. Still . . . you shouldn't be forever living alone. Nothing's ever certain with the stars, of course, but it does look like you'll be living here with us for some time to come." Mrs. Wassermann turned her head upwards, saying, "That empty flat, so big and sunny. But people look at it and never come back."

Of course they don't, thought Jury. Carole-anne is actually being *paid* to show it. The landlord hasn't twigged it yet.

"Well, to tell the truth, Mrs. Wassermann, I think it's nice with just the three of us—"

Shouting down from the top floor came the voice of Carole-anne. She was waving and calling words lost in the spring breeze. Jury saw she'd changed; now she was sporting a dark dress buttoned right up to the neck. Long sleeves, no ornament. The spellbinding hair was pulled back. She could have played the role of the housekeeper in Max de Winter's burning mansion.

They both waved upwards, and Jury turned away, thanking Mrs. Wassermann again for the wonderful food.

Actually, Jury hated eating in the car.

He was a dreadful dawdler on holiday, and would probably hit every service area with a Trusthouse Forte on the M-1.

4

————— 🔔 Following a brief and unlovely
prayer that the man would burn in hell, Joanna
Lewes slapped the carriage return of her Smith-
Corona and stared at the scene she was in the middle of writing. Far from springing to life before her,
the characters lay there sculptured in concrete like
effigies on a tomb.

Joanna had discovered long ago that the only way
to keep from thinking was to write, since her own
writing did not even tip its hat to muses who had
long past fled the scene.

She kneaded her shoulder, and wondered how
much nudity was allowed. And should Matt *push*
Valerie down on the bed roughly? Or lower her
tenderly? These questions were not prompted by
any desire on her part to make the novel "good," or
even a snappy read. They were merely points that

had to be borne in mind in light of whichever editor she planned on sending the completed manuscript to. At the moment she had three—three editors, three separate publishing houses, and three pseudonyms in addition to those books written under her own name. Now she was bringing out her fourth, the "Heather Quicks," a new and innovative series, though in her genre, innovation was unlikely to be looked upon kindly.

Joanna rustled through the mess of papers on top of her desk, found an apple core in the pencilholder and a satsuma peel doing duty as a bookmark, but couldn't find her Requirements List. She yanked out the desk drawer, stuffed like a turkey with balled-up, coffee-stained papers, several cigarette butts, a fruit scone hairy with mold, a vial of Valium, and a small screw of jelly babies. Finally, she found the list of publishers' guidelines she had compiled. Number one was Bennick and Company. She read: *5 hot lips scns, min; 150 pp. TOPS; nude allwed—brsts expsd hfy.* Hfy? What had she meant? *Halfway,* that was it. Breast exposure. Number two on the list was Sabers. The Big Bang scene midway, three-quarters, and last chapter but one. Nudity, to waist. Two hundred pages.

There were five other publishers singing subtle variations of those requirements. She decided to write this one for Bennick because it would save her fifty pages of mind-numbing boredom and because she had a stockpile of love scenes, any of them ripe for transplantation into *London Love,* thereby sav-

ing her another possible thirty or forty pages of
work.

As she pecked away at the ancient typewriter,
she wondered how these people could have the gall
to tell you to read at least thirty of their romances
before you even put pen to paper. To read even one
or two was a torment beyond imagining; she had
got halfway through one. That, plus the last chapter, had given her a complete education in writing
romances. Simply looking at the cover of the book
would have sufficed.

Joanna sighed and typed. Like Trollope, she kept
a watch on her desk—in her case, a stopwatch. Her
goal was the same as Trollope's, two hundred and
fifty words every fifteen minutes. If she was short,
the slack would have to be taken up in the next
quarter-hour and so on. Thus the end of her writing
day was often a race to the death. In these sprints
she sometimes forgot the names of her hero and
heroine, which didn't bother her at all, since her
characters, except for considerations of age and sex,
were interchangeable. If there was one thing
Joanna didn't believe in, it was artistic integrity.
Artistic integrity was a luxury for paupers. All she
wanted was money.

Occasionally, she stopped. Not to think, but to
light a cigarette, which she inhaled and then lay,
coal-end out, on the edge of the desk. The edge was
notched with a row of cigarette burns, like notches
on a rifle for each dead body. Valerie and Matt were
wrestling on the bed, Valerie with breasts halfway
exposed. She wondered if she dared drag the neck-

line down just a wee bit farther. No, this was no time to deviate from Bennick's requirements for the sake of sex. She still had three thousand words to go before the end of the day.

One rule she always hewed to was that revision must be kept to an absolute minimum, generally an exercise in proofreading just to make sure Valerie and Matt kept to their Christian names throughout the book. As for polishing, forget it. Why dress a dog in diamonds?

For the next two hours she tapped away, coming up with the requisite two thousand words and feeling quite pleased with herself. Unfortunately, she wasn't sure what she'd written, having put the plot on automatic pilot while her mind dealt with more pressing concerns.

One of which was that self-appointed guardian of literary taste, Theo Wrenn Browne. She had not set foot inside his shop ever since he had refused to carry her books; that was nasty enough without his also discouraging his customers from reading them. Joanna had been enjoying a considerable reputation in the area. To be one of the first to have "the new Lewes" was a feather in one's cap. After all, how many villages could boast a top-selling author, never mind the quality of what she wrote. Oh, *she* knew her books were mindless, and probably a number of people to whom she gave presentation copies found them a bit thin (to say the least), but when money talks, readers keep their mouths shut. Except for Theo Wrenn Browne.

The trouble was that when you owned a bookshop, especially one that dealt not just in new, but in falling-apart, fox-paged first editions, customers tended to believe that you must have taste and discrimination. Joanna knew the reason for all of his carping criticism: when they had still been on speaking terms, he had asked her, casually, to "have a look at" his own novel. Naturally, he hadn't asked outright that she send it along to her publisher, but that was clearly his intention.

After she was twenty-five pages into it, she wouldn't have sent it to her publisher on a bet. It was one of those terribly avant-garde antinovels, just the thing Theo Wrenn Browne would be expected to write, with no dialogue and no characters save for the narrator, a paranoid South African guerrilla whose life scrolled before him as he was watching the last race at Doncaster. That was the name of it: *The Last Race.* The title was the only intelligible thing about the book. The story had something to do with apartheid, but what it had to do with it was a mystery. Nor was it ever explained how the South African guerrilla had got to Doncaster. Add to that the Afrikaner could not speak the Queen's English and the reader was left to wallow in strange syntactical circles. The theme was the death of Africa and the death of the novel. Joanna had told him his book was abundant proof of at least one of those. Her own publisher, known for its intellectual clout despite its concupiscent sideline (romances with half-bare-breasted heroines published on the sly under another logo), would have dropped *The Last Race* in the dustbin like a dead mouse.

There had been a distinct chill in the air when she had handed Theo Wrenn Browne's manuscript back to him, saying that she doubted her publisher would be interested in a book about horse-racing. That of course had torn it. Theo Wrenn Browne had come down from the rarefied air of his intellectual mountain peak for as long as it took to tell her *she* was merely a hack. He had then made the mistake of submitting it himself. According to Mrs. Oilings, who charred for Joanna when she wasn't leaning on her mop drinking tea, the manuscript had got shot back to Theo Wrenn Browne so fast she wondered who'd had time to lick the flap. So Theo Wrenn Browne had taken to establishing another persona when the Dedicated Artist one had fallen through. He wore seedy tweeds, smoked small black cigarettes, and made Miss Ada Crisp's life hell. Miss Crisp was the unfortunate who owned a second-hand furniture shop next to his cutely christened bookshop, the Wrenn's Nest. He was over at Miss Crisp's whenever business was slack, trying to bully her into selling up so that he could have the premises to expand his own. So far she had withstood this onslaught, but she had become more palsied than ever, twitching down the High Street as if she were plugged into an electrical outlet.

When he wasn't deviling Miss Crisp, Theo Wrenn Browne was across the High Street, being quite open (especially when there were customers in Trueblood's shop) in his criticism of the jacked-up prices and the so-called authenticity of a silver-smith's stamp. As if Marshall Trueblood had gone about stamping all of his silver himself. According to Mrs. Oilings, Theo Wrenn Browne had even taken to dipping into books about antiques. Trueblood, however, was made of sterner stuff than Ada Crisp; he'd have to be bludgeoned with one of his own antique coshers before he'd rise to the bait.

When it came down to it, there wasn't a person in Long Piddleton who had altogether escaped the waspish tongue of Theo Wrenn Browne. . . .

Joanna slammed the door on this counterproductive line of thought; it was only leading to the real reason for her dilemma. She was painfully aware, as she tapped the keys, that her characters' wrestling on the bed was small potatoes compared to her own inner writhing.

* * *

Theo Wrenn Browne watched the single-knife guillotine descend, make a cut, and then return. He held his handkerchief to his head like a compress, soaking up beads of perspiration. At his bench press in the rear room of the Wrenn's Nest, Theo Wrenn Browne, with a certain reverence, pulled over his latest acquisition, a volume that he was in the process of rebinding. He had glued up the sections. Now he was pasting the folds of an endpaper. Finishing that, he placed the endpapered book between boards and weighted it down.

The work kept his mind off the previous night, at least for moments at a time. But still he could feel the cold sweat prickle as it ran between his shoulder blades, and he immediately turned to another book and started applying some edge-coloring.

No one would suspect, not even Marshall Trueblood.

Marshall Trueblood was a man he detested. He brushed aside the uncomfortable feeling that his dislike might arise from a hidden spring of totally different emotions. There was no doubt that Trueblood could easily stand him on his ear when it came to knowledge of antiques, but that the man would humiliate him in front of—

Put it straight out of your mind, old boy, he told himself.

He thought instead of Diane Demorney, who served wonderfully as friend, and as smokescreen, to boot. And adviser. "The trouble with you is, you try to learn too much," Diane had told him. They'd been having drinks in her living room. "What you ought to do is simply stick with one period, no, not even a whole period, just part of it. Better still, part of the part. Say Victorian salt cellars or something easy. You'd make Marshall look a bit of a fool, wouldn't you? He has to *sell* the damned stuff—all he knows he's learned through being in the trade, and you can't stop and read great gobs of books if you're working at the same time."

It made, he supposed, some sort of Demorney sense. Although Trueblood's "being in the trade" was precisely the problem: Marshall Trueblood had gone from rags to riches by selling the stuff. It's impossible (she had said, pouring another of her ten-to-one martini cocktails) to think of Marshall ever wearing rags. The way she'd laughed had unnerved him; one would think the exquisite Diane Demorney saw Marshall Trueblood as another world to conquer.

Holding the cotton wool over the edge of the book, he stared into space and carried on with his mental dismemberment of Marshall Trueblood. He did not see how anyone in Long Piddleton could take the man, and consequently the man's wares, seriously. Melrose Plant, for example, actually seemed to *like* him. And there was nothing, absolutely nothing, to intimate that Plant's sexual persuasion was anything but normal. He clutched at the book, his knuckles whitening.

He unpacked the box and then tore open another. These were current best-sellers, five of each, ten of the one that had won the Booker Prize. There were also two that he'd ordered, not to sell, but for himself to read. Theo pulled out the latest Lewes: *Lisbon Lust.* Odious titles these romances had, and he'd never lower himself to sell Joanna the Mad, an equally odious woman. But he enjoyed reading her; settling down in bed with a cup of tea and a box of chocolates was sheer heaven. Too bad they were warring, or he'd ask her to autograph it. Might be valuable some day, that. As he thought about her refusal to send his own novel to her editor, along with some sort of billet-doux recommending it strongly, he could feel the blood rise to his face. A perfectly wretched person. It was only decent to let your friends have a crack at your editor.

His head started to throb; he rubbed his temples. It was mortifying, having sent the book out himself and having it returned with nothing but a printed rejection slip. They weren't interested in *art*, these publishers; they only wanted Lewes-trash. He enjoyed reading trash, everyone needed a bit of trash in his life, but that didn't excuse them for failing to recognize the Real Thing. *The Last Race* would walk away with the Booker if only he could land it on an intelligent editor's desk. It was experimental, grand. One thing he could say for himself (amongst other things) was that he took chances. Not like so many other writers, who wrote to the same prescription—Joanna the Mad, for one; or that mystery-writing hack Polly Praed, whose books Melrose Plant was always snatching up. No, that wasn't his way. He didn't give a pile of beans for money.

On the other hand, he wasn't averse to making it. He'd been trying to run the Crisp woman out of her distressed-furniture business next door, again, to no avail. But he knew if he kept up this war of nerves, he could break her. Crisp didn't have the pseudosoigné, laissez-faire attitude Trueblood affected. Tremors would shudder through Crisp's wiry frame; her hands shook whenever he walked in the door of that dusty, Dickensian shop. But when he walked into Trueblood's Antiques, the man merely raised one of those painted eyebrows and stuck another of those rainbow-colored cigarettes in his holder. What affectation! Rich affectation, to boot.

He plugged a black cigarillo into an elegant eb-

ony holder and continued musing. Diane
Demorney might be on to something. Although her
little bits of knowledge reminded him of a shabbily
cut quilt, still, what she knew she appeared to know
all of. It was quite damned clever, he thought; instead of attempting the Herculean task of boning
up on history, one just chose a snippet of it and then
cut it to even tinier bits. He'd heard her talk Richard the Third to smithereens and the other person
would simply have to give up, especially when it
came to that murder in the Tower. And Diane
hadn't even bothered cracking a history book.
She'd simply read *The Daughter of Time* twice
over, and it was certainly easier reading a mystery
novel than dry-as-dust history. If only someone
would write a mystery novel set in a bookshop! No,
a bookshop *and* an antiques business, Theo thought.
Trueblood, of course, had a speciality—all those
floggers of old furniture did, or pretended they did.
Trueblood probably really *did* know, he'd have to
credit the man with that. He might be whirling
through life with all his bright scarves flying like
Millamant, but when it came to his business he was
serious. Theo thought again, raising his eyes to the
mouse-colored ceiling and stroking his throat. Millamant. Now, that was an idea. He could kill two
birds with one stone—antiques and the theater—by
reading up on William Congreve. No, reading *The
Way of the World* several times over, the way Diane
had read *The Daughter of Time*. God! *The Way of
the World* he had tried to read and couldn't: the
dialogue was so brittle with wit, every line snapped

like an icicle, every riposte cut the quick like a
knife—

He wiped his forehead again and went back to
the book.

* * *

Diane Demorney was indeed thinking at this moment of other worlds to conquer, having swept her
sword over every battlefield of this one that she
could find. She sat in the sumptuous sitting room of
the house she had purchased from the Bister-
Strachans in London, smoking a cigarette, drinking
a martini, and plotting. She considered her greatest
virtue to be her amorality; she was hardly dismayed
by anything that had happened. A man who
thought he could throw her over deserved what he
got.

Her present campaign had to do with her next
husband; when she found herself getting bored
(which was often), she usually ended up getting
married, knowing that that would, after several
months or a year, be more boring still.

Diane Demorney had been married and divorced four times by the time she was thirty-five.
Then there had been a five-year hiatus, when she
settled for love affairs, but that too had begun to
pall. Theo Wrenn Browne was amusing and acerbic
to the point of viciousness, qualities that Diane
Demorney had in abundance. It might be pleasant
to marry someone who was like oneself, if not quite
as clever. Unfortunately, he had little money. Not
that Diane needed money, she had plenty. But she
believed in excess. If one Mercedes coupe was suffi-

cient to meet one's needs, then why not have two? Consequently, Melrose Plant was odds-on favorite, for he had enough money to buy three without turning a foil of his checkbook. And then there were the titles. She thought it rather reckless of him to abandon them like so many babies (which would not have been reckless at all), but she imagined he could get them back. The Countess of Caverness suited her.

The correct name was almost as important as the correct ensemble. Only her mother (wherever she was) knew that she was not Diane Demorney of Belgravia, Capri, and the Hamptons. She was actually Dotty Trump of Stoke-on-Trent, two names that made her sit up and pour herself a double martini. Especially when she remembered that Melrose Plant had commented on the character in the Sayers book and said the names were an odd coincidence and gone back to reading one of those wretched books by his friend, Polly-Something. The one with the remarkable amethyst eyes. Amethyst and emerald-green. Between the two of them they could beam all the traffic on the M-1 safely through a blizzard. She pushed the two sets of eyes from her mind and absently stroked her showy, copper-eyed, flour-white cat. The cat promptly gouged her hand and she slapped him on the rump.

Her thoughts trailing like long skirts over the grounds of Ardry End once again, she frowned. The trouble with Melrose Plant was his tiresome generosity and humility. When her query about his expected guest brought her no information, she had tried the ploy of telling him that she knew who it was, favoring him with one of her most seductive smiles. He had also smiled (though not seductively) and said, Fine, then I needn't tell you.

Diane thumped the velvet pillow in her lap. She also had no use for that triumvirate that met every day in the Little Shop of Bores. Marshall Trueblood, Plant, and Vivian Rivington. The in-crowd of Long Piddleton. That Melrose Plant might be fonder of Vivian Rivington, or she of him, than was necessary, Diane put out of her mind. Vivian was, she supposed, pretty in a well-bred way; however, no woman had ever been able to compete with Diane.

She turned the cloisonné cigarette lighter over and over in her hand, leaned her head back on the velvet sofa, and allowed part of her mind to drift to the music of Beethoven. It did not compel all of her mind to listen, any more than the music of Mozart or Bach. But she had forced herself to digest medium-sized portions of one famous and one nearly unknown name in music, art, and literature. She learned enough about the famous one to keep her head above water; about the less-known she knew everything. She also delved into one small chapter of other fields—history, antiques, the habitats of tropical birds. It was astonishing what only an hour in the library could do. To know everything about a minor poet about whom no one else knew anything soon established one as an intellectual giant. It was all really so simple. She had widened her scope to take in other fields that often came up in social intercourse—cocktail parties, theater evenings, coronations. Diane knew the value of Time. Why go to Trinity College to study over the Book of Kells—when everyone knew a little about that—when one could pop round to the British Museum and take in one page of the Book of Dimma, which no one seemed ever to have heard of, except experts. Diane merely smiled and smoked silently when she came up against expert opinion. It unnerved them.

She could speak with authority on the Crown Jewels (and had even humbled the guards in the Tower of London); on Richard the Third (holding to the theory that it was Edward who had done in the Princes); on haut couture (Remy Martinelli); on haute cuisine (cuisine minuet); on antique silver (neffs); on American football (Phil Simms, although she had to keep going back to find out what team he played for). And then there were what she called her trivial pursuits—a collection of arcane facts and Demorney theories that she could always trot out for those not interested in Richard the Third. There was the foolproof way of making lemon curd, which endeared her to her husbands' mothers. There was her one paragraph of knowledge about Henry Fielding and the Bow Street Runners that she liked to toss in Constable Pluck's direction. And she had once convinced a compulsive gambler that he cure his habit by attending Sotheby's auctions. It had worked. Unfortunately, he had then become a bore with whom she had nothing in common, being a compulsive gambler herself.

Her adopted name was the product of her pursuits. Leafing through *Murder Must Advertise*, she had read a few chapters dealing with the Dian de Momerie character, a woman she became so fond of she had actually read whole chapters of the book. She had time, after all, to do this. She wasn't wasting it writing books like Dorothy L. Sayers. De Momerie was beautiful, drug-addicted, shark-like, and decadent. Diane had promptly adopted the name with a slight change.

And the Sayers character was without conscience.

If one could be said to lack something in abundance, Diane Demorney's lack of conscience was scandalous.

At least, she hoped so.

5

────────────⚠ "RECOVERED completely, Alice," said Lavinia Vine in answer to Miss Alice Broadstairs. The question was in regard to the health, not of Lavinia, but of her Blue Moon rosebush, which had been drooping by Lavinia's door for days. "But isn't that black spot I see?"

Miss Alice Broadstairs, games mistress of Sidbury School for Girls, looked shocked. "Not on *my* tea roses, I assure you!" In her huge sunhat, she resumed her snipping.

"I mean there and there," said Lavinia smugly, pointing at a coral tea rose with the small antique spyglass she always carried in her pocket when she went for her walk past Miss Broadstairs's gate.

Miss Broadstairs and Miss Vine had ridden every metaphorical horse in an attempt to beat each other to the ribbon, medal, and cup at the Sidbury flower show. In odd years, Miss Broadstairs won, in even, Lavinia Vine. And of course at the flower show each year they had gritted their teeth and shaken hands (both sun-brown and dry and with a trickle of liver spots) harder and harder across the years until Melrose was sure he had heard the sound of small bones breaking.

Having sighted Miss Broadstairs and Miss Vine, Melrose Plant was telling Richard Jury all of this as they walked slowly down Shoe Lane, the last little path curling off from the green and the duck pond. They were enjoying the sublimity of a fine spring morning, drenched in the scent of hundreds of roses—tea, musk, perpetual; bedding, climbing, hedging; claret, crimson, lavender, coral, yellow; climbers cascading down brick walls and climbing up them; floribunda hedging the walk.

The dogs and cats they had passed were all sprawled in various states of drunken delight, the effect of the roses, the sun, the glittering air, as if Melrose's old dog Mindy were back there at Ardry End, beaming out signals to *sleep, sleep, sleep.* Miss Crisp's Jack Russell, which usually took its naps on a weathered chair outside her secondhand furniture shop, had struck out on its own from the High Street, looking for action round the duck pond. But it was now collapsed by the small stone pillar atop which sat Miss Broadstair's oafish gray cat, itself too lazy to do anything other than lie with its face against the warm stone, its paws dropped down the pillar. All dreaming of roses.

"Good morning, Miss Broadstairs, Miss Vine," said Melrose.

The two rose-enthusiasts turned their deadly frowns on him, and then realized they were not looking at each other. They smiled brightly as Melrose introduced them to Jury, who commented on the marvel of the Broadstairs garden to the displeasure of Lavinia, who immediately invited the superintendent to take tea with her in *her* garden.

Jury thanked her, and then remarked on the several roses Miss Broadstairs had cut that now lay in her woven basket.

"*Souvenir d'un Ami,*" said Miss Broadstairs, proudly, holding out a glowing copper-colored rose.

Lavinia looked at them with disdain. "Coals to Newcastle, if you sent those to Watermeadows," said Lavinia, immediately shifting the subject to her own Blue Moon rosebush, and a lengthy discourse on aphids.

Plant flicked a crimson petal from his shoe with the cosher he had taken to carrying about and wished them a good morning, adding a good-bye for Desperado, the gray cat, still with his nose mashed on the stone, and still sleeping.

"That's an appropriate name," said Jury, yawning out the last word.

"*Desperado* is just another specie of rose." They had turned the corner and were nearing the tiny village park (if one bench beneath a willow and a pond could be called that). It lay lush and green under the eye of the Church of St. Rules, situated on a rise of ground behind Betty Ball's bakery. The ducks were motionless as decoys, wings folded, hemmed in by sleep.

Melrose yawned and checked his watch. "In another moment you'll find me on the pavement with Miss Crisp's terrier. The pub's not open yet." Melrose thought for a moment. "Speaking of falling asleep, why not get your obligatory visit to Agatha over with?"

* * *

Plague Alley lay at the other end of the High Street, a twisting little lane among a jumble of little lanes that spread off, vine-like, from the Sidbury Road. Cubes of white-daubed and dark-windowed cottages seemed to have landed among these narrow paths like tossed dice, with no particular plan or scheme to their arrangement. If Long Piddleton could be said to have social strata, this particular stratum was somewhere in the middle of the ladder, although Agatha was constantly upping it a rung or two.

Indeed, the only one who seemed concerned with Long Piddleton's high and low society was Agatha herself. The lines she drew were constantly changing and shifting as she went about laying them out like someone making an ordnance map. Her line of demarcation was the Piddle River. When Diane Demorney, and then Theo Wrenn Brown, had come to the village, she was actually less concerned with the contents of the removal vans than with deciding whether they were on the right or the wrong side of the river. Since the Piddle River was an extraordinarily egalitarian body of water that narrowed in some spots to a trickle, had a way of actually stopping midstream and then springing up again virtually at one's feet, and another way of turning itself to mud and marsh (near Agatha's cottage), she had her work cut out for her. Which was, of course, the way Agatha liked her work. Her study of the ebb and flow of the Piddle added nothing to her knowledge of its vegetable or marine life, but did assist her in putting people in their social places. Since the river disappeared after it shot the rapids under the humpbacked bridge, that more or less left the shop owners along the High Street out of the social swim. It also had an annoying way of twining in and around the Withersby enclave (of which Mrs. Withersby was materfamilias), all of whom lived in a little row of derelict cottages several hundred feet to the rear of Miss Crisp's secondhand shop and Jurvis, the butcher's. These were once almshouses (and still were, if one considered the principal employment of the inhabitants) with just the sort of mild historical interest that moneyed tourists loved to get their hands on and sink the kind of cash into that would have renovated Manderley.

Thus, Lady Ardry, fifteen minutes after her nephew's and the superintendent's arrival in her front parlor, was filling him in, quick stroke by quick stroke, on the new inhabitants of Long Piddleton, while Melrose, putting on his gold-rimmed spectacles, was scrutinizing the eclectic furnishings of the cottage. He came here only on duty visits—such as the one today—or whenever some small, valued bit of his personal junk had gone missing. There was such an overflow of bits and bobs that any little thing from Ardry End could have gone missing for decades. She was living, Melrose had often told her, in a time capsule.

One would never have known it was spring sitting inside this cottage where a shadowy, winterlike darkness seemed to swallow up people and furnishings alike. Objects winked at him out of the gloom —the glass-eyed owl on the mantelpiece, the stuffed parrot glued to its perch by the door to the pantry, the pair of caged parakeets that Melrose assumed were alive, but he wasn't sure. The room had that deathly, airless stillness of a Hitchcockian landscape before the sudden onslaught of beaks and wings.

The woman who had come in to "do" for Agatha since the accident had materialized out of the shadows to bring them a plate of cakes and biscuits. Mrs. Oilings was one of the Withersby clan, and liked to work about as much as the rest of them. She could hold her own, however, in any gossip competition, which probably explained her presence here now. Agatha, being unable to get round the village on her own, could always send Mrs. Oilings to pick up greengroceries, meats, library books, and rumors.

". . . the Demorney woman's living in the Bicester-Strachans' house and has completely redone it in some inappropriate modern—Melrose, *do* be careful of that!"

He intended to be, since the jade Buddha belonged to him. His mother had been fond of smiling Buddhas.

". . . and those books Joanna the Mad writes. Of course, she makes a tidy fortune, but then who wouldn't?"

"You wouldn't," said Melrose yawning. "I wouldn't. Joanna Lewes makes no bones about art; she's perfectly honest in saying that she writes to a formula and the formula was never any good to begin with."

Jury bit into a ladyfinger, looked at it dubiously, and said, "She sounds interesting."

"Well, she isn't. Stop fidgeting with that figurine and pour the sherry," she said to Melrose. Turning from her lackey-nephew to Jury, she said, "I would do morning coffee for you, Superintendent, but as you see—" Her tone was long-suffering as she tapped the cast on her ankle with her cane. "You do know how this came to happen, I expect. Mr. Jurvis—"

"He knows," said Melrose, to avoid the long story of the accident between her secondhand Austin, Mr. Jurvis's plaster pig, and Betty Ball's bicycle. No one had seen this accident since Betty Ball had been in Miss Crisp's shop at the time and Jurvis was back in his frozen-food locker. The plaster pig that graced Jurvis's butcher shop was, according to Agatha, "the perpetrator" in this criminal affair, since it had been put right in the center of the pavement. The bicycle was also at fault as it had been left leaning against the shop front so that Agatha's right front wheel had grazed it as she had run the car up over the curb. All of this she had explained to Constable Pluck, adding that the pig had really been the cause of the damage to the bicycle, since it had fallen directly onto its rear wheel.

Thus the unmanned bicycle and the inert pig had divided the blame between them and Agatha was suing for damages, having got Constable Pluck on her side. Melrose said, "I saw Pluck leaving Plague Alley yesterday." Agatha and Constable Pluck seemed to work hand in glove. "Has he been running at the mouth again?" Melrose selected a small slice of porter cake, which he assumed had come from Betty Ball's bakery, feared it might have been from the past Christmas lot, and picked up a digestive biscuit instead.

"I had just been giving him a bit of advice."

"It was parking meters on the High Street last time. That was nipped in the bud, I'm glad to say." Melrose tested his front tooth with his finger; he thought he might have chipped it on the Eccles cake, hard as a rock.

"Naturally, I can't divulge information," said Agatha, as she set about divulging it. "But it concerns the Leans. They live at Watermeadows; you don't know Watermeadows, Superintendent. It has fabulous gardens. Hannah Lean is the granddaughter of Lady Summerston; both of them are recluses—like me, you know. That's why we get on so well."

"What's all this 'Hannah' business? You don't even know Mrs. Lean."

"I certainly do. I saw her in Northampton two weeks ago; we nearly had luncheon."

For Agatha a near-miss with the reclusive Mrs. Lean was as good as nine courses with anyone else.

Sitting forward, she whispered, "According to the grapevine—"

Of which she was chief pruner and waterer—

"—something's been going on between Simon Lean and that Demorney person."

"Well, as the grapevine hasn't throttled me with its news, I can't say." He squinted into the darkness where one of the shadows separated and pounced. Agatha's one-eyed cat had made a four-point landing on top of her chair. Three-point, for part of its fourth leg had got in the way of a tire-iron some time ago. Melrose checked his watch. The Jack and Hammer was open, thank heavens. He had sat here this long partially out of ingrained politeness and partially because he meant to pay obeisance to whatever god was responsible for not having Agatha break her ankle on the steps of Ardry End.

"Smirk if you like, Plant," she said, tapping her cane three times on the floor, their local wizard about to wave her wand and transform pedestrian facts into fantasies. "Something is going on." She turned to Jury. "Watermeadows is an extensive estate. Finest in Northamptonshire." She bethought herself. "Second finest. At least, no *finer* than Ardry End."

Melrose sighed. Difficult for Ardry End not to come out on top, since she had expectations. It did not appear to occur to Agatha that she would die before Melrose; her twenty-five-year headstart did not put a crimp in her designs.

"The grounds and gardens are quite fabulous; Lady Summerston owns the lot, you see, and Hannah will come into a fortune. Probably what the husband's hanging on for."

"You've never even seen Watermeadows. All you know is what you've heard from Marshall Trueblood when he went up there to negotiate for that fall-front desk."

"*That* opportunist! Only gave half what it's worth, I expect." Leaving out the Withersby family, the person she loathed most in Long Piddleton was Marshall Trueblood.

"Don't be silly. He's perfectly honest. For an antiques dealer, that is. Speaking of him, we're supposed to meet at the pub. Come on, Richard."

They said their good-byes to Agatha, who lost no opportunity to make them feel as if they were the last of the medics deserting the sick and wounded. Even Jury's promise to return and the appearance of Mrs. Oilings with a fresh batch of cakes and gossip did not suffice.

As they left the shadowy fastness of Plague Alley, Melrose related the story of Agatha's accident.

"Are you telling me that your constable let her get away with *that* fabrication?" asked Jury.

"Agatha and Constable Pluck are on very good terms; she drowns him in sherry and gossip."

As they rounded the corner, Melrose said a good morning to a thick-set woman with a frown and a bulldog standing hard by her heels. The frown seemed perpetual since the skin appeared to have set in thin ropes across her forehead, and the corners of her mouth were victims of the pull of gravity. She strongly resembled her bulldog, Trot. She was hanging over the gate of her picket fence and Trot was glaring out between the rails.

"Visitin' yer auntie, was ya, m'lord?" The frown deepened and Trot made an unearthly noise in his throat like the sounds from bad plumbing. The accusation in her tone was clear, as if Melrose had been neglecting his familial duties for too long. "Well, and ain't it a fine thing when shopkeepers can endanger the lives of innercent folk. That Jurvis thinks he owns the High, he does. Just clutters up the pavement so it ain't even safe to walk."

That people had been walking past the butcher shop for a good thirty years without incident made no odds, apparently. Melrose bowed slightly, and they strolled on.

He said to Jury, "You can bet Agatha's going to be groaning with pain until this is settled. Why do you think she's staying off that foot of hers? Except for coming into the pub yesterday to check on your progress, she goes nowhere, and Long Piddleton is getting its first respite in some fifteen years. Would anything keep her from making her daily rounds but the threat of losing her small-claims case?" They had just crossed the Sidbury Road, which ended now where the High Street began. Melrose pointed with his stick to the butcher shop between Miss Crisp's and the bicycle shop. "Let's drop in. I can pick up the chops for Martha and see how poor Jurvis is keeping his sanity."

"So it's between the pig, the bicycle, and the Austin. That it?"

"Yes. The pig and the bicycle managed to move themselves to the edge of the pavement and assault the Austin."

Jurvis the Butcher was located in a cramped little building between Miss Crisp's "Better Buys" and a bicycle shop, the owner of which would probably be called as an expert witness about the possibility of a bicycle's running down an Austin. Behind the plate-glass window lay a suckling pig, mouth agape round an apple, splayed on a metal tray encircled by lettuce leaves and slices of minted apple rings.

"Be careful: it might rush through the glass and throw you to the ground."

Mr. Jurvis was delighted to see Melrose, no matter who his relations were. "The chops—oh, yes. I'll just get them. Would you be wanting anything else? That's a nice silversides, there. And the mince is especially good today."

Melrose was gazing into the case where the assortment of meats was as splendidly arranged amidst parsley snippets and candied cherries as a Cartier's display. The whole shop was clean and neat and gave no indication that knives were set to hew and hack in the back rooms. It reminded Melrose of an operating room washed free of blood.

Jury was looking at the big plaster pig, supposedly the perpetrator of this "accident," standing inside the door. It was a happy-looking pig, painted a bronzy-gold, with a chain of daisies and bluebells twined about its head and ears, drooping over one huge eye. Below its flowery countenance the pig was holding a little tray with a long slot for a sign. This one announced the price of pork as the daily special.

Mr. Jurvis returned with Melrose's chops wrapped in butcher's paper and explained to Jury about the pig. "It was sitting outside to advertise the special. Beef mince, it was. One pound thirty. I paid more than a penny, I can tell you, for this pig here. Disgusting that someone could just drive right up on the curb, run over whatever's there—thank God my little Molly was upstairs, not out here playing with the pig like she likes to do—and then This Person blames it on everyone and everything else. Mind, I'm reasonable. I'd've let it go, only charged damages like to get the pig mended, but This Person has to get shirty about it—sorry, Mr. Plant." Jurvis colored slightly.

"No need to be. Looks like you got the pig patched up." Melrose pointed to the fresh plaster of the leg.

"Might have been better to leave it, Mr. Jurvis," said Jury. "If you mean to collect damages."

Jurvis's hand flew to his face. "You mean that pig might be needed as a witness?"

"Well, not exactly. But as evidence, quite possibly." Seeing the butcher looking sadly at the evidence, Jury added, "But I doubt it'll come to that, Mr. Jurvis. Who'd be dotty enough to make a court case of it?" Jury smiled broadly.

Who indeed? thought Melrose.

6

———————🔔 A removal van sat with two wheels on the curb in front of Trueblood's Antiques, a smart Tudor building next to the Jack and Hammer. Marshall Trueblood was too busy wringing his hands and shouting after a beefy man to *please* be careful of that urn—

That the removal men were paying no attention was evident from the thud and clatter and the wail of Trueblood. "Let's not stop," said Melrose.

The Jack and Hammer was suffering from its usual midday tedium, the stillness punctuated by the staccato snores of Mrs. Withersby. Having earned her char money, she was drinking it up and sleeping it off at the bar, her head propped against the snob screen. An elderly couple sat at a table in back and neither spoke nor looked at one another, in that way of survivors of long-standing marriages.

56

They looked alike with their thatched gray hair and dressed alike in their dark broadcloth despite the pleasant weather. They sat solemn as seals and stared at the door.

Perhaps he was a sadist; still, Melrose always enjoyed watching Vivian Rivington's reaction when she encountered Richard Jury. The meetings were rare and accidental, and it was only the one in Stratford-upon-Avon that Vivian had managed to handle with anything approaching self-possession. And that, thought Melrose, probably had something to do with her being on the arm of—more or less propped up by—Count Franco Giappino. That, or else the clothes she always dragged out of mothballs whenever she'd just returned from Italy. Probably it would give any woman an edge, standing there with someone slim and expensive, with that Mediterranean patina and its sinister implications, the sort of dilettantish air that so beguiled Henry James into wanting to scrape it off. That the count's aura was not nearly so seductive as the superintendent's, Melrose was quite sure Vivian had known for some time.

After she returned from one of her Venetian excursions, she would for a time wear the outfits she'd acquired during the trip, many of them exquisitely expensive-looking and artfully shapeless. But then the old Vivian would reassert herself, turning up in twin sets and good wool skirts. Today she had opted for the frankly feminine; she was quite lovely in a frock of flowered georgette with a coppery background just the shade of her hair and Miss Broad-stairs's roses. She sat at a table in the Jack and Hammer, hands folded neatly, purse beside her, looking as if she were waiting for a bus.

Jury leaned down and kissed her cheek and she blushed and floundered, searching the empty table for something to rearrange. There was only the tin ashtray, so she went for that, turning it in little circles.

"Well, it's too bad about your car, but you finally got here." The tone was almost fractious.

"My car?"

"You know—"

"All right, all right," said Melrose in an unnaturally loud voice. "Drinks, drinks, what're we having?"

Vivian paid no attention to him and said to Jury, "Still, things have a way of working out, don't they? I mean, if it hadn't been for the breakdown, you'd never have met your old friend, would you?"

"My friend?" Jury frowned.

Melrose was calling to Scroggs and rubbing his hands with enthusiasm. "The Thunderbolt, you must try it. Vivian, what's the removal van doing sitting in front of Trueblood's place? Isn't he coming over? Dick!" he shouted. "The superintendent will have a Thunderbolt!"

Her voice was getting testier as she said to Jury, "I'm surprised you didn't go to Woburn Abbey, I mean, as long as you were almost there. She'd probably have liked that, the weather being so beautiful and all." Her face was burnished as if she'd been sitting too long beside a fire.

Jury was searching her face as one does when one is looking for signs of mild lunacy, as Melrose was leaning across her to get a better look, over the stained glass that said "Hardy's Crown," at the shop next door. "There's Trueblood, directing the removal men. He's pulling his hair and shrieking. . . ."

Trueblood's shrieks made no difference to Vivian, who by now had got herself in so deep she couldn't pull herself out, as if her wellingtons just kept sucking mud. She was talking about the lions at Woburn Abbey. Jury was fascinated, his chin propped in his hands, staring at her and smiling as she made her mental journey with him and his old friend through the safari park.

Fortunately, Dick Scroggs's enthusiasm for his Thunderbolt matched Vivian's apparent enthusiasm for wild animals. He interrupted and told Jury all about the new pub that probably wouldn't stay in business long, not where it was located. If that didn't kill it, it would be snapped up by one of the big breweries and sell nothing but the Yellow Peril. "Sly's only a manager, now. You can always tell them what's managed, I mean there's not the extra little bit of trouble took to have things just right, is there, sir? An owner now, he can't let up a minute, that's what I say."

Jury agreed wholeheartedly, and Scroggs left with a big smile and went behind the bar, stuck a toothpick in his mouth, and started reading the local paper, the *Bald Eagle*.

Marshall Trueblood walked in, dressed in his usual rainbow fashion—Italian silk shirt, splotch of russet neckerchief, spread of pale yellow cashmere cap. In his kaleidoscope of colors, he reminded Plant of one of the Tiffany lamps in his antiques shop. His greeting to Jury was as effusive as his costume. Melrose thought for a moment Trueblood might be going to hug him, but he settled for a handshake, catching Jury's in both of his, and making a little moue with his mouth as if he were blowing kisses. It was all such an act on Trueblood's part, though Melrose had no idea who the intended audience was—probably Trueblood himself.

"What a pity about your breakdown, Superintendent. Well, you're here now—"

Said Vivian, "I was just telling him—"

"What's the van doing in front of your place?" asked Melrose hurriedly.

"Delivering my furniture. You really must see it. Cost me four thousand and I expect I can only get six or seven for it."

"That's hardly worth your time," said Vivian.

"Wouldn't you like to see it? Come along, come along."

"No thank you," said Vivian, her mind still on Woburn Abbey.

The other rose and trooped next door.

* * *

Crammed as it was with what Melrose calculated to be a million quid's worth of silver and gilt, display cases filled with Lalique and Georgian crystal, inlaid firescreens, commodes, mahogany shelves filled with leatherbound books, Trueblood had still found space for his prized acquisition, a rosewood fall-front desk with brass handles.

His manner notwithstanding, Marshall Trueblood was nobody's fool; excepting Melrose himself and Vivian Rivington, he was the richest person in Long Pidd. He had a feeling for the marketplace that seemed more an act of grace than of business perspicacity; when no one would touch Empire, he snapped it up everywhere and made a tidy fortune; when everyone else was buying oak, he stored his in a back room and waited for it to go out of fashion in order to come in again. He had the nose of a bloodhound and the methods of a stockbroker.

Trueblood was showing Jury the *secrétaire* when Melrose wandered back, past a collection of jade and a syllabub table he considered purchasing.

"You've no idea what I had to go *through* to pry this from Lady Summerston's claw-like grip." He inserted a small key into the brass escutcheon at the top of the closed writing surface.

"It's a fall-front desk, is it?" asked Jury.

"A *secrétaire à abattant.* There was a matching commode, but she wouldn't part with it. She lives in this great peeling but noble villa called Watermeadows," said Trueblood, lowering the writing surface to expose an array of pigeonholes and tiny drawers.

"Very nice. It needs some refinishing," said Melrose. "And a few of the pigeonholes could do with fixing. Looks like dry rot—" He stuck his finger in one of them.

Trueblood sighed. "Four thousand I paid, and all you can talk about is dry rot."

Melrose peered closer into another of the pigeonholes and then stepped back. He blinked and shook his head. "I think—" His voice broke. He cleared his throat. "—you've got a little more there than dry rot. Have a look, will you," he said to Jury.

Bewildered, Jury peered into the pigeonhole, paused, and then quickly pulled the blossoming yellow handkerchief from Trueblood's pocket.

Astonished, Trueblood said, "What in the *hell* . . . ?" He shouldered his way between Melrose and the bank of pigeonholes and quickly turned round, his back to the *secrétaire*. "An eye. There's an *eye* in there."

With both hands holding the handkerchief, Jury slowly pulled out the whole array of holes and drawers.

The pale blue shirt of the torso was stippled in blood. The head fell forward with a thud onto the writing surface of Trueblood's four thousand quid's worth of *secrétaire à abattant.*

7

🔔 "Simon Lean."

Melrose and Trueblood said the name simultaneously, and all three of them stepped back, Melrose nearly toppling a Lalique vase, which he managed to catch before it hit the floor.

Jury looked at the neck and upper arms. Rigor had passed off, which might have meant he'd been dead for twelve hours, since late the night before or early morning. Jury knew how unreliable such estimates of time of death were. "Ring up your local doctor."

"Carr? God, you don't want him. He's half blind—"

"Nevertheless," said Jury, frowning.

"All right, all right." Melrose moved to the telephone.

"His name is Simon Lean?" said Jury to

Trueblood, who had collapsed on a love seat so deeply cushioned in down he looked as if he might never rise again.

"Watermeadows. Yes. That's where he lives. Lived. Lived. Why isn't he *there?* What in the *hell* is he doing in *my secrétaire?*" Trueblood seemed trying to make some further objection to this desecration of his premises, couldn't, and merely flailed with his arms. "I bought the desk, not the body; send it back."

"Where was this *secrétaire*, then?"

"Where?" Trueblood's eyes were still hypnotized by the sight of Simon Lean's torso lying on the writing surface as if he'd fallen asleep over a boring piece of correspondence. "Watermeadows, of course. Not in the house proper; in what they call a summerhouse. Gathering dust. I just happened to be walking by and took a peek inside. The old lady is loaded with the most priceless pieces of late-eighteenth-century stuff—"

"Just a minute, Marshall. You were 'walking by,' you say? . . . What are you doing?" This was directed to Melrose, who was now redialing.

"Doing? Ringing Pluck."

"Hang up, will you?"

"But he's going to have to get Northampton—"

"Leave it." He turned to Trueblood. "Go on."

"After I saw this *secrétaire à abattant,* which is something I've been on the lookout for for years, I thought I'd just go along to the main house and try to talk Lady Summerston into selling it to me. The old dear is so sentimental about her possessions, given they all belonged to her late, beloved husband, it's like trying to pick barnacles off a ship's hull. Do you know what I had to give for a limited edition of *Ulysses* she'd got squirreled away—"

Trueblood wheeled around. "My God, the books? Where are they, and where is *it?*"

"Never mind them for a moment—"

"Never *mind?* You must be out of *yours* if you think a book by Joyce with etchings by Matisse—"

"And a body by Trueblood," Melrose said, with a gracious smile. "I'd forget James Joyce for the moment."

"And get back to your visit," said Jury.

"There's nothing more. We had tea on her balcony and chatted, mostly about the past. Hers, not mine. And after she'd knocked up the price by a thousand, I fixed up about having the removal men fetch it this morning." Trueblood's glance fastened on the body in the *secrétaire* and he shivered. "And so it was. Let's send it back." He smiled weakly.

"Nothing else?" asked Jury, who was examining the wound. It was a stab wound, but it did not have the appearance of one made by an ordinary knife. "Who else knew it was to be collected this morning?"

"Possibly the old butler. The granddaughter, perhaps, though I doubt it. She doesn't seem to be around much."

"But the removal men had to call in at the house."

"No. There's a sort of lay-by and a short road that

leads to within a hundred yards of the summer-house. They'd have taken it from there."

"It borders my property," said Melrose. "I mean the Watermeadows acres more or less join up with mine. There's no dividing line except for that dirt road. Then there's the footpath."

"In other words, public access."

They both nodded.

Jury turned from his inspection of the wound. "Okay. That means anyone could conceivably have got into this summerhouse fairly easily, if Marshall here simply walked in. Why, if there were valuable pieces, wouldn't it have been locked?"

"This isn't London, old sweat. People don't bother things much about here."

"Really?" Jury nodded toward the corpse. "You could have fooled me."

Trueblood went on: "Lady S. isn't an especially acquisitive person. Except for certain things that belonged to her late husband, I don't think she cares much about possessions."

Jury nodded to Melrose. "Call the constable."

"About time," said Melrose. "You're holding up a murder investigation, you know, whilst we get our stories straight," he added with a grim smile.

"Have you got hold of yourself enough by now to tell your story, Marshall? Where's the bill of sale?"

Trueblood went to a handsomely carved knee-hole desk and started jerking open drawers. Melrose, in the meantime, had sat down on a rose velvet settee and was trying to find a comfortable position in the cramped space.

"Be careful!" said Trueblood, "or you'll break the Spode." Then to Jury, "Wait a moment. You seem to be taking the tack that I, *I* am going to be looked upon as a *suspect.*"

"It would be a little careless of you, wouldn't it," asked Melrose, "to have the corpse delivered to yourself like a parcel?"

* * *

Superintendent Charles Pratt stood staring at the body of Simon Lean, waiting for his medical examiner to finish. To no one in particular, he said, "I must admit I haven't seen a corpse in such an unwieldy position as this since the last time I was called to Long Piddleton." It was as if Long Piddletonians were particularly adept at arranging bodies.

The Scene-of-Crimes officer had been no less surprised as he had gone about adjusting and readjusting his camera to get shots of the body from every angle. The medical examiner, a sprightly man named Simpson, had completed a cursory examination of the wound and now asked the Scene-of-Crimes man if they could set about dismantling the desk so that the body could be removed to a stretcher.

The word *dismantle* seemed to throw Trueblood into further paroxysms of distress, but at least the noise from upstairs had stopped—the sound of furniture shoved about, of legs scraping hardwood— and the two uniformed police had come down, together with the fingerprint man. Dusting for fingerprints amongst the crystal and cloisonné had finally

been given up in the circumstances, since it was
highly unlikely that although Simon Lean might
have been delivered here, he was killed here. . . .

. . . Although Pratt's inspector seemed to want
to make a great deal of that likelihood.

"He had nothing to do with it," said Melrose
Plant, who was sitting on the edge of the fauteuil,
his chin resting on his hands, and his hands clasping
the end of his walking stick.

MacAllister had his notebook out, and his smile
was not friendly. He was one of those policemen
who took an abundance of delight in his authority,
unlike Charles Pratt, who did not necessarily believe the rest of the world was guilty until he himself proved it innocent. "And how do you know
that?"

"Superintendent Jury and I were here when that
secrétaire was opened."

"But not when it was *delivered,*" said MacAllister.
"No reason the body couldn't have been secreted
somewhere in the shop and put in that chest there
afterwards." MacAllister was eyeing an old sea
trunk.

"Not 'chest,' " said Trueblood, *"secrétaire à abattant."* In his book, murder—even one on his own
doorstop—appeared to take second place to educat-
ing purblind civil servants.

Charles Pratt did not hide his impatience. "I'd
give it up, Mac. It would hardly seem worth the
trouble to secrete a body in one piece of furniture
and then move it to another."

The writing surface had been carefully unhinged

and the cabinet doors at the bottom removed after the position of the torso had been chalked in. The body of Simon Lean was lowered to the floor. To Simpson, Pratt said, "Very little blood."

Simpson grunted. "Internal hemorrhaging, it must have been. I can't tell precisely until I get him to the mortuary, but the thrust of the weapon—and it doesn't look like the entry wound of a knife— appears to be upward. Longer than a knife, would be my guess." He thought for a moment. "Sort of wound that could possibly be made with a sword or a dagger, possibly."

Melrose Plant, who had been leaning on his walking stick, looked a little ashen. "This isn't a sword stick, doctor. It's a cosher. I don't care much for sword sticks."

Pratt smiled slightly and, seeing that Trueblood had put his head in his hands, said, "Something wrong?"

Through his splayed fingers, Trueblood answered caustically: "What could possibly be wrong?"

"It must have taken a hell of a lot of strength to shove the body in and up," said MacAllister.

"Not necessarily," said Pratt. "People under stress usually find what strength they need. Any ideas as to time of death?" asked Pratt.

The doctor shrugged. "Rigor's already passed off in the face, the jaw, the hands. But not in the lower extremities." He shrugged. "There's the movement of air to be considered in that thing"—he nodded toward the secretary—"that might speed it up. And then there's the stabbing itself—the violence of the death might speed up the rigor and make it pass off more quickly. Say, as a guess, thirteen, fourteen hours." He stripped off the rubber gloves, put his instruments back, and asked dryly, "Could you deliver the corpse minus the coffin? Thanks." He walked out.

Two attendants came in carrying a stretcher and a polyethylene sheet. Trueblood closed his eyes as they made their way down the narrow aisle, one leg of the stretcher scraping against a rosewood breakfront.

* * *

Constable Pluck, having given over his desk to Superintendent Pratt and his one-room station to the Northants constabulary in general—not to mention Scotland Yard—had positioned himself like someone shouldering his way to the center of a photograph and seemed to be enjoying the situation immensely. Thus when Pratt asked him if he knew Simon Lean's wife, the constable said he'd known the people up at Watermeadows as well as anyone. The statement was the perfect truth; however, since no one really knew them, apparently, Pluck was caught in the uncomfortable position of middleman.

Pratt pushed the phone toward him. "Then call— what is it? Watermeadows—and inform them the police would like to talk with Mrs. Lean and her grandmother."

Then he turned to Jury. "You've said precious little, Superintendent."

"Precious little call to. This isn't my patch. And," he added, smiling, "I'm on holiday."

MacAllister gave him a look that said he'd wished he'd stay on it.

"More or less a busman's holiday, I'd say." Charles Pratt leaned his chin in his hands and gave Jury a piercing blue glance. "You'll make one of the best witnesses it's ever been my luck to round up." He sat back, still smiling, and rocked a little in the swivel chair. "We've just been called away from a messy domestic killing in Northampton. Time-consuming, half of the constabulary is on that job." He paused. "I'm taking my men there, and I'll break the news to her. It would be nice if you could just stop by later on. . . ."

" 'Just stop by.' " Jury sighed. "Either that or I am to make myself available for questioning—as we say in the Job—at any old hour of the night or day. Charles, aren't you ashamed of yourself? Anyway, it'll have to go through headquarters—"

It was as if Pratt were simply completing Jury's sentence for him: "—and Chief Superintendent Racer, after one or two acerbic comments about a murder having occurred the moment you turned up, said that the least you could do would be to assist. As he put it, you're at the disposal of the Northamptonshire constabulary, and he expressed regrets—"

"—that my holiday would be interrupted. A policeman's life is full of grief, Superintendent Pratt."

Pratt was unzipping a ten-packet of Benson and Hedges. "His very words. Cigarette?"

8

─────────🔔 "WAS the killer," asked Melrose, studying the ragged hindquarters of a pewter-colored dog curled on Marshall Trueblood's hearth, "trying to conceal or reveal? Good Lord, it must have been obvious Marshall here would discover it as soon as he opened that writing desk."

"Truer words have never been spoken, old sweat." The words were muffled, coming as they did from a face pressed against the back of an ivory brocade sofa. He was lying there, arms hugging his waist. "And to top it all, I haven't got my *Ulysses.*"

"Oh, stop it," said Melrose. "Sit up like a man." Melrose punctuated this statement by rapping his walking stick several times on the coffee table.

"First time I've ever been asked to do *that.*"

Jury smiled as Trueblood sighed hugely, unwound himself from his fetal position, and sat up.

His hair was ruffled, his silk shirt wrinkled, his scarf hanging limply.

"And *this,*" said Melrose, "is the first time I've seen you looking anything other than sartorially perfect. Why are you letting all of this mess get to you? *We* know you'd nothing to do with it." He looked innocently at Jury. "Don't we?"

Trueblood nearly strangled himself with an adjustment to his scarf, mimicking Melrose. " 'Don't we, don't we?' " He looked accusingly at Jury. "Nor did I hear you answer him. Well?"

Jury pulled at his earlobe as if considering. He was sitting on the arm of the couch from which Trueblood had now risen, since all the chairs in the room with their gilt legs, fretwork, or little claw feet looked entirely too delicate to bear his weight. It was a room as sleek and silky as its owner, and nothing in it was less than a hundred years old, he bet, except for the rough-looking gray dog coiled on a flimsy bit of rug before the fireplace screen, and he even wondered about it. Occasionally, it yawned, creaked up on all fours, turned and turned and collapsed again.

"Thanks. Couple of mates you two are." Trueblood gave them as black a look as the Black Russian he was taking from a cloisonné box. "Why am I letting it *get* to me?" he asked, standing with head bowed, the very picture of tragedy. "The Northants police have practically turned my cottage into one of their incidents rooms, have questioned me round the clock—"

"The clock hasn't gone round; only a couple of hours—" said Melrose helpfully.

"—*And,*" said Trueblood, "they are on the verge of reading me my rights. I can't *imagine* why that makes me nervous."

"Come on, now," said Jury, who'd slid onto the sofa vacated by Trueblood. "You wouldn't hurt a fly."

"Neither would Norman Bates."

Melrose went on: "The body could much more easily have been disposed of in the lake or in the grounds or downriver. Even fetched over to *my* property . . . now there's an interesting possibility. . . ."

"Let's not explore it, if you don't mind," said Jury. "Instead, the body was stuffed into a chest that was to be collected almost immediately. Hmm. You don't really think it was Browne, do you?" he asked Trueblood.

"Why not? The man can't abide the idea that he's a mere dilettante and I'm an expert. I don't write, of course, but then neither does he. Joanna the Mad told me about that manuscript of his. Now there's a thought: why didn't he kill *her* instead of Simon Lean?"

"What manuscript?" asked Jury.

"About an hallucinating terrorist at Wimbledon. Or was it Doncaster? He thought Joanna might use a little clout. Send it to her editor, I expect. She said her editor would hire a terrorist to kill her for forcing Theo's manuscript on him. Well, T.W.B. hasn't spoken to her since, of course. Won't carry her books in that bird's nest of his . . . Stop prodding my dog, damnit."

Melrose drew back his walking stick. "Sorry. Didn't Simon Lean have something to do with a publishing house? Did he work at one?"

"Work? Him? . . . Or do I recollect that he said something about a publishing house that the Summerstons counted amongst their investments?" Trueblood raised his foot, shod in Italian leather, to inspect the shine.

"So you did know him, more or less?" asked Jury.

"Less, much less. He came into the shop once . . . well, Pratt's going to find out anyway."

"Find out what?"

"That I sold him a dagger-cane. He collected stuff like that." Trueblood nodded toward Melrose's cosher. "Tried to buy that, too, but I was saving it for Melrose. It was some time ago, two months, three." He sighed and slid down on the sofa. "How grim."

Jury helped himself to a Black Russian, which he looked at with some suspicion before lighting up. "Don't worry; that won't count for much except to MacAllister."

"He's a sweetheart, isn't he? Thick as two boards and probably can't *stand* one of my sexual persuasion." Trueblood rose and started pacing.

Melrose said, "I didn't know you had one."

"It would be interesting if Mr. Browne had approached Lean about his book."

Trueblood stopped to study himself in a cheval glass—adjusting his cravat, smoothing back his hair, his flirtation with the gallows apparently over for the time being. "I'm *sure* T.W.B. approached him, but I doubt it was just for a manuscript."

"You're not suggesting Lean was gay, are you?"

"Lord, no. That was the trouble, as far as T.W.B.'s concerned. And then to have his sister-in-arms, that Demorney person, meeting him on the sly . . . The more I think of it, the better Theo Wrenn Browne looks as a candidate. Kill two birds with one stone. Simon and yours truly. What a coup. It would fire the imagination of an hallucinating terrorist turf accountant, or whoever the idiot is in his book."

Jury checked his watch and rose. "I'm on my way to Watermeadows; ring there if MacAllister turns the thumbscrews."

9

◮ ITS silence, its absence of life in the midst of what had been splendor were the things that struck Jury first about Watermeadows.

The gardens covered acres and encompassed pools, reflecting ponds, statues now crumbling and patchy with moss all surrounding a baroque house. In the front was a formal pond from whose center-piece of marble children and dolphins, Jury imag-ined, water must have gushed up and outward, fall-ing round an elaborately carved basin in a curtain translucent and shimmering in the May light of an-other year. No water gushed from it now. And on the sloping hill behind the large house were ter-raced gardens. Thus in the midst of what was other-wise a splendid English arrangement of yew and box hedges, beds of grape hyacinths, long borders of aubrietas and wallflowers, there had been at one time an attempt to bring to the English formality something of the Italian, water springing up from hidden reservoirs and cascading down the hillside.

Around the drive were yew trees; beyond them, paths winding through herbaceous borders, row after row of pink and mauve and blue, beds and carpets of flowers, bushes, sumach shrubs, low and high walls, and what looked like an ancient cupola, some sixteenth-century ruin, nearly overgrown with moss. Out there in the distance, beyond a screen of beech trees, he glimpsed silvery water and the roof of a small building that might have been the Watermeadows summerhouse.

Watermeadows was a splendid rotting beauty, but Jury saw no one about to enjoy its splendor.

The servant who opened the door was a frail old form who fit the grand design of the estate. This was Crick (he told Jury), older than Plant's butler Ruthven, thinner and dustier, as if he, together with the broken marble figure in the foyer, a faded painting of Malvern, and a worn Antwerp carpet, needed a good touching up.

He asked Jury if he would be so kind as to wait, that he would tell Lady Summerston that he was here.

When Jury said that it was Mrs. Lean that he had come to see, Crick simply replied that Mrs. Lean was resting—after all, it had been a dreadful shock —and it was Lady Summerston that he would see first in the circumstances.

That the butler, in his old-world and excessively

polite way, took it upon himself to decide what circumstances best fit whom, so amused Jury that he simply did as he was bid—waited in a large room off the rotunda-like entry-room.

The room was huge, shadowy, high-ceilinged, and nearly empty of furniture. At the far end was a Regency sofa whose gilt was peeling, flanked by armchairs in worn tapestry. They sat near a fireplace with a green and black marble surround. The floor was inlaid, the doorframes marble, the mirrors enormous. A massive crystal chandelier hung from a frescoed ceiling and there were in each corner Doric columns of the same green and black marble, as if the size of the room needed this extra support. Long windows behind the sparse furnishings, uncurtained, overlooked a terrace that served almost as a stage for the sweep of the gardens. Beyond the terrace were also formal pools, but these were now only drained concrete. To the side of each was a statue of a partially clothed maiden, one with a garland, one with a bouquet, both with their skirts slightly raised, toes pointing forward, as if they'd meant to dip them in the pool, marble harbingers of spring.

He turned from the light and looked into the crypt-like darkness of the room. Soothing to the eye, depressing to the spirit. It reminded him of those palatial rooms he used to see in old war films, apartments from which the wealthy had fled, taking what possessions they could, before the enemy closed in.

To Jury it was an environment he had come to dread more than any other, though he was not sure why: the ghostly elegance, the remnants of beauty, the fragmented past.

Crick returned to say that Lady Summerston would see him now.

Like the rest of him, Crick's voice was thin and reedy. As he led Jury to her room, he spoke of Lady Summerston as a rather frail person, "bit of a heart problem there, sir," who seldom left her room. Nothing terribly serious, you understand, but that was the way it was when one got older, continued Crick, exempting himself—he whose wafer-thin lips, sunken eyes, and dewlaps would surely have made him, in the physical sense, at least, fit company for the lady he so devotedly served.

He told Jury all of this while preceding him up the broad sweep of staircase. As they labored upward, he murmured about "this business, this business," without actually directly referring to the murder of Mr. Lean. "This business" was quite naturally taking its toll on her ladyship, what with police here with their questions and taking over the old summerhouse. The formality of his dress—the old, black cutaway and starched collar—did not in the least reflect his manner, for Crick was as chatty as could be, although his breathing was growing raspier toward the top. He was, indeed, quite voluble about the murder and quite voluble in his own assessment of Mr. Lean, "with all due respect," of which, Jury decided, there was little. During their alpine climb (would they never reach the top?), Jury pretty much decided it was Upstart Simon, and that Crick, for one, wouldn't miss him and wouldn't miss the furniture. . . . "That *appallingly* poor example of eighteenth-century *secrétaire à abattant.*"

They had acquired the heady heights of the upper floor and Jury was glad that Trueblood hadn't heard him.

Jury congratulated Crick on negotiating this stairway several times a day and with a tray in his hands. Crick told him then that there was a lift, but that he disliked this newfangled technology and that a bit of exercise did wonders to keep us all in the pink, didn't it? The contraption (as he called it, pointing down the hall) with its old ironwork cage, giltpainted, hardly seemed much of a technological advance. Near the top of the stair in a shadowy enclosure was a portrait of a young woman with dark hair and eyes, sitting on a bench in the grounds of Watermeadows. It was Mrs. Lean, said Crick, done ten years ago, but she never seemed to change.

Down the dark hall they walked. A quick rat-tat on the door at the end was answered from inside. "Come!"

* * *

Lady Summerston's room, or suite of rooms (for he was shown into a sitting room), was a clutter of Victoriana, completely out of keeping in both size and ambience with the rest of the big house.

She herself was sitting outside, on the balcony,

which overlooked the rear gardens and the crescent of lake that showed in the distance.

"Superintendent!" she said gaily, looking up from a huge leatherbound book in which she'd been pasting stamps. On the chair beside her were several other albums, probably containing photographs, and a double deck of cards. She had, it would seem, enough hobbies to keep her going through many an afternoon on the balcony, for the balcony had an oddly lived-in look, despite its openness to the elements.

Her voice, when she fluted his rank, was as gay as if she had been waiting for him all the day long, and made it appear that the death of her granddaughter's husband was an event that made a change in an otherwise routine day of looking over albums or playing solitaire. She was positioning a stamp in her book and bringing her fist down on it with a force that could have cracked the glass-topped table. Another dozen or more stamps had been dropped like confetti from a japanned box on the table before her, waiting to be pounded into her book.

Lady Summerston was probably somewhere in her seventies, with fine, parchment-like skin and crisp brown eyes. But if Lady Summerston was frail, that fragility would have to be unearthed from what looked like dozens of pieces of clothes—a dragon-embroidered dressing gown, a ruby-colored Burmese shawl, a Victoria Cross on a chain round her neck, a palmetto fan, which she swished with the gusto of one waving off flies, and a pink turban-wrapped band to which was attached a weeping veil such as a certain caste of Indian women wear. Lady Summerston wore the Empire on her back.

"Sit, sit," she said, with a fluttery gesture, indicating one of the white ironwork chairs, which was, Jury found when he tried to adjust his tall frame to it, as uncomfortable as those chairs always appear to look, sitting clustered on the patios of the rich.

Lady Summerston seemed in no hurry at all for him to explain his presence on this balmy afternoon on her balcony as she relentlessly thwacked another stamp into place. Since police had already appeared, perhaps she thought one more would make little difference.

Jury smiled at the intensity with which she went about her pasting-up. "Got any special system, Lady Summerston?"

"System? Good Lord, no. They're just stamps. You stick 'em in any old way." She turned the frown from Jury back to the stamps as if the beastly little things might have loosened and jumped to other squares while she looked away.

"I thought perhaps you might be doing them by country," said Jury. "All of those in front of you seem to be British Commonwealth."

"Of course they are." (*Thump!*) "They're Gerry's —my late husband's—collection. I found them amongst his belongings. I keep all of his things"— here she nodded off in a direction meant to indicate the hallway beyond her door—"in a room at the end. Sometimes I go in there just to have a look round. Most people would say that's morbid. We're supposed to get rid of anything that reminds us of the dead, I expect. Give it all over to charity or the church fête or Oxfam. As if we could rush headlong into forgetfulness." Another stamp was aimed at its square. Bull's-eye. "That seems to be what Simon thought." She sighed, closed the album, and tapped her heavily ringed fingers on its surface. "Well, you've come about Simon and find me totally unrepentant."

"Is there something you should repent, then?"

"My lack of feeling, I daresay." Her look at him was shrewd, but in the brown eyes was still a film of sadness. "I absolutely disliked him. Except for Hannah's sake, I'm glad he's dead." She shrugged. "I expect at the inquest the coroner will make something of *that.*"

"You're very straightforward about it."

"A lot of killers are straightforward. Look you right in the eye"—and here she leaned toward him, fastening the glittery eyes on him—"and say, 'How I loathed the man.' "

Jury laughed. "You're making quite a case for yourself as a prime suspect."

Now she had picked up the deck of cards and was handling them with swift, sure strokes. "It's merely being clever. I had motive, opportunity, no alibi. *And* could easily have seen him go into the summerhouse." Here she reached to the chair and picked up a pair of Zeiss binoculars. "I'm also a birdwatcher. These are quite powerful."

As he watched her switch a black king to a red queen, Jury asked: "And what about the weapon?"

"A dagger-cane. Fourteen inches long, tempered

steel, knobbly walnut casing." She swept up the rows of cards, shuffled, reshuffled, and started slapping them down again in rows. "Have you met Hannah? No, Crick would have brought you here first. Hannah is probably taking it very badly—"

" 'Probably'?"

"Well, I haven't seen her but for a moment—she looked totally drained—but she has an astonishing way of guarding her feelings." Lady Summerston looked up and off. "Like her mother. Like Alice. Strange, because both Gerry and I wore our emotions on our sleeves."

"Your daughter's dead?"

The hands stopped fluttering over the cards and there was a silence as full of regret as all of her words had been lacking in it. "Yes. When Hannah was very young. It was dreadful, especially since the father had walked out. The Summerston women never seem to choose the right man. The men fared better." She gave Jury a sharp little smile. "I'm quite fond of Hannah: she keeps to herself; she occasionally comes up to play a game of cards; sometimes we dine together."

To Jury it sounded as if they afforded each other little companionship or consolation.

"She was crazy about her grandfather—Gerry; she adored her mother. There were the four of us, then the three, now just the two."

Simon Lean had apparently not come in for consideration as the fifth.

"Gerald—my late husband" (she explained again) "—loved this place and brought nearly everything in it piece by piece back from his travels. So I hold on to things as long as I can. As if—for heaven's sakes—there weren't enough money to go round, as if we might all end up with begging bowls. Simon was hideously extravagant. Gambling debts, the lot. But he *was* the poor girl's husband, and I'm sure she adored him. Some women are born to be victims, I think." Her tone made it clear that she wasn't one of them.

"Was he running through her inheritance, then?"

"No; she hadn't got it yet. Oh, of course she has money, but not the *reál* money." Her smile was a knife-flash. "Gerald saw to that when she married Simon. But he certainly got enough from her to buy whatever he fancied. Including women, I expect. When I die she'll come into an enormous amount, of course. She's not interested in money; Simon was interested in nothing else."

Jury smiled. "It doesn't sound as if you need to sell your furniture, Lady Summerston."

Her glance was quizzical. "I don't. It's the bargaining I like. I sold off a Vermeer to Sotheby's and, as you know, that marvelous old *secrétaire* to Mr. Trueblood. Worse luck for him, I expect. Can you imagine how he must have felt when he found not books but a body in it?"

"The books must have been unloaded before the body—well . . ."

"Was stuffed in? If it hadn't happened here, I'd say it was quite marvelous. But it's too bad about the books. I knocked the price of that *Ulysses* up, but not as much as I would have done for that little swine, Theo Browne."

"Did Mr. Browne make you an offer?"

She grimaced. "He's always trying to get at Gerry's library. But I find Mr. Trueblood rather a pleasant young man; first-rate poker player and a poker face. Naturally, he didn't give half what I asked for the *secrétaire*, but then I asked twice what it was worth, so we both got what we wanted. How damned unpleasant for him now." She held up the metal cross. "Do you know what this is, Superintendent?"

"The Victoria Cross."

She let it drop. "It was Gerry's. Just let me get his photograph from my desk—"

Jury half-rose, but she was already out of her chair, moving quickly and purposefully toward her target. All of her movements were quick and purposeful, thought Jury. If this was Lady Summerston sick, he'd be almost afraid to see Lady Summerston well.

Her voice preceded her as she returned with the picture. As if reading his mind, she was saying, "I imagine Crick told you I had a heart condition, a lung condition, a liver condition. The last might be true, but not the first two. There's a decanter of whiskey on the bureau. Get it, will you? And"—she called after him—"get the toothbrush glass from the bathroom."

As Jury searched the darkened room that smelled of very old and musty scents like lemon oil polish, pomegranate, and musk, Lady Summerston kept on talking away. What he heard of it was largely concerned with Lord Summerston's experiences in France. From the glimpse he had got of the photograph, her husband had left the Second World War with a chestful of medals. Finally, he found the decanter—the room had more than one high bureau —on a tray depicting a brightly scarved Balinese dancer. The tray nearly hid from view a collection of model soldiers, a circlet of kneeling ones in front, armed with bayonets, another mounted behind as if defending the decanter-fortress from invasion. There was nearly an entire platoon of the Royal Field Artillery, lines of Zulu warriors, the Royal Home Artillery, Sudanese soldiers, Bedouins. All sorts of wars were being fought across this bureau. It was the sort of collection he would have given his eyeteeth for as a boy, and he stood there gazing at them, remembering the shop down the street from the Fulham Road flat. . . .

"What're you *doing* in there?"

Jury shook himself from memories of the Fulham Road and dreams of boyhood glory and collected the tray. On the tray was one very fine crystal glass. He got the other glass from the bathroom. "I was looking at the model soldier collection," said Jury, setting the tray amidst albums and cards.

"You've certainly been *long* enough about it. Hannah loves them. Especially the Bedouin. Well, I've finished for the day!" She stacked the cards in the box, sat back, and took a deep breath, apparently pleased with the fulfillment of some odious task. "I'll have the toothbrush glass; you have the good one."

"Do you want water?"

She rolled her eyes. "When Gerry and I drank, we *drank,* Superintendent." She accepted her glass from Jury's hand.

He smiled. Given the dust on the decanter, she mightn't have had a drink since Gerry died. He paused then in the pouring of his own, feeling sad. It might have very nearly been true.

Raising her glass she looked at the triple-framed photos of Gerald Summerston. It was clearly a toast, and Jury joined in. The Summerston on the left, sitting as he was with a glass in his hand, his long legs outstretched on just such a chair as this somewhere out there on the lawn, could easily have made a third at their party. The picture on the right might at first glance have seemed to be of an altogether different person, until one noticed the expression was more sheepish than serious, as if the medal-bedecked uniform weighed rather heavily. The one in the middle was poignant; it was taken when he was an adolescent, and the uncertainty in his expression showed how difficult it was to be young.

"Why, incidentally, is Scotland Yard in on this? Unless Simon was doing something international, which wouldn't at all surprise me. Drugs, forged documents, white slavery, the odd jeweled falcon from Malta. Or would that sort of thing be Interpol? Isn't this just a local murder?"

"I happened to be on hand." Jury looked up at the

placid pale blue of the sky, not a cloud, not a patch of gray in sight. "You have a devious mind, Lady Summerston."

"Living round Simon, you'd have to."

"He must have had more than his share of enemies."

"Any number would be 'his share.'"

"In particular?"

"You'd have to ask Hannah that. I've always given Simon a wide berth. I prefer not to know of his exploits." She was still shuffling through the photos. Jury wondered if her squinting over the pictures and in positioning the stamps resulted from her being too vain to wear glasses. "Gerry was dead set against Hannah's marrying him, naturally. The man hadn't even seen any military service—"

Jury couldn't help laughing here. "Not much for him to have seen."

She looked up smartly from the box. "There was the Falklands, Mr. Jury."

"True, but let's not fight it out here on the balcony. Much too pleasant."

She was leaning toward him, squinting again. Curiosity must have won out over vanity, for she drew from her voluminous layers of materials a hinged spectacle case. Looking at him through the rimless eyeglasses, she said, "Are you married? I expect so; all the good-looking ones are."

Jury smiled, shook his head, and changed the subject. "I heard that Mr. Lean worked for a while for a publishing house."

"Gerry thought he should have a job; it would be

less embarrassing for Hannah, even though it wouldn't be a treat for Bennick Publishing. Gerry had a large holding of stocks there, and, I daresay, even Simon could read. He worked in the accounting department; that's the best place for juggling books, I believe."

"Had they friends around here? In Long Piddleton or Northampton?"

She smirked. "Simon had 'friends' everywhere. But not Hannah. She goes into Northampton to exchange her library books. Or to one of the bookshops. She's a great reader. *He* was friendly—so the rumor reached me—with a few of the local women. The locals I wouldn't know, though I'd heard him mention one or two. It's no use—" She was looking at Jury's small notebook. "—I never paid much attention to anything Simon said. Unless it had to do with money. Since any money he talked about was either mine or Hannah's, one had to turn a sharp ear."

"Didn't your dislike make it hard on your granddaughter?"

"She knew when she married him we neither of us approved. Though Gerry would never have cut her out of his will; he wasn't mean and he wasn't melodramatic."

Out toward the lake Jury saw the figure of a woman standing on the bank, back turned. "Is that your granddaughter?"

Her eyes followed his gaze, squinting again. "Yes, I believe it is." She wasn't even looking in the right direction, but she was too vain to admit she couldn't see.

"I think I'd like to talk to her." Jury rose.

"She's got steel in her spine, that girl. It's only been a few hours since that policeman was here. But, then, Hannah always was the picture of composure. Do you play poker?" The cards were being shuffled deftly.

"I'm not very good at it."

"I am. So come back and bring some money."

10

—————◢ As he walked toward her across the lawn, Jury had the impression of an ordinary girl muffled in clothes that were too big for her, as if she were trailing around in her mother's things. The oversized sweater might be, these days, called fashionably sloppy. But she didn't give the impression of caring at all about fashion. Her wrists were bony, jutting out from sleeves that she kept pushing up and which came falling right back down. The skirt was too long, hemline uneven, as if the band listed at the waist. Her body was angular and moved inside the loose clothes like a bird in a covered cage.

But the image of ordinariness was quickly dispelled standing now a foot from her. Her skin had the flawless look of a bisque doll, and her expression gave away just about as much. The mouth was immobile, the eyebrows as smooth and delicate as if they'd been painted. Her hair was very dark and unevenly cut, as if she'd taken the scissors to it herself in a moment of anger. It lay around her oval face in little licks, falling unevenly across her high forehead. When a breeze came up, she had to shove the strands from her eyes. They were hazel eyes that in the portrait had looked gray, but here the color shifted with the reflected light—green from the grass, blue from her sweater. A lack of makeup and the awkward clothes made it appear that Hannah Lean was dressing down, that beauty embarrassed her.

"I'm terribly sorry about your husband."

She turned her head, looked off across the lake. She did not answer him except to say, "Would you like to walk by the lake? I feel the need to keep moving."

Jury nodded.

They walked through beeches, on a narrow path bordering the lake, the water crisscrossed with light, a golden net cast over it by the late sun. Through the trees he could see both the summerhouse and a small boathouse. Two rowboats, one green, one blue, were moored there, bobbing in the wind-ruffled water. Jury could see two men on the pier, two others coming round the side of the white cottage.

"When will we be rid of them?" she said in that strangely flat voice, as if the Northants police were some annoying variety of insect infesting the gardens.

"And here I am, too."

Hannah Lean turned to look at him squarely for the first time. "Yes. Here *you* are." She looked away again, but said nothing else.

Her body was tense, her fingers interlaced and straining at one another, as if she felt she should be able to do something with her hands, make an appropriate gesture, lash out, hit something. Hannah Lean was bearing up remarkably well. Then she said:

"Why is tragedy often grotesque?"

The death of Simon Lean was certainly that. As to the tragedy, her voice bore no stamp of it, nor her face the mask of it. And then he thought of the other thing Lady Summerston had said: that she was masterly at concealing her true feelings.

But such coldness in the face of her husband's bizarre death rankled. Jury had no business feeling this way. It was just that she otherwise seemed a woman with few defenses. Child-like, almost. Perhaps it was the clothes, the young, clear face in a woman of thirty-odd that seemed contradictory. Perhaps her seeming detachment was a form of denial, a psychic numbness.

"I expect you'll ask me the same questions as that Northants policeman."

"I expect so, yes."

"Why?" she asked curtly.

Not *Why must I be put through it again?* "Things sometimes get missed out." He smiled, but he couldn't keep the chill out of his voice.

They were sitting on a stone bench. She leaned

forward, elbows on knees, face cupped in her hands. The movement pulled the outsized sweater down from her shoulder. It was a sensual pose; he could, with little effort, visualize the slim body beneath the clothes that masked it.

She did not object; she did not reply. The lack of response to his implication that she might be hiding something made him wonder. He broke the long silence by reaching down and pulling a forget-me-not from the bank. Could any flower be so richly blue? he wondered, handing it to her.

Turning it round and round, and without waiting for his questions, she said, "I was probably the last person to see Simon alive. Last night at dinner. He was going up to London."

"Why would he be going there that time of night?"

"I imagine to see his lady-friend. He wasn't the ideal husband, as you've no doubt heard from Eleanor. I've seen more than one woman out for his blood after he dropped her. Of course, police would think, including me." She turned, smiling slightly, pulling the sweater back up on her shoulder. Then she looked off across the lake and her voice was doleful as she shrugged and said, "I was used to it."

Jury watched her long fingers, turning the drooping flower. "I wouldn't think a wife could ever get used to betrayal."

Ruefully, she looked round at him. "You sound a little like Eleanor. 'Betrayal' is a rather melodramatic notion these days, isn't it?"

"No. Do you know who he was seeing?"

"Indirectly. There was a letter that came for him from London. E-one or -fourteen. The mark was blurred. No return address. Pale blue paper and smelling faintly of musky toilet water. Do women still do that sort of thing? Perfume their letters? And besides that one, there might also have been someone local. I saw him in Sidbury one day in the Bell, having a drink with a woman from the village. Her name's . . . Demorney, something like that. She's very good-looking, *haute* everything—you know: couture, coiffure, London polish." Hannah Lean looked down at her own costume, as if making a mental match.

"And this letter? Did you read it?"

"No. It's been months ago." She nodded toward the summerhouse. "He'd burned it. In the grate."

She seemed unaware of the tears that had come to her eyes and that were silently spilling down her face. No sobs, no facial contortions, no attempt to wipe them away. Jury handed her his handkerchief and she dabbed at the tears listlessly as if the face were a stranger's.

"Did you see him drive away? Why would his car come to be parked in that lay-by near the summer-house?"

"I heard him go. And he did sometimes leave the car there. He liked to—stay in the cottage. To get away—from us, I expect." Her look at Jury was hard. "The point is, Mr. Jury, that Simon couldn't take too many liberties. I have the money."

"You mean he wouldn't have wanted to jeopardize his position with you." It sounded like a business venture, not a marriage. "Why would you put up with that sort of treatment, Mrs. Lean?"

She smiled. "Why would I? Because bounders have tons of charm. I loved him." She handed back the handkerchief, folded and refolded. "The point is, though, that this time I really felt I had enough. I meant to divorce him. Simon would do anything to prevent that—*anything.*" She turned her placid, ivory face with its tiger eyes on Jury. "When I told him, he was mad enough to kill me."

* * *

Two borders of black tulips in a carpet of silver-white dead nettle led to the door of the summerhouse. Jury looked behind him, back toward the main house. Little of that baroque villa could be seen—only the upper part, where Lady Summerston had been sitting on her balcony.

The Northants police had cordoned off the cottage and the surrounding garden with white tape and a constable had positioned himself in a chair at the door. Sergeant Burn, one of the uniformed branch, had an intimidating build and a granite face. He acknowledged Jury's presence, but looked suspiciously at Hannah Lean.

"I'm sure your lab technicians have covered every inch of the place, Sergeant. I'd like to have a look."

Burn nodded and resat himself by the door, unrolling a *Private Eye* magazine from his back pocket and picking up his mug of tea.

* * *

It was small, almost diminutive, like an architect's model of a larger house. At the opposite end of the living room, which was furnished in country English, were french doors that faced the lake. Off to the left, through the angled opening of a door, Jury could just see the foot of a four-poster, large enough to take up most of what space there was. The kitchen, he imagined, was the sort where two people would have been constantly bumping into one another. Sergeant Burn had apparently been making his afternoon tea.

On one side of the fireplace with its marble overmantel was a sofa, on the other, two matching lounge chairs, all of them covered in a faded, flowery chintz in a rather fussy design of peonies and nasturtiums crawling up a latticework of pale blue striping. To one side of the french windows sat a small table nearly overwhelmed by the four highbacked antique chairs of carved mahogany.

If two people enjoyed living out of each other's pockets, it would be a pleasant arrangement—and with the right companion, the right woman (he thought), wonderfully cozy. From what he'd heard of Simon Lean, he doubted he went in much for coziness, and apparently hadn't found the right woman. Jury looked at Hannah and wondered why. That combination of adolescent dreaminess and hard-mindedness was very fetching. What a word. He hadn't used that one in years.

Here Simon Lean had come for five years, his eye forced to look on the splendor of the villa-like house

in the midst of acres of fabulous, romantic gardens
and pools, wondering, no doubt, when he would be
up there as lord of the manor. It was more a place
for overnight guests, or a place to isolate oneself. Or
the perfect setting for a rendezvous, and his wife
seemed to have been suggesting just that. The
french doors opening onto the pier and the lake
expanded the room and the view in an extraordinary way.

Hannah stood quite still, her eyes fixed on the
corner by the french doors where it was clear the
secrétaire had stood. The bloodstained carpet was
still crushed with its weight. Beside the empty
space were two piles of books. Jury hunkered down
to have a look. They would have had to be removed
to make space for the body. He looked up at her: the
empty square of carpet seemed to affect her suddenly more than any of their walk or talk had done
and she shivered and hugged herself.

Jury said: "It looks like Burn has helped himself to
tea. How about us?" She turned toward the kitchen,
turned back, and smiled weakly. "Would you mind
getting it?" Her look was helpless. "But you don't
know where things are—"

"I'm a detective, remember?"

It was the first truly spontaneous smile he'd seen,
and it was radiant. It illuminated her face like the
sun going down over the rim of the lake, turning it
to a slick of fire.

The kettle stood on the cooker where the constable had left it, and Jury went about heating the
water. Mugs were in the last cupboard he opened;

Burn had left out the sugar and tea. When the water was ready he heated the pot, tossed it out, put in the tea. When he walked back into the sitting room, she was studying a sketch on the mantelpiece beside a small, double-framed photograph of her husband and of the two of them together.

Again, that nervous mannerism of pushing up her sweater sleeves. "I was beginning to feel, well, panicky. In just two minutes." Her laugh was strained as she thanked him for the mug of tea.

He looked at her, said nothing for a moment, and then picked up the sketch. It was rough, the sort of preliminary thing an artist does for a portrait. "The painting at the top of the stairs?"

She nodded. "I don't care for it."

"Funny. I think it's beautiful."

"Then I doubt it looks much like me." It was a flat statement; she was not the type to fish for compliments. "It's too bizarre to be believed. Did someone know that fall-front desk was going to be removed to Trueblood's Antiques? Why would someone . . . hide him in there?"

"The killer might have wanted to make things difficult for Mr. Trueblood."

She seemed to be turning that thought over. "Do you really believe that?"

"It's possible."

Seated now on the sofa beside the fireplace, she had her back to him. He could not see her expression and went round to sit on the facing sofa. "Did you know the arrangements for the pickup?"

"Is that one of the questions you want to see if I'll answer the same way twice?"

Jury said nothing.

Carefully, she put down the mug. "What did Eleanor say? Her memory's none too good, you know." She paused. "Yes, I knew the *secrétaire* was to be collected either today or tomorrow."

Jury held his cup with both hands, not drinking from it, watching her intently. "You said your husband went to London—"

"He often did," she said quickly.

"—sometime around nine, was it?" Her nod was puppetlike. "And did you see him off?"

The smile she gave him was as bitter as a smile could be. " 'See him off.' What a pretty picture. The devoted wife, getting a kiss, waving from the doorway—"

"Oh, you needn't embroider." Jury's smile wasn't as chilly as hers. "I meant, simply, did you see him go? Out the door? Across to the stable-yard down the drive?"

"I saw him leave, yes. I was still sitting at the dinner table and he'd gone into the hall and collected his coat and gloves. Yes, he went out the door. As I was having my second coffee, I heard the car going down the drive. As I told you before." The look in her eyes was steely.

"Where was Crick?"

That seemed to disconcert her. She looked about confusedly. "I—well, he wasn't serving me coffee, if that's what you mean. He was upstairs with Eleanor. Serving *her* coffee."

"That was usual?"

With a sigh, she sat back. *"Everything* that happens is 'usual.' Her dinner is taken up to her at eight-fifteen; her coffee at nine. They chat for a while; the routine never changes." Abruptly, she rose, went to the mantelpiece, and opened the silver cigarette box. Empty.

Jury took out his own. "Here, have one of mine." He got up and lit hers, then his own. "You don't like her, do you? Lady Summerston?"

She closed her eyes, exhaled a long stream of smoke as if she'd been dying for a cigarette all this time, and said, "It's the other way round: she doesn't like *me.* Somehow I think she resents me being alive when my mother is dead."

As she smoked her cigarette with quick little jabs, the tears ran down her face carelessly, as if they were standing in the rain. No sound came from her, no attempt to wipe them away or hide them.

Jury put his hands on her shoulders, pushed her down gently to the sofa again. He himself remained standing, hands in pockets after tossing the cigarette into the grate. "That's not at all the impression I got from your grandmother. If anything—" Jury stopped. He was saying too much.

" 'If anything'?"

What he thought was *She was trying to protect you.* What he said was "It wasn't especially kind of me to bring you here, to the summerhouse, but I frankly wanted to see—"

"My reactions." She set down her mug of cold tea and rose.

That she knew this so clearly made him feel—guilty. He wondered if Hannah Lean didn't have this effect on most of the people she knew. It was, he suddenly saw, a dangerous quality to have. It put people off; it made people want to throw up their hands, figuratively speaking, and let her be. He said, "We understand each other, then." The smile he had meant to be genuine felt false even to him.

"No. No, I don't think we understand each other. I thought we did, but not now." She was walking toward the door, where Sergeant Burn was making a fuss with his chair, assuring the visitors he was fully awake. There she turned and said, "You haven't given thought to the fact that this morning my husband was murdered. I've been questioned by the Northampton police and now you drag me here to see my reactions. My reaction is that the police, number one, have decided I'm the prime suspect—because, I assume, I'm the wife deceived. My reaction, number two, is that both the Northants and the London C.I.D. are goddamned sadists." She picked the framed snapshots from the mantel and let them fall on the tiled hearth. The glass shivered like a broken windshield. "Good-bye, Superintendent."

He looked from her departing back to the small photograph. Hannah and Simon Lean, smiles fixed on their faces that gave no clue as to how they felt about one another. Why had she broken it? Perhaps to symbolize the wounds this inquiry was causing her? In any event, it hardly seemed a gesture of affection toward her late husband.

He cleaned up the bits of broken glass and deposited them in the dustbin in the kitchen and pocketed the photographs. Then he stood looking down at the cold grate. Perfumed blue paper.

Why would Simon Lean have waited to burn it?

"Sir!" said Sergeant Burn, quickly rising and rolling up the *Private Eye*, which he jammed in his back pocket.

Jury smiled. "At ease, Sergeant. Where're the men who were here twenty minutes ago? Have they gone back to Northampton?"

Burn pointed to the left-hand path that followed the stream going in the opposite direction from which he'd come. "Inspector MacAllister and two others said they were going to have another look at where the car was parked. The Jaguar," Burn added with a note of truculence.

* * *

"They're fresh tracks," MacAllister told Jury with much the same truculence, snapping shut his notebook as if Jury were looking over his shoulder. He gave out his information snappily, too—as little as possible and testing the current of every reply to Jury's questions. "New radials, cost a hundred apiece, I'll bet. They would do, with the money this lot's got."

As if he'd said too much, he snapped his mouth shut as he had done the notebook.

"So it looks as if, when Lean came back from London, he parked the car here."

MacAllister tried looking down his nose; since Jury was nearly six-three and the inspector was five-eight, it presented a logistical problem. "Of course. This is where his car *was.*" Scotland Yard couldn't put two and two together. "The ground's a muck-up of tracks. One of them's Mrs. Lean's Mini."

"Oh?"

"They're old ones. That car hasn't parked here in some time. Most of them are the Jag's and the odd lot here and there, could be anybody. If you're checking the odometer—" Jury was walking away up the road slightly to where the Jaguar was parked. "—I've already done. He kept a logbook."

Jury had no doubt there'd be a record. The book in which Simon Lean noted mileage was in the pocket on the inside of the driver's door. He took out a tiny torch, got in, shoved the seat back away from the steering wheel, and ran the torch down over the book. The mileage checked with the approximate mileage between Northampton and Victoria Street. Seventy-five minutes to Euston Station by train. In this car, even less if you were an intrepid driver. Jury added on a bit for the traffic, the extra distance to the E-14 postal district. Limehouse was a possibility. The other London entries covered the same number of miles, and had been made at regular intervals.

"Find anything we didn't?" asked MacAllister, looking up from the cast the two policemen were taking of one of the treads.

Jury smiled. "Well, I don't know. Who drove the

Jag up the road?" Jury nodded to where the car sat about a hundred feet away.

MacAllister's face reflected the suspicion of a man being led into a trap. "I did. Nothing wrong with that; it'd got a thorough going-over, especially the passenger seat, if that's what you're thinking."

"Why would I be thinking that?"

"Why? Evidence he had a lady with him. We found hairs, fibers, the usual, but that stuff's been sent along to the lab."

Jury lit a cigarette, offered one to MacAllister, who hesitated, then shook his head, as if even that would put him under some obligation. "Why do you think Lean left the car here? I mean, instead of going to the main house."

"So no one'd know what time he came back, possibly. Or just because he liked to sleep in the summerhouse. According to his wife, he often did. Liked to get away from them, she said." Given that MacAllister disliked saying any more than was necessary where Jury was concerned, Jury was surprised when the inspector added: "No love lost is my guess. And that wife—widow—cold as hoarfrost."

Jury asked, "You didn't move the driver's seat?"

Perhaps from self-consciousness of his shortness, his *no* was snapped out. Then MacAllister knelt on the ground again and said, "Of course, she probably killed him, so no wonder she's not shedding tears, right? You'd think she'd try to fake it, though, wouldn't you?"

* * *

The voice might have been coming from the marble maiden in the fountain. It said, "I'm sorry," as Jury was getting into his car.

Hannah Lean came through a thin opening in the high yew hedge, looking about in that undecided way of hers, as if it hadn't been herself indeed who had said it.

"I wouldn't worry too much about apologies. Not in these circumstances."

It was as if he'd thrown it back in her face, the apology. Once again, her face took on that glazed look, one of the things about her that had probably caused MacAllister to judge her. "You mean because you've all decided I killed Simon. In cases like this it's usually the wife or the husband, isn't it?"

Jury closed the car door and leaned against it. "You know, you and your grandmother are putting guilt up for grabs. Are you competing for prime suspect, or something?"

She turned to look down the drive. "Who else would have done it? Who else had a motive?"

Jury laughed. "My God, you think we work fast, don't you? It's early in the day to be answering that question. But I can certainly toss out one or two possibilities: the women he knew. Or someone who had it in for *both* your husband and Marshall Trueblood. *Or* someone we know nothing about as yet. But go back to the women. The summerhouse is accessible to anyone, isn't it? A disappointed lover —a disappointed anyone—could have come along that path without being seen."

"But if he was in London—"

If he was. Jury looked at her. According to the doctor, death probably occurred between nine-thirty and twelve. That would not have given Simon Lean time for a return trip to the East End. Yet with all the factors that could affect the time span, there was some uncertainty even here.

And there were other considerations: that the last person to have driven the Jaguar was short, a woman, possibly.

She had been watching him carefully as these thoughts ran through his mind. "You're thinking perhaps he wasn't? In London, I mean? Simon kept a record . . . at least I think he did—"

"Oh, yes. The car had been driven the same mileage as before. On his other trips. The lab would know if the odometer had been messed with, or if any entry had been forged."

They had been standing there, before the fountain, sundrenched from the light reflecting from marble and Italian tiles. Her face lost all of that tint, went pale again, and she said, "Forged. You surely can't believe that's possible?"

Jury hated the anxiety on her face so much, he looked away, up toward the facade of the house, wine-gold in the late afternoon. A curtain dropped. Crick, he supposed, having little else to do, watched from windows, narrowed himself into corners, stood as if about to knock outside of doors. He saw nothing sinister in any of this, only sadness.

How could anyone, he wondered, have thought Hannah Lean marble-cold? He answered her question: "I don't think it's likely, no. The entries all looked to be in the same handwriting."

He would have thought she hadn't heard a word he'd said.

"It's still me, isn't it? I would have wanted police to think Simon had gone to London."

For a moment, he was puzzled. "It wouldn't have been an alibi, not one at least that could have saved you. If you killed him, Mrs. Lean, you could have done it when he returned."

When she looked up at him, her complexion had regained its translucence. Her smile was slight, but Jury felt its impact. "I think it's very funny to talk to a possible murderess and call her 'Mrs. Lean.' I'd think such a dreadful suspicion would at least come on a first-name basis. My name's Hannah; I don't know what yours is."

As she left him, as her small heels hit the tiles beneath in her hurry, Jury saw the curtain fall again.

The dry fountain, the elaborate loggia crusted with sun, the flowery walks and wind chimes, so many flowers they might have fallen from the sky.

And yet an inexpressibly lonely place. Jury drove away.

11

───────────🔔 LOOKING more draped than dressed, Diane Demorney opened her front door.

The former owner, Lorraine Bicester-Strachan, had fit the doorway in much the same way as Diane Demorney fit it now. Both the past and the present mistress had much in common: dark hair, good bones, a haughty tilt to the head, and an equally wolfish desire to get Jury inside. That was certainly the impression he was getting, as she held the door wider even before he'd got out his warrant card.

The house had been completely revamped (as was its owner, he imagined, several times between dawn and dusk). The room into which she led him was now an Arctic glare, where before it had been full of horsey stuff and paintings of driftwood and Cornwall-like coastlines. Yet it had been just as chilly-looking then as it was now, since there are some people who can suck the warmth out of anything. The only thing that had looked lived in was Diane Demorney.

In the case of the present owner, he detected something nearly humorous in the way she'd stuck herself in her setting: it was an ensemble look, the lady and the room, as if one would be lost without the other, like foreground and background. Everything was white—carpets, sofa, chairs—right down to the painting on the wall, which was white on white. What didn't look like Arctic snow looked like Arctic ice; the several tables were glass, with a vaguely blue tint. A martini pitcher and glasses nearly as wide as umbrellas waited on one.

Thus the foreground—Miss Demorney herself—supplied the only stroke of color. And it was quite a stroke, at that: her crimson dress was composed of folds of georgette. From the shoulder-padded top, resembling the hilt of a knife, the material draped across the breasts to an undefined hipline, and from there to the knee, in increasingly tighter folds. It narrowed like a blade, cutting a swath of blood-red across the white walls, as if the room had been stabbed.

As she poured a small Niagara of gin into the pitcher, Jury said, "I'm sorry. Were you expecting a friend?"

"Only you, Superintendent." She filled the cap of the vermouth bottle, poured half back in the bottle, and added this breath of vermouth to the pitcher. "Olive? A twist? I prefer a bit of garlic rubbed round the glass myself. Or would you rather have vodka?"

"The search for the perfect martini, is that it?"

"The perfect martini, Superintendent, is a belt of gin from the bottle; one has to be slightly civilized, however."

As she started to fill the second glass, Jury said. "Not for me, thanks."

Diane gave him a pained look. "God, it's not really true, is it, about not drinking on duty? I thought that only happened in those dreary mystery stories. 'Thank you, Lord Badluck, but I'm on duty.' How boring, though I'm sure Fielding would have approved, had you been a Peeler."

"I'll join you if you have a little whiskey. Pretend it's vermouth and measure accordingly."

She reached round to the end table, a thing composed of glass and mirrored doors, pulled out a bottle of Powers. "Will Irish do?"

"Fine. If you knew I was coming, then you know why."

"Simon Lean. I knew him." She handed Jury a tumbler so wide that the level of whiskey was deceiving. Then she crossed her legs, and the slit necessary to allow for walking gave him a pleasant view above the knee. She screwed a cigarette into a long white holder ribbed with thin, frosty-looking stuff.

A very glacial lady, thought Jury. Intelligent? Perhaps yes, perhaps no. He'd liked that comment she'd worked in about the Peelers and Henry Fielding. In her head, it probably passed for panache.

"As I understand it, you knew Mr. Lean rather well."

Again, the beautiful wing of eyebrow moved upwards. "And *how* do you understand it, then? From *whom* do you understand it?"

"Mrs. Lean says she thought you saw him—rather often. I believe she said she'd seen you having a drink at the Bell in Sidbury."

"Sitting in the bay window on a main street does not strike me as secrecy. Does it you?" Over the wide rim of her glass, she regarded him.

"I didn't say you were being 'secret.' You could be having an affair and nothing secret about it."

"Is *that* what she told you?" She didn't stop for an answer. "Well, Simon was certainly attractive enough, but always broke. I believe *I* had to pay for the drinks."

"What's money have to do with it?"

"God, do you live on a star, Superintendent? Is there anything money *hasn't* to do with?"

"Were you having an affair with Simon Lean?"

From pursed lips she blew a rapier-like stream of smoke and watched it float and disperse. "Perhaps I shouldn't be answering your questions. Aren't you supposed to warn me, or something?"

"Yes; I'm warning you to stop fiddling around and to answer my questions." Jury smiled. "Let's leave Simon Lean for a moment—"

"Let's."

"I'm surprised someone like you'd choose a place like Long Piddleton to live."

" 'Live'? Oh, but I keep my flat in Hampstead;

insofar as 'living' is concerned, I do that in London. One must simply have a place in the country, also. For weekend parties, that sort of thing." She poured herself another drink and drew her skirt up another inch with a casual twist of the hand.

"Must one? Do people still go to parties?"

He wanted to laugh at the instant look of alarm, as if she'd missed out on the newest trend. Then she pretended to misunderstand. "I don't expect policemen have time for them, no."

"So you party in London and more or less slop about here, that it?"

The look was so hard he thought the face would splinter, but it lasted only for the instant it took her to work out that any show of anger would disturb the carefully wrought façade of ennui. Ennui shot through with glints of humor, like the silver ribs on the white enamel cigarette-holder.

When she didn't answer, he said, "Simon Lean?"

The look of ennui back in place, she said, "We met in London two or three times. Nothing serious."

Jury smiled. "Your idea of 'serious' might be different from mine. Or Hannah Lean's, for that matter."

She was well into that second martini, which in these glasses, would make it easily her third or fourth. Jury got up, raised his own glass. "Mind? No I'll get it." He hadn't drunk any after the first sip, but thought the act of freshening his drink (which he did with soda) might make her more convivial.

He resettled himself on the cool white sofa that seemed, like Diane Demorney, incapable of retaining body heat, and asked, "What about his wife, then?"

Shrugging, she turned away. "Well, *you've* seen her."

In other words, one look at Hannah Lean should have sufficed to explain her husband's infidelities.

"She's pleasant; she's attractive."

Attractive? Her glass poised in midair and then she waved it slightly, dismissively, as if Jury's taste in women was to be pitied. "She's dressed by the Army and Navy Stores."

"Mmm."

"The *only* reason she snagged Simon was because of the money. She's got piles."

Jury wondered if it had occurred to her that the only reason *she'd* snagged him was because of the money.

"And I wish you'd explain what you meant earlier about 'indiscretions,' plural." She turned the lazy look on him. "I was under the impression that *I* was the indiscretion, if we still use that word. Are you married, Superintendent?"

"Would it disturb you if you weren't the only woman in his life? Besides his wife, I mean." Thus far Jury knew of three women in Simon Lean's life. There were undoubtedly more. How many women, he wondered, did a man need? All he himself wanted was one.

"He could have had a little something going with Joanna the Mad, for all I know."

"You mean Joanna Lewes? Where does 'the Mad' come in?"

That she absolutely relished giving him this nugget of information was clear: her eyebrows went up, her glass stopped at her lips. "Why, because of her ex-husband, Phillip. Phillip of Spain. You *have* heard of him? Drove his queen Joanna insane. She's the one who calls *herself* that."

One would almost think she'd read history. Jury doubted it.

"Why are you smiling, Superintendent? Brilliantly, I might add. That smile must make women absolutely incendiary. You didn't answer me either. *Are* you married? Or just living with someone?"

"What makes you think I'm either?"

"What makes me *think* it? Well, if you're not, I'm thoroughly ashamed of my sex. As to Simon—look, I know I should have met you at the door with a hankie wadded to my face and wearing an old bathrobe—the distraught mistress, the one left out of things, she who must bear her burden alone. Bloody hell, I wasn't all that fond of the man. Nor would I mind if he indeed had 'others'; heaven knows he had enough stamina for it. I don't like the look on your face. Though I love the look *of* your face. You think I'm lying?"

"If you are, you're doing it beautifully."

"Ah. As long as I'm doing it beautifully, I don't much care what I'm doing."

Jury leaned forward, turning—almost caressing—the tumbler. "And what about murder? How would you do *that* beautifully?"

Her intaken breath was not prompted by fear, he knew, but by her liking for the star role—

"I certainly wouldn't *stuff* someone in a Regency breakfront."

"*Secrétaire à abattant.*"

"Pardon?"

"Not a breakfront."

She seemed amused. "I *do* know antiques."

"So do I." The corners of Jury's mouth twitched. Shallow as she was, and silly, he was developing a perverse affection for Diane Demorney. "How would you do it, then?"

"It depends on the circumstances." She unplugged her cigarette, put down the holder.

"We've got the circumstances."

"Simon? What motive would *I*—"

"I'm not talking motive, just how you'd do it."

"Will this incriminate me?"

Was he supposed to say, Yes, but go ahead? "No. It's just a game."

"Ha! I imagine the last game you played was when you were five." She leaned back and looked up at the ceiling, as if she were reflecting deeply on the puzzle. "First, one wants to avoid *blood*. God *knows*, one wants to avoid it on an Armani silk suit—"

"Was that what he was wearing?"

She sighed. "You don't really think you'd catch me with that old trick? Simon *always* wore Armani, and one of them's sand-colored silk. I merely threw that in for color."

"Mmm. Go ahead. What would your method be, then? Garroting? Poison?"

"Drowning. Just drug him and overturn one of

those rowboats." She leaned forward, chin on fisted hand. The martini warmed in the glass she seemed to have forgotten, now. "I'm telling you what I wouldn't do. I *wouldn't* do something so absolutely bizarre as put the body in a piece of furniture."

"But if you wanted to hide it—?"

"Oh, really, Superintendent. There's a perfectly adequate lake just beyond the cottage. Dump it there. Faster and simpler and safer. A dead body in a *secrétaire* would begin to pong the room up in a couple of days, surely. Although my acquaintance with dead bodies is minimal. As for the method, yes, strangling would do, I expect. The details, naturally, I'd have to think about. I'm merely filling in the brushstrokes, taking the larger view."

"Tell me, though. You've never been to Watermeadows. How'd you know about the position of the cottage?"

She just looked at him. "All you're trying to do is trap me. How disgusting, after I've done half your work for you. Simon *described* the place, of course."

"Right down to the rowboats?"

She sighed. "Oh, very well. Yes, we'd had an assignation—I'm sure that's the sort of word you like—in that summerhouse several times."

"What did he tell you about his wife?"

"Same things all men tell me. A bit of a frump, a bit of a bore—but with"—her teeth flashed whitely—"a bit of the ready. So obviously he preferred to put up with boredom and frumpdom instead of give up the lolly." She stared at him. "Good Lord, Superintendent, you've brought out the shopgirl in me. I haven't used language like that in years."

"You've got a bit of the ready yourself, Miss Demorney." He smiled. "He'd give up his wife for *you,* surely."

He was amused she took this buttering-up as a serious compliment. Diane Demorney did not have quite as much of anything as she wanted to think— brains, money, beauty. "Well, thank you. I, however, didn't want Simon. And anyway, I'm not talking about my kind of money. I'm talking about serious money. The sort that's been around so long it looks specially made for the Leans, like a new wardrobe. *Money,* Superintendent. You know."

"Not on my salary."

She leaned forward so that he could light her cigarette and get a better look at the cleavage. "What do you have, then? Two up and two down?"

"Nothing nearly so attractive. One up and one beside it."

"That must be difficult."

He was glad Wiggins wasn't there to take notes. "Did he tell you anything about her divorcing him?"

"Hannah? Divorce Simon? Don't make me laugh. But what makes you think I was the only local who went to that summerhouse?"

"Who're you hinting at?"

"I'm not about to name names, Superintendent."

"That's obstruction."

"Do policemen really say things like that? Now, if you're absolutely dying for a murderer, I might go along with it for a bit of fun. But how do you like my theory?"

"Seems perfectly plausible, Miss Demorney."

The martini pitcher pressed to her breasts as if she were the nubile maiden about to be anointed, she said, "Oh, call me Diane, won't you? And my theory's far more plausible than what happened, that's certain." Annoyed now, she retrieved her glass, tossed the contents into the fireplace, and refilled it from the pitcher. "I can't imagine anyone's doing what someone did; it simply *screams* for attention. You'd think someone simply *wanted* the body to be found."

"Yes, you would, wouldn't you?"

* * *

Constable Pluck had grown (in his own mind) several inches in stature in his role as Long Piddleton's single policeman and therefore keeper of the keys to Trueblood's Antiques. Even though Superintendent Pratt had been disposed to return them and let Trueblood open up shop, Pluck was hanging on to them as long as he could, the massive ring strung through a loop in the waistband of his uniform trousers.

Right now he was jingling them, as he tilted backward on two legs of his chair and planted his feet on his wooden desk very near Jury's downturned face. "Bit of a cipher, inhn't it, sir?"

Jury was reading what remained of the blue page found amongst the cinders of the summerhouse fireplace. The documents expert at the Home Office lab not far from Northampton had managed to virtually reconstruct the letter. Deducing the size of the burned-off bottom portion from the singed upper part had further enabled him to calculate the spacing between words, working with the few letters that remained. These he had placed in what must have been their original position. The characters and words had been lined up—the word *pub*, followed by an *n*, the rest of whose letters were burned out, followed by a *th*, followed by the word *church*.

"Do you know where Mr. Plant is?" Jury asked, head still propped in his hands, studying the words through the protective coating. "Ring Ardry End, would you?"

That Pluck did not like being reduced in rank to mere secretary was clear from his huge sigh and his being in no hurry to pick up the phone. When finally he got Plant's butler, Ruthven told him that he had gone to Plague Alley.

Pluck returned the receiver to its cradle and said sagely: "I'd let him have a look at that, if it was me. Mr. Plant does crosswords; he's good at filling in blanks."

* * *

Which was what Melrose felt he was doing, sitting here listening to his aunt and drinking tea he was sure had been wetted from this morning.

"Twenty-seven thousand pounds!" She was sitting in the same chair, rattling a newspaper clipping in Melrose's face.

"What's that to do with me?"

"Haven't you been listening? Paid for a *title*, Plant. *You* are worth far more than that!"

"I've never before heard you express such a sentiment. I'm touched." He studied the dregs of his tea.

"Not *you!* Your titles. If titles are bringing that sort of money at auction, think what you could have done with yours!" She adjusted her half-glasses and read off sums and buyers. An Egyptian had made off with the lordship of Mumsby and Thrysglwnyd Manor for sixteen thousand, five hundred. An American had topped that with thirty-six thousand for something that had to do with Abraham Lincoln. "And you simply *gave* yours away." She glared at him.

"Not to an Egyptian, as I recall. And I didn't give them away, I gave them *up.* There's a difference."

The difference meant not a jot. "You could have been *rich.*"

He yawned. "I *am* rich. Somehow the idea of putting my titles on the auction block strikes me as a bit too trendy. Is that what you got me over here for? You made it sound to Ruthven as if you'd run into that pig again."

"Well, it *is* to do with my case." She leaned over to adjust the bandage on her ankle. "I thought you might like to get hold of Angus Horndean—"

Of Horndean, Horndean, and Finch, the very proper and very pricey firm of solicitors that had taken care of the family for a hundred years. Melrose sat back and studied the binestem choking the small windows, then the low-beamed ceiling and the cobwebs there that Mrs. Oilings had included in her live-and-let-live cleaning program. He was merely trying to think of a sensible response to this silly request. "Angus Horndean's success in writing briefs to prosecute papier-mâché pigs is limited, Agatha."

"I should have known you'd take that tone."

As he once again reminded her it was either no case at all or, at most, a small-claims case, the telephone rang. He nearly jumped to answer it and was relieved when Jury's voice came on the line. "Immediately," said Melrose, nearly dropping the receiver in his haste to collect his walking stick and raincoat.

*   *   *

"Pub near a church," said Melrose. "Pub near *the* church." He and Constable Pluck were leaning over the blackened letter. "That should narrow it down to about a thousand possibles."

Jury told Pluck to get a facsimile of the letter from Northampton and said, "Maybe not. It's either E-one or E-fourteen, so we've narrowed it to Wapping, Stepney, Whitechapel, Limehouse." He put the letter away and said to Melrose, "That new pub you mentioned. Let's have a go at the manager, shall we?"

12

—————⚠ THE sign of the Blue Parrot hung hawklike over the Northampton Road. Anyone out for a cheerful carouse might have taken its artwork for a band of gypsies dancing on top of a caravan. Up closer, the figures were clearer, but still life-sized. The Blue Parrot (the eastward-pointing arrow told the driver) was located down a furrowed dirt road that no one would be tempted to investigate except a farmer searching for strayed cows.

" 'The Blue Parrot.' Wasn't that Sydney Greenstreet's pub, the one in *Casablanca?* And the only parrot I can make out is in the background there, sitting on someone's head," said Melrose.

"How does he do any business, then, out here?" Jury studied the huge, bizarre sign, meant to represent one of those cafés full of smoke and beaded curtains, flimsily draped ladies, and swarthy-faced men with eye-patches or knives in their teeth—the sort meant to suggest Tangier and the Casbah—that probably never existed, anyway.

Melrose accelerated and the Silver Ghost ran smoothly down the dirt road as if it were spinning on satin. "He does quite well. He's got all of the youth of Dorking Dean and many from Northampton convinced it's an opium den. No, no, he doesn't push the stuff. It's just a self-fulfilling prophecy, that's all. They go there and smoke whatever they smoke and drink some of his home brew and think they're in Cairo, or one of those places Peter Lorre was always turning up in in dark glasses. The place was empty, nearly derelict for years. I'm sure Sly bought it for tuppence, tarted it up out here in the fields, and joined the campaign for real ale."

The pub lay ahead, a bright-blue-washed, but otherwise undistinguished building, poking out of acres of stubble turned gold by the setting sun. In the strange light, and without the screen of trees through which they had just passed, the Blue Parrot shimmered like a mirage.

Plant stopped in a circular courtyard consisting of almost-buried bricks around a dry basin in which birds were having a dust bath. The silver sheen of the Rolls, a ray of sun sparking its roof, contributed to the mirage-effect. Above the dark-beamed doorway was another sign, this one appreciably smaller, but no less suggestive, depicting a veiled lady with a jeweled forehead and a turbaned man in bloomers about to enter what was surely meant to be a den of drug-laced iniquity. A camel, like an afterthought, was tethered to one side, as if they'd just tied it up for a bit while they went shopping.

"Is this Mr. Sly an Arab or an Alexandrine?"

"He's from Todcaster. Years ago this used to be the old Pig and Whistle. He took down the pig and stuck up the camel. He appears to favor the desert."

An understatement if there ever was one, thought Jury, who was almost ready to believe everyone came here on camels. In the shadowy environs of the Blue Parrot, ceiling fans churned creakily in the cool darkness, fake palm trees were stuck in the deserted corners, and a camel train threaded its way in gold across the top of the long mirror over the bar. Each of the cane tables spotted down the length of the room was adorned with a small, plastic camel that held a box of matches on its back like a tiny howdah. There was also a large cardboard cutout of a camel just inside the door, its hump a chalkboard on which was written the day's menu. Jury wondered if Miss Crisp had a strong sideline going of plaster and cardboard animals. The only thing missing, oddly enough, was the blue parrot itself.

"Maybe he sent it out for stuffing," said Jury.

"Just so long as it's not the special of the day," said Melrose. "Look at that—" Melrose tapped the tip of his walking stick on the chalked-up hump. "It's written in Arabic—well, let's say something that vaguely resembles Arabic."

Jury squinted, trying to make out the translation. " 'Kifta Mishwi'; what the devil's that?"

"I'm having the camel custard myself," said Melrose, wandering to the bar.

"That's 'caramel custard,' " Jury called after him, noting that macaroni cheese was safely there, as were a few sandwiches. He followed Melrose to the bar.

From beyond the beaded curtain at the far end, a tall gentleman had emerged. Not so much tall as long, perhaps. Trevor Sly had associated too long with camels, for he had a face a little like the dromedary back there—long and lantern-jawed, and with a brown, ubiquitous eye whose focus was slightly off-center, giving the eerie impression that it could take in everything at once. His thin hands flopped at the wrists, for he carried his forearms slightly raised, in that sleepwalking way of some people. Jury could imagine him in one of those fields out there, a scarecrow keeping limp watch over his acre. Though from the sharp look, Jury doubted Sly's head was stuffed with straw.

"Gentlemen, gentlemen. So glad. Ah, it's Mr. Plant from Ardry End. Delighted, delighted. We don't see enough of you, do we?" Sly could waggle and *tut* his words as well as his long finger.

"No," said Melrose.

"And whose acquaintance might I have the pleasure of here?" asked Trevor Sly, offering a dead-fish handshake.

"Mr. Jury," said Melrose, looking straight in Sly's eye as if he meant to correct its alignment with the rest of the world.

Jury smiled. He imagined that Plant's own penny-wise speech was meant to weigh against Sly's over-spending, thus keeping a balance. "I'm with Scotland Yard C.I.D., Mr. Sly." He showed his warrant card.

The man threw up his long hands and said, "Oh, God! Isn't it *awful?* A murderer right here amongst us?" His expression did not reflect the awfulness of the situation. It seemed to make him feel quite spry.

"Just a few questions," said Jury.

"And food," said Melrose. "I'm starving."

"Certainly, certainly, my dear people. Now, our special this evening is—"

"Something I've never heard of." Melrose was studying the bar menu. "I'll have it. And an Old Peculier. Mr. Jury would probably like the Kibbi Bi-Saniyyi." Melrose slotted the menu between the mustard pot and the napkin dispenser.

"Roast beef sandwich and horseradish sauce," said Jury. "And a pint of your Tangier."

Melrose frowned. "Then bring me both of them."

"Good choice; I like a man that's adventurous. Are you sure, Mr. Plant, you won't try the Cairo Flame?"

"No, thanks. That's one adventure I can do without."

Trevor Sly was obviously enjoying this badinage, probably soaking it up like his own strong brew, to tell his customers Scotland Yard drinks on the job with the nobs of the county. "I'll just get your food, then." He drew their pints, the stout rising to its feathery heights, the Tangier with only the barest trace of bubble looking flat as death.

Jury took a long drink and nearly fell off the stool. "Strong stuff."

As Melrose studied the mirror-camels, Jury turned to look at the wall opposite. Among the pictures there was one of the handsome profile of Lawrence of Arabia, closely placed to a big poster of the equally handsome Peter O'Toole, a montage that showed him in one scene walking across the tops of a black line of train cars against an endless waste of sand and sky. Trevor Sly must have thought Arabia and India were hand-in-glove, for the second film poster was an advertisement for *A Passage to India*, showing the long caravan with Dame Peggy Ashcroft seated in a howdah wearing that expression of empathy and invincibility that only Peggy Ashcroft could. The posters were side-by-side, the camel-train oddly resembling the line of boxcars; yet though the dark caravan and train seemed to be moving inexorably toward one another, the lines were so placed on the posters, it was clear that Peggy and Peter would never meet.

Jury found this terribly sad and turned back to the bar.

At that moment, Trevor Sly came down the bar with their plates of food and condiments held on his arms in lieu of a tray. Long as they were, the arms could probably have accommodated a service for six. He set it before them, with napkins and cutlery, and drew himself a Cairo Flame. When he sat on the high stool, he could twist and twine his legs round each other like rope. His writhing and churning made Jury think of a restless spoon in a stew pot.

Melrose frowned at his plate. "This is nothing but beef mince and chips. *This* is what they eat in the Sudan? And this other one—" He poked moodily at the second plate. "—is just like this." He prodded the first plate.

"Basically, it is. Too bad, but I ran out of grape leaves, pita bread, and charcoal."

"Can't imagine why," said Melrose, unrolling his cutlery.

"Did you know Simon Lean, Mr. Sly?" asked Jury.

"Yes. He came in here several times. Lends a bit of tone, doesn't it, someone from up at Watermeadows."

"By himself?"

"Two or three times, yes. Once with his wife, once with that writer-person, Joanna Lewes." That he expected this to be quite a meaty morsel was clear.

It was. Melrose stopped pushing his mince around the plate and stared up at Sly. "What? Are you sure it was Miss Lewes he was with?"

"Certainly. I've read all her books and her picture's right on the back." Sly took another mouthful of his Cairo Flame. "I never forget a face; customers like that." He hitched his stool a bit closer and re-wound himself. "It'd just gone three and no one else was here. They sat way over there"—he nodded toward the far corner to a table by one of the fake palms—"and I couldn't hear them, but I'd say she was a bit unhappy. Yes, I'd go so far as to say she wasn't happy at all. Not at all." He twined his fingers tightly while his high forehead pleated like an accordion in his effort to find the cause of the Lewes woman's unhappiness. "I'm not saying I heard anything, mind you. It was just the look of her, see; ever so taut she was, sitting there."

"It was only the one time?" asked Jury.

"That's right. To tell the truth, I couldn't help but be surprised. I mean, she's not exactly dishy, is she? Nice enough, I expect, but he's the sort—well, you hear things, don't you?"

"What sort of things?" said Jury, finishing off Plant's highly spiced dish.

"Mr. Lean likes his women, that's what." His smile was like broken twigs, thin and tiny at the corners, spliced in the center.

"Any particular women?" asked Melrose, who had shoved his barely tasted food to one side.

"I've heard talk of something going on between him and that Demorney person."

"Do you know her?" asked Jury.

"To see, I do. Come in here two or three times by herself. But she never come in with him. Awful cold, that's what I think. Still, I expect that's what some men like." Here he smoothed back his thin hair, disturbing the artful arrangement of strands that covered the bald spot, and went on about Watermeadows. "There's just the three of them, you know. No proper live-in staff, and with *that* big house. Only that old butler and the gardener that comes in now and again for a taste. Lives down the road, here. Name's Joe Bream. And then there's his Jewel that comes in to cook for me when I'm in a bit of a rush. She goes to Watermeadows four times a week and I guess they eat leftovers the rest of the time. Right spooky, she calls it. Mostly she never sees a living soul. The wife keeps to herself and so does the old lady. Jewel, that's Joe's missus, told me once it put her in mind of that horror film where everybody talks about Mother but there's not one. It's just people's souls get sucked into this room, or something."

Jury smiled at the notion of Lady Summerston's rooms sucking up people's souls. "Tell Mrs. Bream that there really is a Lady Summerston. You say this Jewel cooks for you?" Jury made a note in his small notebook. When Sly nodded, he asked: "Then did she cook up this tasty dish?" Jury nodded toward the plate and pocketed his pen.

"No, indeed. That's me does the Kibbi Bi-Saniyyi, and to my mind you'd have to go all the way to Lebanon to get better."

"I'll crawl on my hands and knees," said Melrose.

Jury smiled. "It's very good, Mr. Sly. Very . . . exotic."

Trevor Sly writhed a bit at the compliment and slid from his stool. "It's a treat to serve them that appreciates good food, Mr. Jury. The British stick too much to their roast beef and potatoes. Now, I insist you just try a mouthful of my Cairo Flame." He was fussing about the beer pulls.

"He's already paralytic," said Melrose, pulling out his cigar case and offering it around.

"A mouthful is all we have time for, I'm afraid," said Jury. "We've got to be off." He picked up his notebook.

The strangely thick-looking brew was set before him and Jury took a swallow too quickly. It felt like Sergeant Wiggins's description of an asthma attack: instead of a column of air, his throat felt like two boards pressing closer and closer together. He said, somewhat laryngetically, "A wonderful drink for sword swallowers, Mr. Sly."

Trevor Sly fairly twinkled at that and said, "I've always said my Cairo Flame is better than medicine. Clears up the sinuses better than Coleman's mustard." He snapped his thin fingers.

"My sergeant'll love it," said Jury.

13

THE Wrenn's Nest Book Shop, according to the gold-leaf cursive beneath the name, specialized in Antiquarian Books and Bindings. It was located in the former premises of an auto-parts shop. The façade of that shop had run to a faded green and greasy garage door, always open; a guard dog, always asleep; a brown tub of petunias, always in their death throes, but put there to spiff the place up by the owner, who had considered himself quite a lad when it came to decor.

Melrose had much preferred it to the prettified black-beamed, whitewashed, bow-fronted look of Theo Wrenn Browne's renovated shop. For Theo Wrenn Browne's purposes the placement was ideal, as it was on the High Street and across from Trueblood's Antiques (also bow-fronted, but nicely mellow and real Tudor), and jimmied right up against Miss Crisp's secondhand furniture shop, where Browne was planning a takeover. Two doors down on the other side was the butcher shop, the course of whose trials had been the talk of the town until something more interesting had now come along.

Melrose had nearly toppled on the huge tub of cyclamen and now stood looking through the window. Jury said that the antiquarian-shop owner might know his first editions but he also knew where the money was.

"He doesn't know anything," said Melrose. "Certainly not books, which is one of the several reasons he loathes Marshall Trueblood." The display consisted of blockbuster novels, some British and some American whoppers; one or two "literary" volumes that were Booker nominees; and absolutely no Joanna Lewes. The Stephen King looked thick enough to break both of Agatha's ankles.

"Here's one of Polly's," said Jury, nodding toward the window. *"The Nine Barristers.* Sounds awfully Sayers-ish."

"Well, it isn't. Oh, I think she *meant* it to be, but Polly's not exactly a dab hand when it comes to style. She says she's dried up after that one. I told her to stop being hysterical and get her hair done. There's the new Elizabeth Onions." He pointed to a pair of books, lined up so that one could see both the title and the madcap face of Elizabeth, whose pulled-back hair was wound far more tightly than her plots. He had become acquainted with her books at a snowed-in house-party in Durham and found them delightfully dreadful. He was sure this one wouldn't disappoint him. Since Polly Praed wrote mysteries, he felt he should keep up with the worst of them, allowing Polly's to absolutely glitter by comparison.

"There he is, worse luck," said Melrose as Theo Wrenn Browne emerged from the shadows of his workshop to sit down near the window as if part of the display.

Theo Wrenn Browne seemed thrilled at the entrance of Melrose Plant and a superintendent of police.

He was perched on a low ladder wearing Italian-leather sandals and a silky patchwork shirt. Smoke plumed from his cigar. "Melrose! I haven't seen you since the binding of *Lady Windermere's Fan*."

Melrose sighed. The man did not date meetings and events by the dull days of the week or Bank Holidays, but by first editions and endpapers. Melrose nodded and nearly yawned. The affectations of Theo Wrenn Browne always made him feel like sleeping where he stood. "This is Superintendent Jury. He wants to have a little talk with you." He drifted back to look at the books.

There were two other customers, a woman copying a recipe out of a glossy-fronted cookery book; and Miss Alice Broadstairs, making a shambles of the gardening section. She managed to nick a page here, tear a dust jacket there, as if her hands were gloved in thorns.

Hitting his head on one of the quaint low beams

and barking his shin against a protruding metal rack for paperbacks, he went into the mystery section. Nooks and crannies and a creaking staircase all lined with posters and dust jackets were Theo Wrenn Browne's idea of a bookshop. Melrose would have preferred the old garage. He should have bought it himself; then he could have left the walls perfectly bald and blank, stuck in functional shelves, and called it Basic Books. He could even have trotted Mindy along as a guard dog. Oh, well, too late now. He picked up *The Maypole Murders* by Elizabeth Onions and found Wing Commander Fisher dead in the opening paragraph. So much for the commander's career.

Melrose moved on to headier stuff bound in leather and gold-tooled.

Theo Wrenn Browne was *devastated.*

Or so he put it, when the subject of the *grisly* discovery of Simon Lean's body was introduced. That the corpse had turned up on Trueblood's premises did not seem to fill him with a similar dismay. "Too bad for Marshall," he said blandly, holding a sample of calfskin up to the light, in the way of a photographer studying negatives.

Theo was still on his ladder-perch, and Jury was leaning against a counter not much bigger than a lectern, positioned by the circular metal staircase.

"Did you know him well, Mr. Browne?" asked Jury, turning over a handsomely bound copy of *The Moonstone.*

"Simon Lean, you mean? No. No, I mean,

scarcely at all. Wasn't much of a reader, you see. I couldn't say that I knew him, no—"

"But well enough to know his reading habits, at least." Jury smiled, lay the book back on the counter.

"What? Oh, not really—" Theo's expression was hidden as he fussed about with some papers beneath the counter. Then, looking up, he said smoothly, "I think it was Trueblood told me that, actually. You see . . ." Ignoring his own sign, he lit another small black cigar, and leaned forward, cozying up to Jury's elbow. "You see, Trueblood's been buying up old editions—most of them junk, but one can't expect an antiques dealer to know simply everything, can one?—and consequently he's gone several times to Watermeadows to look over the library. I might say that I don't believe in making a nuisance of *my*self. Lady Summerston's very possessive of her husband's books. Trueblood does rather put himself forward, though." He wiped a bit of stray ash from the counter into a dustbin and continued. "Anyway, I was talking to Trueblood, giving him a bit of advice on a foxed first edition, and he happened to mention that Lean read very little, what a pity to waste such a fine library. The old lady can't read much at all because of her eyes—" Jury heard the beginnings of rancor creep into the voice. "—and as far as the wife goes, well I think thrillers might be more her style. I abominate them myself. But one does have to please one's customers."

"So you know Mrs. Lean."

"No, only him. Simon."

"Did you know him well?"

"Not very." He was looking toward the rear of the shop, rising from the little ladder to crane his neck. "The Broadstairs woman is an awful nuisance. Never buys, only takes notes. You'd think it were a lending library."

"I understand that Miss Demorney was a friend of Mr. Lean's. You know her, don't you?"

The effect was electric. Theo stiffened, the knuckles of the hand holding the calfskin going white. "If you're implying that Simon and Diane were . . . I take it you've been listening to the gossip. . . ."

"Policemen tend to do that sort of thing." Jury smiled. "But I'm not implying anything. Just trying to get relationships straight." And Theo's calling Lean by his first name certainly suggested a stronger one than the man had admitted to—and was trying to hide. "You've got a writer here in Long Piddleton. Joanna Lewes, isn't it? I didn't see her books in the window."

Jury liked the whiplash reaction as Theo snapped his face first to the window, then back to Jury. Jury was looking at the porcelain replicas of Beatrix Potter characters and the stuffed and cuddly versions of Maurice Sendak's friendly-looking monsters, all larded in amongst the shelves to lure parents. "You've got a grand business here, Mr. Browne. I imagine Long Pidd's glad to have a bookshop. A service to the community, I'd say." Jury looked up at a china Tom Kitten and felt just about as mewlish, but smiled inwardly.

Theo Wrenn Browne went right for the bowl of cream, his manner changing from ashen-faced anger to pleased surprise. "I'd say that it's done something for the village. One doesn't have to go all the way into Sidbury or, for that matter, Northampton, which is far preferable to Sidbury. The shops there seem to cater for the newspaper–greeting card–magazine readers. People standing two deep in W. H. Smith's having a free read of *Private Eye.*" His glance strayed to Melrose Plant, having a free read of his own.

Only, Melrose's free read was far more interesting than anything he might have found in W. H. Smith's. He looked from the Matisse sketch to the fresh binding, the floral borders, the beautiful endpapers. He shook his head slowly in wonder. Well, he certainly had to give the man credit, having the nerve to hide it in plain sight.

The several sketches were original Matisse. That would have made it valuable enough.

That Matisse's signature was one of the two on the flyleaf would make it worth a small fortune.

The other signature was James Joyce's. That would make it priceless.

"You don't care for Joanna Lewes's work, then?" asked Jury.

Theo made a strangling sound. "Those formula

romances could be written by monkeys and they wouldn't need infinity to do it."

"But she's very popular. You were talking about catering for different tastes."

"*Taste* is the word. Joanna the Mad's stuff is completely without it." His eyes seemed to take in all of Jury's face, clutching it in their embrace as he leaned closer. "Do you know the woman has contracts for as many as four, *four* books a year?"

"And here I am plodding along on a cop's wage." Jury was studying one of the Sendak Wild Things. "I don't know, I guess I have some respect for anyone who can actually finish a book. It's not easy."

Theo's laugh was shrill. "I assure you it isn't. It took me five years to write *one* novel."

"Nothing ever came of it?" Which, Jury knew, was just the way to put it if he wanted to see Theo Wrenn Browne turn about the same shade of green as the stuffed monster smiling through its fangs like a kid with overbite. How did Sendak always make them look so friendly?

He seemed actually to crumple, to thin out before Jury's eyes. "It would have done, had Joanna had the decency to . . ." He stopped, took another cigar from its metal tube, and lit it.

" 'Decency to'?"

Fidgeting with his lighter with a shaking hand, he said, "She refused to pass it along to her publisher. It's Bennick's. They've a cheap line of romances—"

"There's a coincidence. Simon Lean had some connection with Bennick's."

"He'd nothing to do with editing—accountancy

or something." Theo smirked. "Simon couldn't have edited the *Bald Eagle*, he was that unaware of language."

Jury put the monster back in its windowed box and said, "Sounds to me as if you were on better speaking terms with him than just nodding good-bye."

Theo crushed out his barely smoked cigar. "If you'll excuse me, Superintendent, I must lock up."

Down the staircase at that moment came a child humping along a good-sized book, whom Theo regarded coldly. She was dressed in a blue pinafore, with sturdy legs, feet tucked into dirty sneakers. The crown of the little girl's head was barely level with the walnut countertop and a mountain's distance from the owner, who looked down upon her from his high peak with an appropriately glacial expression. "I didn't know you were up there; thought you'd gone hours ago. This isn't a library, you know."

She neither looked at him nor spoke, and laid the large book on the counter. Then she opened a plastic purse from which she lifted a handful of coins. The book was a Maurice Sendak. Jury thought he had read all of Maurice Sendak, but the little girl's book was unfamiliar. The cover showed a young girl with a face so pale and hair so flaxen that the resemblance to Carrie Fleet made him physically ill for a moment. An open window with wind gusting the curtains and a blanketed baby had produced on the heroine's face a look of piercing sadness.

The little girl, though, looked anything but sad as she fingered the book, and put her money on the counter. Theo Wrenn Browne sighed and, with exaggerated labor, started counting through the ten- and twenty-p coins.

Jury saw that the little girl was watching him watching her book, and, perhaps sensing acceptance, picked it up and opened it to a center page that must have been her favorite, so quickly had she found it. It showed small, gray-hooded figures with black blanks for faces coming through a window carrying a bundle that, on the next page, turned out to be an ice-baby. She said nothing.

"I think the other baby will be brought back." He smiled.

Standing there, still oddly on tiptoe, as if reaching for that strange peak from which adults conferred their favors and punishments, she frowned. For the picture had made her momentarily fretful; after all, the baby had been taken away by creatures in cloaks.

"Maybe she needs to be taken somewhere. For some reason," said Jury.

The girl's eyes widened. Here was a point she must verify against her previous experience of cloaked creatures. Her look was a mix of wonder, expectancy, and a world of clouds and winds that didn't follow any earthly rules of behavior.

Her feet hit the floor, and so in a sense did Jury's, when the thin-reeded voice of Theo Wrenn Browne announced that she hadn't enough money. "You're a whole pound fifty short. Run along to your mum, then. I'll just keep it here for you. But mind you come back first thing in the morning or I'll have to put it back on the shelf." For resale, it was clear. "This is the last one," he added, to make matters worse.

It was as if through the open window on the book's jacket, something had flown from the room —the glimmer of mahogany, the slants of moted light—something.

Jury had the sudden and momentary feeling that he was falling through ice. He was sure, no matter how irrational the thought, that Theo Wrenn Browne could have murdered anyone without turning a hair. He reached in his pocket, said, "Well, mums aren't always at home, are they?" and tossed a pound coin on the counter. He could find no more change and called over to Melrose for the loan of fifty p.

Melrose carefully reshelved the book and pulled out his money clip. He walked with the new Onions over to the counter and thrust a fifty-pound note into Jury's hand.

"Fifty *p,* not pounds."

"Take it out of that," he said, nodding toward the note, while reading of the gardener and the constable raking through the roses of *The Maypole Murders,* destroying every inch of evidence. A police constable who didn't immediately get in touch with his superiors . . . ?

The little girl was having a delightful time, it seemed, more or less surrounded by Jury and Plant. She gazed from one to the other in perfect silence.

Melrose's eye left the page to fall on the child and he was pleased to see that she had been properly (that is, silently) brought up. He even smiled at such golden silence. And he was of course aware that Theo Wrenn Browne would have liked to swat the lot of them out of the store, but he could hardly do that to police or to the lord of the manor. And here was that lord with his money clip.

"I don't believe I can change that note, Mr. Plant," he said with a false smile.

"Oh. Well, let's just open an account then," said Melrose, brightly.

"An account?"

"We can just put the fifty p on the account." Melrose returned to the petunia patch.

Theo Wrenn Browne's mouth was tight as sticking plaster. "Never mind. Effie, just bring along the rest of it later." And with his hand he waved her off.

"That's settled then," said Melrose, wondering if a merger of Austin-Rover and British Leyland went this way too.

Effie hugged the book, ran to the door, circling round as she did so, waved to Jury, and set the delicate blossoms of cyclamen quivering as she ran out.

"I'll have this, I suppose," Melrose said wearily. "There've been eight murders already, and I think it's neck-and-neck to see whether it's the reader or a character who turns out to be number nine." Melrose slapped open his checkbook, and then his eye hit on the shelves on the right. "And that Beatrix Potter figure, there."

"Little Pig Robinson?"

"Yes. With the telescope. Doesn't miss a trick, I'll bet. What've *you* bought?" he asked Jury, picking up the box. "Good Lord." He set about writing his check as Theo, pleased with this last-minute bonanza, wrapped up the pig. "I meant to ask you about your aunt. I hope she's on the mend."

Purchase a pig, and thoughts of Agatha spring to mind, he supposed. "Umm. On the mend, yes."

"Well, I certainly hope she wins her case. Frankly, I've been more than once discommoded by Jurvis. Why the High Street need be cluttered up with pigs and chamber pots is beyond me."

The chamber pots belonged to Miss Crisp, next door. She must have got in a rather large shipment. Cats were curling up in them and sunning themselves.

"Yes," said Melrose tearing out his check and thinking of the tub of cyclamen he'd nearly fallen over.

Jury handed Theo Wrenn Browne his card. "I'll be going to London tonight, Mr. Browne. When I come back I'd like to put a few more questions to you." That should give him time to reconsider his relationship with Simon Lean.

Unhappily, Browne took the card and, more happily, closed and locked the door behind them.

"Must you carry that doll-thing?" asked Melrose. "Couldn't you at least have him wrap it or put it in a bag? Why did you buy it anyway?"

"Why're you so cross? All you did was hold up the wall and read that idiot thriller."

"Not quite all. Theo has just rebound a quite valuable book, thereby reducing its value, I expect; but I also expect it's not one he means to sell."

Jury stopped, his arms holding the big-fanged monster to his chest. He frowned.

"You look absolutely ridiculous; I wish Vivian were here. Oh, you want to know about the book?"

"It would be nice, yes."

"It's one of the most valuable I can imagine. *Ulysses*. Sketches by Matisse, signed by both of them. Matisse and James Joyce, I mean."

"In other words, Trueblood's."

"In other words, Trueblood's. Yes. I don't imagine there are two of them in Long Piddleton."

"It's Darrington's old house," said Melrose, as they turned the corner. "Perhaps there are ghostly emanations, an aura, left by Oliver. Considering that he didn't bother writing his own books, I'd at least give Joanna the Mad credit for *hers*. As she said to me once: 'Steal? From whom? Who in the hell else would write this crap?' "

Jury was beginning to like her already. "What possible reason would she have had for meeting Simon Lean at the Blue Parrot?"

They were now on the outskirts—if Long Pidd could be said to have them—and Melrose said, "Walk more briskly. Plague Alley's just across the way."

"What of it? Agatha's laid up with a bad sprain."

"Even if she were, which she isn't, she'd follow us till her legs turned to stumps."

Before them lay the Sidbury Road, running white between the darkening fields, past a run-down inn placed back from the road.

"What's happened to the Cock and Bottle?" asked Jury. A weather-worn sign sat propped against a rusted pole.

"After the body was found on the road, they weren't doing very much business."

"That was six years ago."

"People have long memories." They were walking up what seemed an endless gravel drive to Joanna's house as Melrose discoursed on the latest Onions. "The killer, or somebody, had to take the stuff out of the trunk—old wedding gown and silk shawls and the usual things one finds in trunks—so that he could stuff the body in." They had come to the front door at last, and Melrose picked up and let fall the huge knocker. "Well, it simply reminded me of Trueblood's *secrétaire à abattant.* The books would either have been there, stacked on the floor, or old Theo might have done the stacking himself. Either way, he was in that summerhouse."

14

JOANNA Lewes pulled open her front door, holding a sheaf of manuscript pages in one arm and a good thousand-page best-seller that Melrose recognized as the one in the window of the Wrenn's Nest.

She peered out at them, trying to push her tinted glasses back on her nose with both arms full. "Just making comparisons," she said.

Whether she meant of the two books or the two visitors, Melrose couldn't say. Before he met her a year or so ago, Melrose had envisioned a writer of romances as being rather plump and peachy, a once-pretty housewife going to seed. But Joanna Lewes was blade-thin and running to gray rather than fat, although he didn't suppose she was more than fifty. Nor was she really unattractive, just a little thin and worn, like one of Theo Wrenn

Browne's antique volumes in need of rebinding. Everything about her was no-nonsense, including her attitude to her books, which were (she often said) utter nonsense.

This was what she was saying now in answer to Jury's questions about her writing, but saying it lengthily as they passed from doorway to hall to study. The library, the former owner used to call it; the only difference in it was that now it looked used. Columns of books and magazines and crooked stacks of paper stood against the walls, and the desk was covered with manuscripts and gimcracks such as a kitchen-frog that should have been holding a scouring pad, but whose gaping mouth was instead doing service as an ashtray. A nearly empty liter of Ribena dripped stickily amongst the mess like a statue in a leaf-choked pond.

She still held on to the manuscript pages as she offered them a seat and herself perched on the fireplace fender. Melrose wished Jury would stop asking her questions about the writing life, as if he meant to take up the quill himself. Standing there as if he had all the time in the world, completely foreign to murder or other nasty business, he remarked on her apparent productivity.

He was getting, thought Melrose, the answer he deserved—one that would stretch from here to Victoria Street and back. For a woman who could be determinedly cryptic, when Joanna the Mad got going, she traveled far and fast.

"Of course, I have difficulty keeping my pseudonyms straight. Ramona de la Mer is for the more exotic settings—Barbados, Montego Bay, Hong Kong, the Himalayas—"

Melrose tried to envision the couple on the cover of one of her books he had picked up tracking through a bunch of mountain goats in search of a guru.

"—Then there's Robin Carnaby; in those the heroines are nurses or doing good work out in the Australian Bush; or well-bred shopgirls whose families have been ruined by something. The other two, Victoria Plum and Damson Duke, I got from jam jars. They're nice for Englishy settings. Ruined castles, country manor houses, et cetera. That's one of the ones I'm writing now: the heroine, Valerie, is an innocent—rich, of course—transplanted American who meets a mysterious—richer, or course—stranger on a plane. A collision, one might say, between two cultures. Although I doubt Henry James would agree, not when it comes to Matt and Valerie—"

Melrose wondered why Jury didn't fall where he stood. He himself slid down in his seat and studied the style.

"How do you manage? Do you ever get your writing-names mixed up?"

"Of course. Once I had Ramona de la Mer writing a hospital exposé where a gorgeous lady doctor of nymphomaniacal inclinations—that was for the publisher who likes them randy—falls in love with a patient. But when I came to the end and realized this was a Ramona book and not a Robin, I simply turned the patient into a handsome Barbadian, stuck in some sand, and that took care of that. Naturally, I don't have time to visit any of these exotic places I write about, but after all, one can see a long white beach quite as easily as a long white corridor, can't one? I am actually working now on an entire new line of Heather Quicks—*that* is the name of the *heroine.* You see, I realized how much less work it would be to keep the same heroine and simply change the plot. Well, a little bit. Although my heroines are largely interchangeable, still this would relieve me of having constantly to go back and see what color hair, eyes, et cetera, each has. A new heroine means different bra sizes or bikinis. One needs a good memory for exposed flesh, but then I have my guidelines to refer to. And also one has to invent boring histories for them—families, friends, background, all of that filler stuff. Now with *one* heroine carried from book to book to book, I'd need only think up some dreadful problem for each story. I'm having her live in the Fens or the Norfolk Broads or Romney Marsh—some sort of place where the possibility of mysterious strangers turning up is increased tenfold." She stared at Jury over the top of her pale rouge-colored glasses and said, "Like *you,* Superintendent! Ah. Now *there's* a hero made to order. Why don't you sit down?"

Jury smiled his thanks, pushed aside a Navajo blanket lying across the back of a wing chair of tired leather, tossed an apple core in the coal scuttle (already filling up with them), and sat down. Then, before another verbal onslaught, he said, "What about Simon Lean?"

A drawn bow could not have tightened more quickly. The question had stopped her cold, stopped all of them—Joanna, Ramona, Robin, Victoria, Damson, and Heather—dead in their tracks. "Oh. Oh," was all she said, looking vaguely round the room, so recently peopled with leftovers from a Pirandello set, and finding it uncomfortably empty. "Absolutely frightful," she went on, tucking a wisp of straying hair back into the bun at her neck.

"Did you know him well?" asked Jury, his face resting against his hand. Casual, almost sleepy he looked.

"Simon? Well, no. No, of course not—"

"But at least well enough to call him by his first name." Jury smiled, as if to say, No harm meant.

Now she was busy tucking up her hair again, the pages on her lap sliding to the floor. Melrose reached to pick them up and she murmured her thanks. "Well, I expect it's because his name's on everybody's lips; I mean, I scarcely knew the man at all."

Jury's smile broadened. "You know, everyone I've talked to just barely knew him, it seems. Except for Miss Demorney."

The expression on her face shifted, but she said nothing. "It's just that Watermeadows isn't really *in* Long Pidd, you see. They've not much reason to come here. As for me, I stick close to my typewriter. An occasional drink at the Jack and Hammer is my social life." As if inspired by this talk of socializing she said, "Wouldn't you all like a sherry?" Without waiting for an answer she went to a drinks cabinet and returned with a decanter and three glasses.

"Invent something, Miss Lewes."

Frowning, she looked up from her pouring. "What?"

"With all of your imagination, just make up a tale in which a corpse is found in a trunk or a closet or, of course, a fall-front desk."

In spite of herself, she seemed fascinated, standing there clutching the sherry decanter and forgetting to give them some. "Something by Ramona, Robin, Victoria, or Damson Duke?"

"Oh, I'd much prefer Heather Quick as heroine."

"Heather discovering a body." She sat down heavily, decanter on one knee, glasses on another. "She could walk across the moor—"

"Fens," said Melrose.

"Or broads. Or marsh. That would be best, I think. I've never been to Norfolk or even East Anglia, but that makes no odds. She could be squelching across—"

"Umm. No, tell it like you'd *write* it. Not 'she,' 'Heather.'" Jury offered cigarettes around. Realizing she hadn't poured their drinks, she did so, in quite a good balancing act. Probably like juggling her various writing names, thought Melrose, taking his sherry.

Joanna was clearly considering Heather's dilemma as she bolted back one glass of sherry, poured another, and stood up, sherry decanter in hand.

"Let's see, now: 'Heather pulled off her wellies; it

had been a beastly tramp across the marsh. She looked round the cottage, the fine old cottage out here in the middle of nowhere, and checked her watch. Ten o'clock. Hadn't David said ten? She was irritated—no, she was bloody *mad.* Had she ever been able to depend on him?' " Joanna sat down on the fender again, and with her eyes closed, continued. " 'Tears began to spill from her sea-green eyes. Angry with herself, she brushed at them, looked at the port bottle, and poured herself a small one. Surely, just *one* wouldn't hurt. . . .' " In her apparent delight that she might have found a new wrinkle in her plot, Joanna smiled slightly and rose, swinging the decanter to punctuate her thoughts. " 'Damn David!' . . . No, let's call him Jasper—"

Just don't call him Melrose, thought Melrose, holding his glass toward the tick-tocking decanter. How on earth could Jury look so engrossed?

" 'Damn Jasper! How long could she let this affair go on? How long would she let him keep taking advantage of her? The promises he'd made . . . Heather's eyes, used to looking out on the world calm and cool as the slate-gray ocean—' "

"Sea-green."

"What?" She came out of her coma long enough to blink at Melrose.

"You said her eyes were sea-green before." Melrose supposed she would describe his own eyes as "sparkling like emeralds." Melrose smiled, avoiding Jury's black stare.

Joanna laughed. "Oh, well, I do have trouble with eyes, hair, and extraneous details like that."

"Mr. Plant perhaps doesn't realize," said Jury, "that distracting comments like that play hell with the flow of creativity."

Melrose saw Jury look at Joanna with real slate-gray eyes, but very changeable gray. At the moment they looked storm-gray.

"Ah, but you do, Mr. Jury."

"Absolutely. I've been thinking of writing my memoirs." He held up his hand when Joanna looked, open-mouthed, about to remark on this. "We'll talk about that some other time. Let's get back to Heather."

"Heather. All right, she's drinking her port, furious with David—"

Melrose bit his tongue. Did Polly Praed work like this?

" 'Heather refused to sit here, waiting. Let him think she simply hadn't come at all. She pulled on her wellies and buckled her Burberry.' "

Thank God she's leaving; perhaps we can too.

" 'She would simply go walk back across the beastly marsh to the pub . . . the inn where she'd booked a room, knowing in the back of her mind that this might happen, that Jasper wouldn't be here. The inn she had disliked immediately; the owner sounded like a gossiping wretch who would go tell the world about her—' "

Who's to tell? wondered Melrose.

" 'It was then that she saw the stain on the carpet. And when she looked more closely, she realized that it was a trickle leading away from the . . . cupboard.' No. . . . 'As she was pulling on her wellies she saw a dark line snaking across the rug from the cupboard. *Blood.* In horror, her slim hands flew to her mouth. The door that had been slightly askew looked *as if it was opening!'* "

In spite of himself, Melrose was edging forward in his chair, and was absolutely astonished when he heard Jury's calm voice asking,

"Were you in love with Simon Lean, Miss Lewes?"

The rug at her feet was thick enough so that the decanter did not break when it slid from Joanna's grasp. It rolled back and forth for a moment and stopped dead. A thin line of sherry oozed across the rug. She looked down at it blindly, then looked from Jury to Melrose and back again.

When she didn't answer, Jury said, "I was wondering how many times he didn't turn up. And how often you went to that summerhouse."

* * *

"But *that* wasn't supposed to be the question!" said Melrose as they walked back to the High Street. Joanna had simply refused to say anything, so Jury had said he would call on her again. Said it like a sympathetic doctor might to a fractious patient. "It was supposed to be 'Was Simon Lean blackmailing you?' Or something like that."

"Why?" Jury looked up at the sky that had begun to darken, at the stars that showed there mistily as if behind a scrim.

"The coincidence of the publishing house. Blackmail or revenge. Perhaps Simon Lean had blasted one of her books a long time ago—"

"Lean was in the business end, accounting. Close to the money, you know."

"I don't see how on earth you deduced all that from Heather and Jasper."

"A shot in the dark. When she gets wound up, even talking about the real world, she seems to forget herself." Jury shrugged. "So I thought she'd get even more involved if she was telling a story. She couldn't help herself. She even had her heroine staying at an inn in the middle of nowhere."

"Like the Blue Parrot. Hell's bells. I *like* old Joanna. I'd hate to think she was under suspicion."

Jury smiled in the dark, shifting the stuffed monster from one arm to the other. "Not to worry, there're no end of suspects." They were nearing the Jack and Hammer. "And I have a suspicion I might find someone else in London. Simon Lean's mistress, perhaps. If I *can* find her."

"You're not really going tonight?"

"Yes."

They stood looking through the amber window of the Jack and Hammer, where Marshall Trueblood and Vivian Rivington were in deep conversation. "He just wanted the money," said Jury, almost absently.

"Joanna's, you mean?"

"I was thinking more of his wife."

"What do you think? Is she the most likely suspect? Isn't that usually so?"

"I expect so," said Jury, watching as Trueblood

collected the glasses and left his and Vivian's table. Vivian was looking toward the window, where they stood in the unlit dark, looking not at them but through them.

"I'm off, then. I'll be back, probably tomorrow. If I don't have a breakdown on the M-1."

Melrose watched him walk off down the shadowed street, the stuffed monster under his arm.

PART TWO

*You owe me ten
    shillings,
Say the bells of
    St. Helen's.*

15

◢ TOMMY stood with his case on the pavement, much as he had stood on the dock at Gravesend. The fancy ironwork streetlamp, made to simulate the old gaslights, veiled him in its cone of light. The narrow, flat-roofed house had been done over in some attempt at Edwardian style; the ones on either side looked like cripples, broken windows boarded up. The first in the line was flush up against a black warehouse, graffiti fading from its slab-like door. Limehouse Causeway and Narrow Street were pocked with such doors.

The address he was looking for was in Narrow Street. Its door had a brass knocker in the shape of a schooner. The house itself was up for sale, but the sign listed as if it had been planted there for some time. And no wonder, thought Tommy. More than two hundred thousand, leasehold. Sadie's place was a basement flat. He wondered what her rent was; he'd have thought she'd more likely be living in one of the council flats across the road. Cap back on, he opened the wicket in the black iron railing and went down the four steps to Sadie's flat, where a pinkish light glowed dimly behind frilled curtains.

He could not understand her absence; she'd known he was coming in late, and she said it would only take fifteen or twenty minutes to get to her place. Take a cab, she'd said; but he said he'd take a bus or the tube. That had made her laugh. Take a cab for once. But he hadn't liked to spend the money she'd sent him on luxuries like cabs—and you always had to give a tip, and he wasn't sure how much.

Now the door was locked, but since the dim light glowed behind the poplin curtains, he supposed she'd just gone out for a bit, gone down the pub, maybe. He lit a cigarette from the ten of Players he'd bought and inhaled as deeply as he could. Tommy hid his smoking habit, not that it was much of one. Aunt Glad was hell on smoking before you were at least eighteen. Why his lungs would collapse between fifteen and eighteen he didn't know. Lungs, lungs, she kept nattering at him. If she ever saw him working side-by-side with Sid, cigarettes dangling out of the corners of their mouths, she'd probably kill him.

Again, he took the wristwatch with its broken strap from his pocket, shook it to see if it was running, wound it though it didn't need winding. Exactly thirty-four minutes he'd been sitting here on the stone step, looking up sharply when he heard the click of heels, which was seldom. It would be another hour or so before the pubs closed, and he certainly hoped she wasn't drinking and forgetting he was coming. He leaned his head back against the brickwork of the enclosure; his cigarette sparked the night as he drew on it. He stubbed it out suddenly, collected his case, and went up the stairs. He knocked and waited, knocked and waited. No one seemed to be in. The only lights were the street-lamp's and Sadie's.

Farther along, where Narrow Street converged with Limehouse Causeway, he saw a yellowish light flick on at the top, in what must have been one of those lofts the rich did up. Probably someone who'd been in bed and got up. Tommy left his case, walked along until he came to the warehouse. He could track the progress of the person up there by the light that moved from window to window, as if it were floating up there like an imprisoned moon. Then the house went dark for a moment until a rainy, rainbow pattern of colors washed over the stair where he stood from the stained-glass fanlight.

She'd been carrying an electric torch; that was what caused the ghostly movement of the light from window to window. Tommy had never seen any woman so good-looking, certainly not as old as this one, who had to be at least thirty, he guessed. Even Sadie wasn't as pretty. This woman was tall and what they called "willowy" and had (at least from what he could tell in the dim light) long hair the color of Altman's ale, Sid's favorite drink.

Smoky was what he'd call her eyes, though he couldn't really make out their color.

When she asked him what he wanted, she frowned slightly.

"Sorry, miss, but that house down there—my sister lives in the basement flat." He stopped, embarrassed because he'd gotten her up.

It must have made her impatient, as if that was all he was going to say. "Yes?" she prompted him.

Nervously, he started wadding his cap as if he were playing an accordion. Bunch, spread, bunch, spread. "My sister's not there, and there ain't—isn't —no one else at home. The thing is my sister—"

"What's your sister's *name?*" Opening the door to arm's length, the hand of her outstretched arm held the door; her shoulder rested against the jamb. She seemed bored.

"Sadie. Sadie Diver. The thing is, she was to be here when I came, and I've been here for upwards of a half-hour, and there wasn't no one else to ask. I'm her brother."

"So I gathered," she said, looking at a little wristwatch. "Probably at the Five Bells. It's not eleven yet."

Tommy frowned too. Ten was late to him; he was always up at dawn, his feet slapping down on cold linoleum. "Well, but . . ." He didn't know what to say or ask. "Do you know her, then?"

"I don't know the name. I may have seen her." She yawned and ran both of her hands back through that old-gold hair, looked at him and blinked. She couldn't have been more bored.

"You mean you think I should go down to the—?"

"Five Bells. But that's not the only pub . . ." Her voice trailed off, uninterested.

"It's strange."

"How, strange?"

Tommy thought a bit. "Well, *really* strange."

"I *mean* in what *way* . . . oh, hell, you might as well come in. Can you fix fuses? All I've got for light is this damned thing." She picked up the torch. "They went out a while ago. But not the whole street, obviously, because that streetlamp's burning." There was a kind of childish resentment in the tone. "*Can* you fix a fuse?"

Tommy was just looking at her. Of course, if you're that pretty you're expected to be dumb. He frowned. "You mean, can I *change* one? You don't exactly 'fix' fuses. You just screw them in and screw—"

"Look, I don't bloody care about screwing *anything*, just can you do whatever needs to be done to get some *lights* on in here?"

She needn't be so sharpish, Tommy thought. *He* was the one who came for help, and she didn't seem to be of a mind to give it. He stuffed his cap in his pocket and his case over the sill and said, "*Any* man can fix a fuse," just to let her know there was a difference between men and women that way.

He wasn't much into what they were calling "women's liberation." He'd never known a girl yet that could change a fuse.

She led him through a room as big as a lake. The huge windows that looked out toward the river reflected the light from her torch, giving the weird impression that someone on the other side was seeking him out. Tommy always carried a small torch clipped to his belt in case of emergencies. There were always emergencies round the house in Gravesend—light bulbs shattering as if someone had shot them, the fridge and cooker breaking down, blinds snapping up as if raised by invisible hands. The light's beam was slender but strong, and it danced on the kitchen's enamel and chrome.

The fuse box was in a larder off the kitchen. He ran the thread of light across the top of it; there were a dozen fuses at least scattered there, different strengths, different-colored tops, probably spent. It was hard to tell in the dark.

"What's this lot, then?" he asked, picking up one and looking at the glass top. She was holding her torch on the box.

"Fuses. They look rusty to me. They were here when I moved in." Impatiently, she shifted the light. "I thought the hell with it and just went to bed."

Tommy shook his head in dismay. Just went to bed. Probably thought little men would come in the night to sort out the fuses and screw in fresh ones. From all the money it looked like went into this place, why didn't she have a circuit breaker, anyway? He asked her.

"A what? Look, you needn't put on that face. *I* certainly wasn't going to stop here all night trying to work them out, putting one in, then another. I had to hold the torch, too."

"You got two hands." Waiting for someone to come . . . In all of this business he had nearly forgotten why he *had* come along. "What time's it now?"

The way she sighed you'd think she was paying him by the hour. She flashed the light on her watch. "Five of. If your sister's gone to the pub, she'll be back soon. Can't you get *on* with it? I'm cold."

Again he wondered at this total inability of women to fix the simplest things. Faced with the easiest of mechanical tasks, like changing a fuse or a tire, or hoisting a sail, their hands turned to clubs. Aunt Glad was like that. She could do anything when it came to cooking or slipcovering chairs, but if he hadn't been around, Aunt Glad would be living in the dark (just like this one) amongst crippled appliances.

"The thing is," said Tommy, "I've come all the way from Gravesend." He squinted down at the little circle of glass and determined that here was a good fuse, at least it looked like. "And I don't see why Sadie'd be going down the pub when she knew what time I was getting—" Lights everywhere sprang up, as if it were Christmas and switches were being thrown all over London.

She looked around, marveling at this sudden display of light. "Well, you're pretty clever!"

Clever. Tommy squinted his eyes in disgust. Sometimes he thought Sadie was the only sensible girl he knew. Probably that was because she'd been on her own for so long. Sadie was the clever one, by half.

"I expect the least I can do is give you a hot drink." She went back in the kitchen, a modern butcher's-block and white-surfaced length of work-space, where she started rattling about with pans.

"I expect you don't have an Altman's or some-thing." He had to give her one thing, she took it in stride, none of this looking him over to check and see if he was old enough. When he sat in the Dol-phin with Sid, both of them smoking, both of them drinking Altman's, he felt comfortable enough. But not if he had to go into a pub on his own, like the railway bar at the station. Didn't *that* one ever stare him practically to bits. And Tommy thought Lon-don would be more worldly.

No Altman's, but she did have Bass. He sat on a high stool, nodded his head in a world-weary way. Sid was cool, calm. Once Tommy'd seen him turn the public bar of the Dolphin pub into sawdust without so much as blinking. Tommy, on the other hand, was always being told he looked innocent as an angel, clear-skinned, eyes so bright they blazed, like the lights that had just sprung to life.

She set about uncapping two Bass's ale and sat down on the mate of the high stool by the kitchen counter. "Well, I don't know your sister—what'd you say her name was?"

"Sadie. Sadie Diver."

"What's yours, then?"

"Tommy."

"You're her brother."

Tommy bit his lip and looked up at a big calendar. If you tried to nail the IQ of this one up there, it'd fill one square, maybe. But he supposed if a person was that pretty, she'd almost have to be dumb. Nodding, he drank his ale and tried not to look at her. Maybe she didn't look the soul of innocence (as he did), but how could she, with those sultry eyes and burnished hair, and thirty.

"What I don't understand is, why she didn't leave a note. That's not like Sadie."

She pulled a packet of cigarettes from the windowsill above the counter, took one, and slid them across the counter to him. This was pretty nice, thought Tommy; being around here was certainly better than sitting on a cold stone step. Though his aunt and uncle would probably argue the point.

"Is she on the phone, your sister?"

Tommy talked round the cigarette that dangled out of the corner of his mouth. "Hasn't got one connected up yet. You know Telecom," he added wisely, recalling some complaint his uncle had made about the time they took.

"Don't I ever. It was four months, *four*, until they did mine." She took a mouthful of beer and seemed to be thinking.

He liked the way she drank right out of the bottle. Maybe she wasn't as stupid as he thought at first. And with the next thing she said, he *knew* she wasn't stupid.

Sliding from her stool she said, "Well, come on, then. We'll have to break in."

Tommy stared. "What do you mean?"

Already she was pulling a black slicker from a peg by the kitchen door, and stuffing her torch in the

171

pocket. "Just what I said. You didn't even try the windows, apparently. And if that doesn't work, we can use a credit card. Have you got one? I hate hunting for mine."

Credit card? Was she kidding? "I pay cash."

"Smart." She let the cigarette drop in a metal bin, and led him back through the wide, glossily waxed room, where she plucked a tan bag from a high-backed chair and rummaged through it, tossing out tissues, cigarettes, loose bills, lipsticks.

"I don't know about this," said Tommy, still talking round the cigarette. "I mean, breaking into my own sister's flat—"

In the wake of bag-debris, she had, in passing, opened a plastic compact to check her hair and bite her lips. Tommy guessed they took any opportunity. "You'd rather break into one that wasn't your sister's?" She snapped the compact shut and tossed it in the little rubbish heap, and went on searching.

Sometimes he felt at a loss. "Of course not; I never broke into *any*body's flat. I guess you have."

"Sure, I'm in the business."

Open-mouthed, he sat down on a row of leather strips that he supposed was a chair. It was about as comfortable as the stone step; indeed *all* the furniture, and there were hardly enough pieces to fill his own room at home, much less this one, had spindly-looking legs and bent chrome arms that looked as if they'd come out of a *Star Trek* set.

Impatiently, she sighed, flipping through a many-pocketed card case. "I'm only kidding. You're looking round like you think you'll find a great big bag with *swag* printed on it. Here it is!" Triumphantly, she held up the plastic card.

On the way out, he said, "Where'd you get all that funny furniture?"

"All that funny furniture happens to be Bonoldo. You were sitting on a chair worth five hundred quid, in case you didn't know."

Tommy didn't. He supposed it must be swell to sit around on her friend's furniture, but it didn't feel like it to him.

The house was still completely dark, the pinkish light glowing in the basement. There were only the two small windows facing the street, protected by an ironwork grille that looked about as strong as lace. He would have to mention this to Sadie; in a pinch he could have taken out the grille and broken a window, but he didn't want to.

As there was no other way of entry on the side or the rear, the only thing to do was to try and get past that lock. He looked around and saw her keeping watch, standing in the same pool of light from the streetlamp, looking up and down the pavement. Her dull gold hair was tucked into the collar of the black slicker, and that and the black boots she'd drawn on made her look mysterious, dangerous even. Her hands were shoved in her pockets.

Tommy whistled and she walked over and down the four steps and drew out not a gun but the plastic card. It wasn't a deadbolt lock, for after a half-minute's jimmying the card eased through and he heard the click of a tumbler.

Just as she opened the door, he was suddenly frightened. It occurred to him for the first time that something was *really* wrong, and he didn't know what they might find in the flat.

Nothing. He let out his breath. The flat looked as if someone had simply stepped out for a while; magazine open on the sofa, mug of cold tea on the end table. Tommy could tell it was a brand-new sofa bed. Everything looked as if it had been taken out of the window and brought here. He saw *her* looking at it, chewing her lip, and could see it through *her* eyes. Even if the weird stuff in *her* place felt hard and looked austere, Tommy could tell that Sadie's looked pretty cheap by comparison.

But she said nothing, just sat down in the pinkish chair by the pink lamp and took out her cigarettes. A cuckoo clock on the wall startled him; from its dark green door in its fake walnut hut, the painted bird sprang out and announced half after eleven.

He sat on the edge of the sofa. The nubby material scratched his rear end. "What's happened, do you think?"

She tossed him the pack of cigarettes, and looked round the room. Then she rose, walked about, looked at the bookshelves, frowned. "What does she look like, your sister?"

Tommy pulled out a snapshot Sadie had sent him over a year ago. Her hair was piled on top of her head; she was wearing what looked like a velvet evening gown, and around her throat was a string of pearls.

She got up, dropped her cigarette, half-smoked

like the others, in the clean ashtray, without comment, except to say, "Now you're in, at least; so you've a place to sleep."

"Well, but I don't know I want to stay here—alone, I mean. I mean, I'm not afraid to. . . ." He was, too.

"I have a friend. I might call him."

He followed her the few steps to the door. "Who?"

Her answer was indirect. "He might know something."

Tommy could tell, from the way she looked at him, head tilted slightly, the eyes half-shut in a considering sort of way, that she didn't want him to know what she was thinking. It was the way Sid had looked at him when he'd said he wanted to come to London.

It was written all over her face that Sadie was missing.

16

──────────── 🜨 TOMMY was dragged from a dream at six in the morning by the knocking on the door of Sadie's basement flat. Breaking the surface of sleep, he felt like someone who'd had to force his way upward against the heavy weight of water.

And the dream he was slowly sloughing off had been about water. A great flow of water bearing dream-images along: Sadie and himself looking out through a watery pane of glass in a house he didn't know, as both they and the house were being borne along in a flood; the two of them floating in a small boat chopping little hard-edged waves, rowing uselessly because the water flow was carrying them. The dream was colorless, a monochrome. Dark gray water, pale house, and their paler skin looking moonlit against the drab backdrop. In the distance, a foghorn sounded.

Thus when Tommy woke his arms were still moving in water-darkness, and the foghorn, he realized, must have been the sound of a knock at the door. He looked around, squinting through a veil of weak gray light that confused rather than illuminated, so that the room looked full of shifting, wavering things, furnishings as fuzzy as the curtain of the kitchen alcove, the room unrecognizable as the house in the dream. He didn't know where he was.

When he realized it was the sound of knocking, he tripped over the little footstool in his haste to answer, the thought coming to him only at the last moment that Sadie wouldn't be knocking on her own door—

Tommy stood blinking at the two men standing at the bottom of the brick steps. They might have come from his dream, standing there shadowy and fixed, yet giving the impression of pursuit although they made no movement.

His eyes widened. Even Tommy could tell police officers when he saw them. And didn't they always come in pairs, like oars? He felt exposed, standing there in bare feet and wearing only this old flannel nightshirt. The two of them were so thoroughly dressed they looked as invulnerable as knights in armor.

They showed him their identification. Sergeant Roy Marsh of Thames Division and Constable Ballinger from Limehouse police station. "Might we come in?" asked the constable, with an embarrassed and shabby attempt at a smile.

"Did you find her, then? Sadie?" He thought if he

kept them outside he might be able to hold back
what he knew, in the back of his mind, was the
truth.

"If we could just come in?"

It was Sergeant Marsh who asked this. Tommy,
for all his thinness, seemed to fill the doorway.
"What happened?" he asked.

"You're related to Sarah Diver, son?"

Tommy nodded. "I'm her brother."

"There's been an unfortunate . . . accident."

Dead. Tommy dropped his hand from the door-
frame and stood back. Dead. That's what "accident" always meant on the telly, but he didn't think
police in real life would actually say it. With the
saying, the two of them, like enormous cartoon
shadows that spring up walls, half covering them,
filled the room. Tommy felt as he had in the dream,
caught up in an unstoppable flow of water carrying
strange images along like household objects: upended tables, broken chairs. Nothing was falling
into place.

The one from the river police, Marsh, said, "I'm
the one found her. I'm sorry."

Marsh was a square-faced, muscular man, and his
voice surprised Tommy, for it was low and soft. It
made Tommy think of the tread of a cat. Slightly
pulling his mouth up at one end was a small razor-
thin scar that gave to his expression an ironic cast.
He was heavy for the small chair he'd sat on, its
fussiness and femininity made even more pro-
nounced by his sitting in it. Ballinger preferred to

stand, propped against a cabinet in which were kept curios and books and magazines.

From a brown shopping bag, Marsh pulled a small woman's purse, one of those things women called "clutches." He handed it over to Tommy, who took it, feeling its clammy wetness. He frowned. Was he being told that this was all that was left of Sadie? Was it some talisman or charm, did they mean? It was wine-colored with sort of snakeskin inserts. Was he supposed to do something with it?

Again from that incongruous bag, as if they'd been out doing the shops, he pulled a compact, snakeskin like the purse, a small hairbrush, a comb, a lipstick missing its top. Sergeant Marsh lined them up carefully on the table, where they lay like ancient artifacts, water-ruined.

The leavings of the flood, thought Tommy, picking each of them up and setting it down again. He blinked. If he shut his eyes and shook his head quickly, they would be gone—purse, lipstick, police. But they seemed determined to stay. "How do you know this stuff's Sadie's?" he asked dully.

"This." Roy Marsh dropped a small plastic case on the table, like a trump card. "This. Library tickets, a credit card—"

Tommy frowned, pushing at it with his finger. "She never had a credit card. Once she bought some stuff on hire-purchase. It's only the nobs have credit cards."

Roy Marsh smiled. "Well, they're pretty common now, Tommy." In that level, soft voice he went on: "We need someone to identify her."

"Thought you had," he nodded toward the line-up on the table, "—with that stuff."

The sergeant leaned closer. "Formal identification. I'm sorry. It's usually done by family. Husband, parents . . ."

"There's no one. There's our aunt and uncle. Mulholland's their name," he added, when he saw the notebook come out. "We live in Gravesend." He glared at Roy Marsh. "You haven't told me what happened." He still couldn't believe anything *had* happened to Sadie, but he might as well go along with this mistake. After all, he'd talked to her only a week ago, hadn't he? Tommy dragged his jeans from where he'd thrown them on the sofa bed and pulled his boots from under it.

Roy Marsh paused. "The body was found on a slipway by Wapping Old Stairs. But we can't be sure it's your sister, yet," he added quickly.

"Drowned?"

Again, Roy hesitated. "No." He hesitated, looked at Ballinger. "Stabbed."

Tommy dropped the boot he'd been about to pull on.

"We found her two hours ago."

"Then it happened last night?"

Roy Marsh shook his head. "The night before."

"Took you long enough." Trying to hedge the raw feeling in his throat that could only mean tears, he took solace in anger.

Constable Ballinger asked, "Do you carry her photo, lad? Snapshot, something like that?"

Mutely, Tommy drew out his wallet, showed them a small, rather cheap portrait-shot of Sadie in a low-cut dress, hair piled high on her head.

"Looks a bit different, sir," said Constable Ballinger.

Tommy stood up. He felt a surge of relief. *Maybe it's not Sadie.*

A tiny knot of the curious had gathered across the street to stare at the police car and the van just pulling up, out of which several men climbed with equipment that might have given passers-by hope that the BBC was doing a special on Limehouse, had the van not borne the insignia of the Metropolitan Police. Except for the action here, the street was deserted and depressing, still basically warehouses, the wide slabs of doors interspersed with little waterfront properties and bulldozed earth. Exorbitantly expensive, the houses still managed to look untenanted and poorly groomed, as if the spirit of the older Limehouse had triumphed. The wrought-iron streetlamps looked out of place here.

Sergeant Roy Marsh was giving his instructions to the crew who'd just appeared, and Constable Ballinger was herding Tommy into the other car.

It was then Tommy saw her, standing outside of her house, wearing her raincoat. In the confusion and shock of the last hour, he'd forgotten her. Then when she started walking toward them, her huge sack of a handbag slung over her shoulder, he felt almost the same rush of relief he had a few moments ago, when he thought maybe the sergeant had got it all wrong, that it wasn't Sadie who'd died, but someone else.

She put her hand on his shoulder and looked past Tommy at Marsh. "Hello, Roy."

The sergeant looked at her, not very happily. "Ruby."

"I think I'll go along. I think I should go with him."

"None of your affair, is it?" His stiff smile was not helped by the scar.

"I think so. I think you could probably use all the help you can get." And as if she didn't notice the flicker of pain in his face, she went on. "After all, you're going to be questioning the neighbors. Why not me? Why not now?"

Roy Marsh was standing by the open rear door. "Second sight, haven't you, Ruby?" He was having a hard time of getting a cutting edge into his voice.

"Clairvoyant. I can take a missing woman, a police car, and her brother being led out and put them together and work out that you might be going to the station house."

Ballinger, in the front seat, did a good job of pretending not to hear any of this, pretending that a strange woman could just keep the door of the back seat open that the sergeant had meant to close, and could also just angle herself in and slide across it.

With Ruby sitting beside him, staring straight ahead, and the door being slammed, Tommy was wondering too.

* * *

The hair was brown, the face bereft of makeup, plain as ashes, barren as sand. He had been going to shake his head—*no, that's not Sadie*— when some tiny ball of memory rolling round in his empty mind made him nod. It was a long-ago image of Sadie's face, right after a heavy rain, when she was drenched and her face clean and pale-looking. But that was years ago. The image formed brightly like a match and then went out.

It had been too long. It looked like her—the white, unsmiling face, glazed over like ice. And yet also the face of someone completely alien, whom he'd never known and never cared about.

He turned away. Roy Marsh had a hand on his shoulder and seemed to be urging him to take another look.

He didn't want another look. "It's not Sadie."

Marsh nodded to the mortuary attendant, who dropped the covering back in place.

Tommy pulled away from the sergeant, walked out the door and down the hall to where Ruby was sitting, waiting. He sat down hard on the wooden bench, locked his arms across his chest, and stared at the grim, police-ocher-painted wall. Ruby, he was glad, asked him nothing, said nothing, until Roy Marsh came out.

"How well did you know her?"

"I'm not sure I did. I saw a woman answering that description in the Five Bells or the Grapes, and coming from Narrow Street. But not recently. Who knows?" Ruby stood up. "Let's get it over, shall we?"

It wasn't until she came back, looked down at him, and said, "I just don't know, Tommy," that he wondered if he'd been fooling himself. He looked down at the snapshot he was as good as hiding in his cupped hands, almost for fear the sergeant or someone would snatch it from him. He'd been waiting for some affirmation from the world beyond the glass bell he felt he was floating in. And now was out of, because it broke.

17

───────── ⚱ FIONA Clingmore sat at her desk wearing a mask of brown goo that hid everything but her eyes and lips, turning the pages of *Harrods* magazine with a wetted fingertip.

"Hullo, Fiona, you could have been Al Jolson's understudy," said Jury. Fiona jumped, slapped shut the magazine, and glared at Jury for his unexpected and unfortuitous entrance into Racer's office at New Scotland Yard. The glare was effective, considering the contrast between the dark green irises, the white eyeballs, and the rest of her face. Her hair, recently cut and silvered, was pushed back by a green band, forcing the usual bright blond curls into gold and silver spikes.

Jury sat down and returned the hard stare with a bright smile. "Well, maybe not Jolson. But you'd knock 'em dead in the Piccadilly station on New Year's Eve."

After her initial shock, Fiona regained her usual cool, calmly drew a cigarette from a pack on her desk, and leaned back in her secretary's chair. No mad dash to the Ladies for Fiona to scrub the stuff off.

The cat Cyril, who'd been nosing at the mudpack pot, shot Jury the same sparky glance Fiona had, as if he resented the intrusion into this new and fascinating look into the world of cosmetic technology. Cyril was no slouch, either, when it came to grooming. His coat had the sheen and shimmer of copper from his constant polishing; it was sprigged here and there with threads of white turned silvery by the morning sun. It was a strange copy of Fiona's own hairdo. Cyril had become Chief Superintendent Racer's nemesis, ever since someone had found him padding through the halls of New Scotland Yard and had handed him over to Fiona Clingmore. Because Cyril could dodge, parlay, and outwit Racer in the chief's devising of all sorts of exotic deaths for the cat, Cyril had become more than a mascot; he'd become chic, trendy, a sort of Platonic Idea of Cat.

"And might one ask what happened to your hols?" Fiona exhaled a thin stream of smoke; she was a study in iron control as she pretended not to notice that talking made the mud crack. "Might one ask what you're doing here?" Not even a finger strayed to the green band working its way up, making the spikes even spikier.

"One might. We had a little trouble in Northants." Jury nodded toward Racer's door. "He can't be at his club this early; it's not even ten."

Fiona was holding out her hand, inspecting the nail art. A tiny fake emerald glittered in the sunlight. "Out on a case, he is. Even took Al with him."

Jury smiled. "Poor Wiggins."

Fiona tried to look bored—difficult in the circumstances, all the while crossing and recrossing her legs so that Jury could get a good view of the rhinestone insets on the black hose. Since she knew she could hardly seduce Jury with a mudpack, she was bringing whatever other bodily components she could into play: skirt above knees, one arm hooked over the back of her chair nearly strangling the black ebony buttons of her blouse.

"What's all this artistry for, Fiona? Racer retiring, or something?"

"Heavy date." She winked.

"I should have known. Too bad, thought you'd like a drink over at the Feathers." He hated himself the moment he'd said it. He knew there was probably no date, and he'd meant only to make her feel better. Now she'd missed a chance with Jury. He could sense the disappointment. Quickly, he said, "Make him wait, then. Come on, one drink . . ."

Footsteps pounding down the hall made the three of them look toward the outer office door. Cyril had his ears flattened back, so it could only be Racer.

"Start typing," said Jury, forgetting that would be a rather ineffective diversion, in view of the mudpacked face. "I'll wait inside wearing a pained look."

When Jury opened the door to Racer's sanctuary, Cyril slid between his feet, streaked snake-like across a carpet the color of his own fur, and was scaling the bookcase set back against the wall to the left of Racer's large desk. His claws were like pinions digging into forensic science, the Commissioner's Report to the Queen, and several other dusty tomes. A government-issue copy of the portrait of the Queen was balanced atop the bookcase, its nail having come out of the wall. Cyril was now sitting behind it, in the dark shadow between wall and painting, waiting.

"What're *you* doing back here?" asked Chief Superintendent Racer, removing his linen jacket and settling into his leather swivel chair. "Supposed to be on holiday. God knows we get few enough of *those!*" A heavy sigh suggested Racer had been shackled to his desk for years, a fact not borne out by the Antigua tan covering his vein-shot cheeks. Already this year he had three times found sunnier byways than Victoria Street, and from the BA ticket-folder stuck in the corner of his blotter, it looked as if he was due for a return trip. Racer was using his office here as a VIP lounge between flights, it seemed.

"Are you off again, then? To the Caribbean?" Jury stretched out his legs, prepared to give him fifteen minutes for the check-in lecture.

"What? How did *you* know? Cleopatra out there been talking again?"

"Of course not," said Jury, who got most of his information from Fiona, her mouth being considerably more fluent than her typewriter. He nodded toward the BA envelope. "That."

Racer grabbed it up, stuffed it in his desk drawer, and said, "One whale of a detective, aren't you?"

"One whale." Jury stifled a yawn as Racer started the ritual lecture about a policeman's life being full of grief. . . .

He glanced up at the Queen's portrait. The frame was moving. Jury watched Cyril's glossy head ease itself out from behind the picture to study the bald pate of Racer's own head. He might have been hiding behind the Queen's skirts, the way the head and forepaws drew in, slid out, drew in again as Racer rambled on. Having worked out that Her Majesty was giving him carte blanche, or diplomatic immunity, or something, he lay down flat, paws dangling over the edge of the bookcase, waiting, daredevil-wise.

". . . and to stop sticking your nose into the business of provincial police, Jury!"

"The body nearly fell on me," said Jury calmly, at the same time helping himself to one of the Havana cigars Racer had been smuggling in from Antigua.

"Next time prop it up and get the hell out! And you've probably deputized that damned earl or duke or whatever he is—doesn't he live in that village?—to do your legwork for you. A policeman's life is bad enough without his using private citizens as partners."

"Sergeant Wiggins is my partner; I came back to get him." He glanced up at the bookcase. Jury could see Cyril was going to sneeze, from the jerky sidewise motion of his head. When he did, Jury crackled the cellophane wrapping from the cigar.

Racer's head shot up. "What's that?"

"Sorry." He tossed the cellophane into the ashtray.

But Racer had too long been competing with Cyril to fall for the cellophane ruse. "He's in here. That is definitely the sound of that cat."

Jury looked all round the floor. "No he isn't. Sir."

"Don't be so goddamned dim; he's smarter than that." Squinting, Racer started scoping the ceiling, then got up and stuck his head out the window.

"Well, he can't be out *there.*"

"The hell he can't. He's a feline fly." Racer sat down again, but uneasily, his eyes traveling to the top of the bookcase and meeting only the jaunty smile of the Queen. Jury could almost see the crown glitter.

Still uneasy, Racer looked round once more, then said, "Just keep that friend of yours out of the way. A fine mess he made of things in Hampshire."

The "fine mess" referred to the occasion when Plant had saved Jury's life. "He's a recluse," said Jury, turning the cigar in his mouth, inebriated with its flavor. "Never leaves the house."

Racer was up, patrolling the room again. "Superintendent Pratt told me the body was shoved inside a chest that was about to be picked up by the local antiques dealer. Well, for God's sakes, the killer wasn't doing much by way of hiding it, was he?" Racer looked down in the wastebasket, shoving his hand round in the trash there. He sighed and started walking again, scoping it as he'd done before, like the captain of a sub, looking out over the close, hard edge of the water and wondering about torpedoes.

The torpedo atop the bookcase quickly withdrew its head.

Jury frowned. "No, not if he or she knew it was to be picked up."

"You can bet your pension, if you get one, it was the wife. You'd think she'd know, wouldn't you?" Racer was pulling books from the shelves and looking behind them.

There was a thin, swishing sound, as if the Queen's skirts had rustled. The frame moved slightly just before Racer wheeled around. "I knew it; he's in here!" He went to his desk and slapped his hand down on the intercom. "Would the Queen of the Nile get the hell in here and get this ball of mange *out! Permanently out!*"

Fiona entered, face pearlescent and seemingly pore-free. Racer told her to call the effing RSPCA and tell them they were out of business unless they came round with a cage.

Jury looked up to see Cyril's back rising, quivering like a diver about to take the plunge. All he'd been waiting for was a sure means of egress.

"Well, they won't come again, will they?" said Fiona.

They had once, three people in extraterrestrial outfits prepared for a rabid cat. It must have seemed rather awesome to them—Scotland Yard calling in the cat-catchers. Cyril, of course, had vanished, in that way cats have of dematerializing, leaving locked-room mysteries in their wake. Fiona had seen him later, outside with the window washer on one of those catwalks, his face against the glass wearing a mashed grin.

Cyril sprang straight to Racer's desk, scooting across it and sending up papers like a watersplash, then diving to the floor and whizzing from the room. One single motion had done it all, from bookcase to doorsill.

In a flash, Jury saw this maneuver like some comic, cockeyed, and surrealistic version of Simon Lean falling from the secretary. Simon Lean, set up and ready to pounce.

18

──────── ♣ "HUMOR" would have been used in its Burtonian sense if one were applying it to Detective Sergeant Alfred Wiggins, who sat in Jury's office ruminating over a row of medicine bottles with the same intensity of Fiona over her mud pots and nail art.

Jury said hello as he gave his jacket a toss in the general direction of the coattree, where it caught and hung as limply as Wiggins's head. "You look like a man who's lost his last Fisherman's Friend." The yellow box of throat lozenges sat amongst the bottles. And Wiggins sat there like an epidemic.

Wiggins heaved a sigh and chose a two-toned capsule that he washed down with dark tea. The sergeant had, bottle by bottle, lozenge by lozenge, made a place for himself in Jury's office. Wiggins's old mates had chain-smoked away until their office looked like something seen through yellow Victorian fogs: crouched shapes, uncharted movements, faces appearing under lights of desk lamps. Jury had watched Wiggins go from gray to moldy green and offered to share this office with him. Jury smoked, but did not invade the sergeant's no-smoking area.

"I've got that list, sir. There's about fifteen pubs and I've ticked the most likely." He reached the clipboard across his desk.

"Thanks," said Jury through the sweater he was yanking off to accommodate himself to Wiggins's controlled eighty-degree temperature. He'd be down to his vest in fifteen minutes. "Aren't you hot?" Jury ran his hand over more than a dozen slips with telephone messages. Two were from Carole-anne; three were from Susan Bredon-Hunt. Over the last year he had been seeing less and less of her; perversely, she had been calling more and more.

Wiggins sat there looking quite comfortable in his brown worsted suit and neatly tied tie. "I'd be glad to turn off the heater-fan, sir." Martyrdom fit Wiggins as well as a cowl.

"Never mind." He nodded toward the clipboard and Wiggins's list. "Which are the likelies?"

"There's the Golden Heart in Commercial Street. That's near Christchurch Spitalfields—"

"E-one?"

"Yes, sir. Then there's the Jack the Ripper, also near Christchurch."

Jury was tossing the calls from Carole-anne into the trash basket, and said, "Let's hope it's not that one; I don't think I could deal with it. What else?"

"In E-fourteen there's the Five Bells and Bladebone—"

Jury looked up. "E-fourteen's Limehouse. What
about the church?"

"St. Anne's Limehouse. There's something else,
here, sir, you might be interested in—"

As Wiggins was handing a file folder across his
desk to reach Jury's outstretched hand, the telephone rang. Wiggins answered, held the receiver to
his chest, and said, woefully, "It's Carole-anne, sir. I
think she's crying."

That didn't move Jury deeply. In the extreme
circumstances of his brief holiday, she would, naturally, need a surrogate cop to talk to. Carole-anne
couldn't get over the romance of living two flights
up from a police superintendent, especially one
over six feet with an "otherworldly" smile (as she
put it, and she should know), a smile that remained
with her even after he'd gone. In other words (he'd
replied), you're looking for a six-foot-two Cheshire
cat.

From the other end of the line came a flood of
details foretelling ghastly events to come. Carole-
anne was telling him, as "Stars Fell on Alabama"
rasped on the old record-player at the Starrdust,
that the Hanged Man had turned up at least half-a-
dozen times, and she hadn't much hope for any
future walks down the Angel with Jury. Exactly
who the mark was here—Jury, Carole-anne, or the
Islington monument—he wasn't sure.

Why was it so difficult to convince Carole-anne
that *his* murder (as she put it), having occurred

right here on earth, on the night of the first of May or early morning of the second—an occurrence fully accounted for by some confluence of time and space, gravity, the rules of logic, and Greenwich Mean Time (in other words, measurable quantities) —why was it that *his* murder should be dismissed as less certain than *her* murder (as she put it), which had not even happened. But *would* (she claimed) at some time in the future (a future controlled by the stars at some universal way-station, some outpost of the planets not accountable to the laws of physics, much less to forensic medicine). The dead body had come to her in a vision or a dream or her Tarot cards, rather than in a seamy London alley.

"The Hanged Man," Jury reminded her, "doesn't mean death, it means life suspended." He was running his eye over the report on Wiggins's clipboard, frowning.

"Well, if you don't care if you see me lying in one of those drawers at the morgue some day with a ticket on my toe . . . !"

"Of course I care, Madame Zostra, but the operative term here, love, is *someday*. The murder hasn't happened yet, and I don't have much evidence to go on except that the cusp of Pluto or something—"

He was having no trouble reading the report as she yammered in his ear that she supposed ordinary police hadn't the imagination to solve her murder. It sounded like something she'd found in a Kubla Khan-esque vision and, oh, how Jury wished that the Gentleman from Porlock who had ruined Coleridge's poem would show up right that moment in Covent Garden and knock on the door of the Starrdust. Unfortunately, gentlemen from Porlock, like cops, were never around when you needed them. Into her voice now crept the best threat of tears she could muster, given she was competing with the molasses voice of Dinah Shore. Dinah and Carole-anne were at this moment living their little drama. Jury smiled and wished that a whole bucket of stars would rain right down on the red-gold head of Carole-anne Palutski.

"Venus! You've not been paying attention *at all!*"

"I have." Jury held out a file folder for Wiggins to take. Wiggins had been sitting there during all of this, entranced. Carole-anne seemed to be able to fascinate men by remote control. Ever since she'd taken that job, Carole-anne pretty much thought she had an inside track with the cosmos. Appointments with destiny—and it wouldn't be so bad if she'd only stop making them for Jury, too—were pretty much crowding out everything else on her engagement calendar. Dentists, doctors, and even getting her nails wrapped had been X-d off long ago. Carole-anne's future was, in a manner of speaking, fully booked. If she'd had as many starts on stage as she had with the stars, she'd be right up there with Dame Peggy Ashcroft.

"Trouble with you is, you don't believe in Evidence of Things Unseen."

"True. I'm having a hard enough time with things seen, much less un."

As "Moonlight Serenade" slid smoothly past in the background, Jury cut off her protesting by telling her gently that the present was all he could handle at the moment and he'd have to ring off.

He did, and turned to Wiggins. "The Town of Ramsgate is one of the pubs on your list. What else do we have on the murder of this Sarah Diver?"

"Nothing but what's there. It's Thames Division's case. They found her on the slipway between the stairs and the bottom of the pub wall. Early this morning, around five. Must have been goddawful damp, I meant being right on the Thames."

"She wouldn't have noticed, Wiggins. Come on." Jury rose to get his jacket and watched Wiggins pocket notebook, capsules, and a packet of evil-looking biscuits.

19

———————♠ "THEY said it looked like a ship with a tall sail coming right at you," said Wiggins as he and Jury stopped for a moment after getting out of their car in Three Colt Street to admire the view of St. Anne's Limehouse. Wiggins sneezed, blew his nose, and continued: "They complained about Hawksmoor's churches for two hundred years, especially this one. Well, he was ahead of his time, that's all." Wiggins held up his hand, squared off between thumb and forefinger, like a painter gauging lines. "Kind of art nouveau-ish, don't you think?"

Jury didn't know what to think. He never ceased to wonder where his sergeant managed to pick up such arcana. "I don't know, except that it's a lovely church."

"Better than Christopher Wren," said Wiggins,

sneezing again. And with this verdict on seven-teenth-century ecclesiastical architecture, he added that it was beginning to rain and walked on.

The bells just then poured out twelve sonorous notes, perhaps exulting in the knowledge that after two centuries of waiting, someone finally appreciated them.

Behind the bar of the Five Bells and Bladebone stood a middle-aged man with a round face and a cupid's-bow smile who bore more resemblance to angel or priest than publican. Actually, he wasn't, he told Jury. He set the lager on the counter for his customer, who paid for the drinks without speaking and who yawned all the way back to the rear of the pub, to a small enclosure whose walls and ceiling were composed of ancient tea packets. There were a dozen or so customers such as the man sitting at the bar, staring at the optics, smoking, and pretending not to be listening.

"Not the owner here, no," said Bernard Molloy. "Got a place in Derry, I do. Just filling in for the owner, who's a bit liverish."

Wiggins was about to open his mouth to offer advice and succor, Jury knew, and he quickly produced the photo of Simon Lean. "If you haven't been here long, then perhaps you don't recognize this man."

But Bernard Molloy was still going to adjust his spectacles, and was not about to take any decision lightly. Here was something to savor, to turn this way and that as if the subject's face would become more familiar by virtue of being turned sideways. "Now, there's that about him makes me think I've seen him—"

The man at the bar, who had flicked a glance toward the picture, said, "You never seen him, Molloy; all's you've been here is a week, and it's a good two month since this chappie's been round."

Wiggins, who'd had his notebook ready at the same time he was staring at the beam behind them and what was hanging from it, asked him his name.

"Jack Krael."

"When did you see him last, Mr. Krael?"

"Like I said, dihn't I? About two months ago." He looked at Wiggins out of eyes like bullets.

"Did he come in often?"

"Mebbe I saw him three, four times." He shrugged and slowly rolled the ash from his cigarette into the tin ashtray. "Wouldn't remember him except he come in with Ruby."

"Ruby?" said Jury.

"Ruby Firth."

A man to his right in a checkered cap said, "Don't she live in Limehouse Road, Jack? Police been creeping about all the morning, ain't that right, Jack?"

Jack Krael appeared to have been chosen as spokesman and guru for the Five Bells. He nodded, tossing back his whiskey. "Same as Sadie." He turned the eyes with black, pinpoint irises, small as currants on Jury. "You must be the fifth, sixth one in here." He looked at his empty glass. "Funny they'd both be living so close."

Jury put some money on the counter and signed Molloy to fill up Krael's glass.

"Bushmill's, Molloy. That Black Bush right over there." After all, he wasn't paying for it. "Pore girl." Krael sighed as if the expression of some sentiment would be thanks enough for the Bushmill's.

Mention of the "pore girl" Sadie drew a few others over to the bar to compare, contest, and redesign their separate versions of who was asked what by police. That there might be a second tragedy to add to the first seemed to perk them up.

A woman who might have been sixty or eighty had slapped through the door to join the congregation. She wore a flat black hat with two plastic daisies stuck in the fraying band and was bundled into so many layers of clothes that it looked as if she'd got dressed without taking off the old outfits before adorning herself in the new. Rummaging about in her massed skirts, she pulled out a dirty sheaf of pamphlets tied with a string and started handing them out.

"Bit mental, that one is," whispered a sallow-faced man they called Alf, "been spreadin' the rumors all over Itchy, she has. Ain't it enough I can't go back to Hong Kong because of them rumors. They know all about me. It's Singapore Airlines that's doin' it. . . ." He drifted off, back to his seat in the tea-packet-lined alcove. But he called over his shoulder, "You been spreadin' the rumors agin, aint'tcha Kath?"

The daisies bounced as she slammed down her glass. "I got no int'rest in what ya done or ain't done, Alf. I got better to do than talk about you. Not with the by-election comin' up." Her voice was a high whine, and reminded Jury of a bad wheel bearing.

Wiggins, Jury noticed, backed off from Kath at the mention of what used to be called, and probably still was by some, Itchy Park. It was a public garden adjacent to Christchurch, in high favor with the tramps who enjoyed sleeping under tented newspapers, bottles nestled beside them in brown bags, guarded while they snored.

"You'll win for sure, this time, Kath," said Jack Krael.

Bernard Molloy's laugh was cut short by a look from Krael.

"How long had Sarah Diver been living in Limehouse Road?" asked Jury.

"Narrow Street. Down there near the Grapes. Said she used to live in one of them council flats—"

Kath broke in. "That's the platform I'm runnin' on. It's them developers that want to fill in the basin and bulldoze anything that don't move and mebbe a few things that does." She shoved her lager glass toward Molloy and gave Jury ten more fliers when he offered to pay.

Jack said, "She's right there. You seen them houses at Blythe's Wharf? Half a million quid them ones cost. Narrow little things all stuck together. People'll pay it for a look at the Thames." He shook his head, eyes still staring at the wall. "Couldn't have earned that in ten lifetimes if I had the job I used to."

"What was that, Jack?" asked Jury, motioning to Molloy to fill the glass again.

Wiggins was staring up at the beam again, and Kath wiped her fist across her mouth and said, "That there's the bladebone if you was wonderin'. Used to slaughter the pigs and such-like below." She stamped on the oak floor and pointed to a sign near the entrance. "Right there's the history." Then she sauntered off to hand out more fliers.

"Waterman," said Jack Krael. "Worked the bargers off the Isle of Dogs. There ain't many of us left, is there? Not with jobs, I mean. The ships stop coming, they pull down the warehouses, raze the land, and parcel it off to the rich or some chain hotel. St. Katherine's Dock, would you look at that now? Big hotel and a yachting marina. Warehouses getting turned into 'lofts' so people can look out their windows and see the Pool. They'll never see what I saw—all of them ships, India, China, the tall red sails, the smell of cochineal—no, they'll not see that again. Common Market." He turned to gaze at Jury. "It's all the Common-bloody-Market, ain't it? They sit round with their fat cigars burning holes in history." His gaze went back to the optics. "On the Isle of Dogs they're putting up a twenty-story building of flats. Probably see a Hilton and a dozen boutiques."

"So Sarah Diver came into some money, you think?"

"Must've."

Seeing that Jack Krael was probably growing monosyllabic, Jury had Molloy refill the glass.

Krael nodded his thanks and said, "We call her Sadie here, but I haven't laid eyes on her in two months. Sorry."

"Don't apologize; you've been more help than most."

Wiggins had come back from reading the sign on the wall. "Butchered them for ships' crews," he said, looking up at the bladebone suspended from a beam on small chains. He went on to give the ghastly details much in the way of the person who finds the sight of a motorway pile-up abhorrent, but who always slows down to get a better view. The sergeant stopped in the middle of his bloody discourse to drink a glass of soupy-looking water, its dark turgidity apparently the result of bits of crumbled biscuit.

"If you can get your mind off the abattoir, I want you to go to Wapping headquarters and talk to whoever's in charge of this Diver case. I'm going to find Ruby Firth."

Any mention of sea, river, or cesspool always brought that pained expression to Wiggins's face. "You don't have to swim in it, Wiggins." Jury hated himself for asking, but he did: "What *is* that stuff you're drinking?"

"Good for all sorts of things, sir. Black biscuit crumbled up. You think these two killings are connected, then?"

"It would be damned coincidental if they weren't." Jury shoved the door open.

"Stranger things have happened."

"Not many," said Jury as they walked out into a thin veil of rain.

20

──────── ♤ Her hair was stuffed down into the turned-up collar of her raincoat and she wore dark glasses even in the rain. Her movements were decisive—the way she shut the door of the police-issue Cortina; the way she appeared to ignore the driver who was halfway out on the other side; the way she simply walked away.

As Jury crossed the old and narrow Limehouse Causeway, he could see clearly the boy who got out and followed her. He was perhaps fifteen or sixteen, thin and rather delicate-looking, but still handsome. A gust of wind tagged his brown hair and, watching him scrape it back, Jury thought he looked familiar. He could not think where he'd seen the boy before.

The car was about to drive off when Jury reached it. "I'm interested in the Diver case. And I'm looking for a woman named Ruby Firth. That wouldn't be her, would it?"

The driver, wearing the uniform of the river police, looked hostile and said nothing.

"Sorry," said Jury, pulling out his identification. "I'd like to talk with you."

The driver's expression changed, but not for the better. The old hostility was exchanged for a new one, better suited to the occasion of having head-quarters C.I.D. minding the business of Thames Division.

"Climb in." He said he was Roy Marsh and the police constable was Ballinger from the Limehouse station. With his head only half-turned and the pretense of a smile, Marsh asked, "Do we need your help?"

Jury studied the profile and the thread of a scar at the corner of the mouth. The profile turned to the front and Roy Marsh looked at Jury in the rear-view mirror. He had eyes like iodine.

"No. But I need yours." Jury took out a fresh twenty-pack of cigarettes and offered them around. Marsh shook his head; Ballinger took one.

"So what's your interest in Ruby Firth?" Marsh asked, drumming his fingers on the steering wheel.

"Who she's been palling around with."

Abruptly the tapping stopped and Marsh turned in his seat to say, "And what's that mean?"

"There was a murder in Northants. A man named Simon Lean."

Roy Marsh's expression shifted. Jury could feel the tautness.

"Who's he, then?"

"You're asking more questions than you're answering, Roy. Was that Ruby Firth who got out of your car?"

Given the look on Roy Marsh's face now, Jury knew he must have been right about the look on his face a few minutes ago. His interest in the woman, Jury suspected, went beyond the formalities of an official investigation. "Yes," was his crisp answer.

"Who's the lad with her?"

Marsh did not answer immediately.

Constable Ballinger, perhaps realizing that the course of the friendship between Marsh and Jury was going downhill fast, broke in. "Name's Tommy Diver, sir. Sarah Diver's brother. Come here just to visit and finds that. . . ." Ballinger inclined his head toward Narrow Street, where Jury could just make out a knot of policemen. "The boy was there this morning when we went round to look over the house. Before the clean-up crew. The Diver woman was supposed to have been there to meet him last night, and never did show up. I guess we know why, now. The lad's bad luck he happened to be on hand to identify the body." Here Ballinger gave Roy Marsh a quick look. Marsh said nothing, so Ballinger went on. "The brother said it wasn't her, not the way he remembered her. This one was thinner, her hair not as reddish, no makeup, plain clothes. It'd been some time since he'd seen her." Ballinger shrugged. "His folks are coming from Gravesend to collect him—"

Roy Marsh had turned to face Jury and cut off

Ballinger. His voice was soft, the kind of soft that sounds like danger, like the muffled tread of footsteps. "We found the body at four-thirty this morning in an old boat covered by a tarp. The slipway by Wapping Old Stairs. We'd been checking the boat to find out who owned it. In the meantime someone'd dumped the corpse in it; it was submerged for a while by the tides." He turned to face the windscreen.

Quite a mouthful for Roy Marsh, who now turned the key in the ignition. Ballinger looked nervous. You don't just brush off C.I.D. superintendents.

Jury wanted to be gone, anyway. Bad enough that Roy Marsh didn't like Scotland Yard trampling through his patch, worse that he was probably uncommunicative even in the best of circumstances, worse yet, he seemed to be involved in a personal way.

Over the engine noise, Marsh said, "You started by asking about Ruby; I thought you were here because of Sadie Diver."

"I am now."

Jury slammed the door and watched the car take a turn on West India Dock Road that would have earned it a ticket.

* * *

"Ruby Firth?"

She glanced from the warrant card to Jury's face and back again. "An endless stream," said Ruby Firth. "Which one are you? Limehouse? Thames Division? Port of London Authority?"

"Scotland Yard." He smiled. "Have you been having a rough time of it, then?"

Looking bored—a look Jury questioned, in the circumstances—she stepped back from the doorway. Under the raincoat now discarded she wore a straight up-and-down cotton frock whose hem met the tops of her fashionable boots. At first he thought it shapeless; then he noticed the cut. Expensive. She was a little too thin, a little too tall, mouth a little too wide, but she was memorable. Her hair was dark gold and her eyes a smoky carnelian-brown that seemed to be looking at him from behind a curtain of fog.

The room in which they stood was enormous, one of those converted lofts Krael had mentioned, the wide floor as burnished and seemingly endless as a ship's deck. It did end, though, at a panoramic window that gave its tenant what must have been a pricey view of the Thames. Weak light fell across old lacquer, when she threw a switch that lit two black, needle-thin torchieres with flat, green bands of light like rings around planets. The fireplace itself was wide green-mottled marble, perfectly plain, the mantel without ornament, not even the usual vase of flowers. The only furniture was a rosewood sofa, on which she now sat, and two modern, Italian-looking chairs across from it, separated by a small lake of smoked glass. There was other light, soft and melting into shadows, but whose source Jury couldn't discern. Hidden illuminations behind moldings, he supposed. She turned on the silk-shaded lamp beside the sofa, increasing the play of light and shadow that marbled the stark white walls. Jury had a weird sense of a Daliesque landscape of which she was the center, a study in contradictions and distorted realities.

Disinterested, waiting for him to begin, get it over with, leave. That was the image she projected.

"It's about Simon Lean."

He had meant to shock her out of that bored pose. Yet her eyes, shrouded still, never left his. Her only movement was to open the clasp of the wicker workbasket and ask him if he wanted some tea or a drink. When he refused, she drew an uneven piece of watered silk from the basket, and asked, "What about Simon?"

"He was murdered," said Jury abruptly, wondering at the self-control of a woman who could sit there sticking pins in material and saying nothing. And then she reached toward a porcelain dish, plucked up two tortoiseshell combs, and pushed her hair back with them. Playing for time, he expected: she must have thought he'd come about Sadie Diver; she would not have expected Simon Lean's name to come up. At least, that was what Jury had supposed. "You knew him."

"I did indeed." Her hands finally dropped away and she settled back.

Jury was a little astonished by the transformation. She no longer looked like a willowy country girl, but like an Edwardian lady about to collect her basket and shears for an hour in her garden. He was annoyed that he couldn't tell whether the serious look she now turned on him was the real thing or the mere mask of seriousness. He could not make out how she felt about Simon Lean's death, nor did she bother to pull from her wardrobe of looks a response to fit the occasion. "How well did you know him?"

"Quite well. But that's history," she said. From somewhere on the other side of an arched doorway came a fluttery sound of music. Harmonica, Jury finally made out. Abruptly leaving her seat, she moved through the arch into deeper shadows.

Jury went to the wide window. Not even two and twilight dark. Below him curved the dark Thames, past Wapping and the London Docks, and he could see Tower Bridge beyond. True enough, it was a fine view of river and city. Yet, he couldn't help but feel, along with Jack Krael, that something was gone, the Thames diminished as the big ships had been replaced by pleasure-craft. That speedboat out there, cutting through the water even in the rain. It fretted the glass, as if uncertain of direction. Spring, yet through the window it looked like autumn's dregs. In a scene in Jury's mind, dateless, snow fell. Like the rain, he felt uncertain what direction to take.

Then she was back. "Just checking on Tommy. He loves that harmonica. It wouldn't be so bad if his repertoire included something except 'Waltzing Matilda.' If you were talking to the Thames police out there, you obviously know about his sister." She threaded a needle, bit off the end of the thread.

"Yes. I'm wondering about the connection."

" 'Connection'?"

"Come on, Miss Firth." Even if Simon Lean was, as his family said, a "bounder," he thought the man at least merited some mild display of bereavement, even a feigned display. He lit a cigarette, tossed the match in a fragile ashtray. "The body of Simon Lean was found yesterday midday in a village near the Summerston estate. The body of Sadie Diver was found this morning around five by Wapping Old Stairs. But they both appeared to have been murdered within hours of one another. She lived in Narrow Street, was seen in the same pub as you've gone to. You've just been back from helping to identify the body, haven't you?" The question was rhetorical. "I'd have to be pretty dim not to think those two killings were connected."

Ruby inclined her head slightly, as if memorizing his face. "You don't look dim at all, Superintendent. But I'm not the connection."

"What were you doing two nights ago?"

She looked round the loft as if some reminder might be written on its wall. "Out. Doing my own little pub crawl."

"Where'd you crawl?"

Again, the pause. "Prospect of Whitby, for one."

There was silence. Jury said, "The Prospect of Whitby is pretty near Wapping Old Stairs. Where else?"

Ruby set down the black obelisk of table lighter with which she'd quickly lit a cigarette. She gave Jury a long look over a long stream of smoke. "Town of Ramsgate."

Another silence. "That's even closer, wouldn't you say?"

She didn't say.

"And you were alone?"

She didn't answer.

"Puts you in a bit of a spot."

When she refused to respond, Jury asked, "When did you last see Simon Lean?"

She shrugged. "About two months ago."

"Where?"

There was a pause as she frowned slightly. "The Five Bells, I expect. It's in Three Colt—"

"I've been there. How did you meet?"

"In my shop. I've a decorating business in South Kensington. Walk-down basement type, but I've a reputation. I'm the citified Laura Ashley, for one thing." Her smile was sardonic as she held up the silk. "Interior decoration is my real line. I did this flat." There was humor in her glance. "Which you don't care for." She tilted her head, regarding him. "I'm sure your own house is quite nice. Suburbs or rhuburbs, Amersham, Chalfont St. Giles. Chintz and huge leafy trees. Pastel woodwork and sprigged wallpaper. Neat as a pin."

"I live in a flat and it looks like hell. How often did you see him?"

"Mmm. Once a week, perhaps. Whenever he was in London." Her voice was flat, expressionless.

"Hard to believe you were in love with him. You seem totally unmoved by his death."

"I wasn't in love with him. And I've been jarred

enough in the last twenty-four hours that I feel a little dead."

"Did Simon Lean know Sadie Diver?"

"I couldn't say."

"Mightn't they have met? Perhaps in the Five Bells? It would certainly have been possible."

She shrugged. "Not that I know of. I've already told you—"

"What about Roy Marsh?"

That *did* unnerve her, enough so that she rose from the sofa and started messing about in a drinks cabinet, rattling bottles. Behind him, her voice said, "I could use a drink. Sure you won't join me Superintendent?"

"No."

Now with her customary composure and a balloon glass with a tot of brandy, she reseated herself. "You're talking about the sergeant?"

"About him and with him. I get the feeling you know him well."

"Yes. Dead bodies aren't all that common in Limehouse Causeway. Or Wapping, to be more exact."

"And did Sergeant Marsh know Simon Lean?"

The whole of her drink went down in one gulp. "They'd met."

Jury smiled. She didn't. The look she flashed him was the first real glint of feeling he'd seen.

"How long had Sadie had that flat?"

"I've no idea. I didn't know her, except to see—or could have done, I should say."

"Then why would Sergeant Marsh ask you to help in the identification? You didn't know her."

"He didn't ask. I thought Tommy should have someone along."

"What do you know about Mrs. Lean? Meaning, what did he tell you?"

"Very little; I don't like men talking about their wives. Simon apparently doesn't mind talking. Did his wife tell you about me?"

"Not really." From his pocket Jury took the copy of the charred letter. "This did, such as it is."

Ruby glanced at the pieced-up bits. "I didn't write Simon letters."

"Mrs. Lean remembered the postmark as E-one or E-fourteen."

Her tone was dry, but her expression more relaxed as she said, "Now that's interesting. Does she do number plates, too?" She handed the letter back to Jury.

"Tell me about the brother."

"He just came for a visit. Her flat was locked, and it was strange, since she was expecting him. So I helped him get in."

In the distance, Jury heard the tread of feet. "How'd you do that, then?"

"With a credit card."

His smile broadened. "My, my." Jury looked up then to see the boy hesitating in the shadowed archway.

His eyes were the shade of brown of the tea packets that lined the rear room of the Five Bells, looked old like them, and worn, and at the moment, the skin beneath was puffed. His lusterless brown hair was uncombed, his shirt wrinkled, shoved carelessly into the jeans. Whatever sense of loss was missing in Ruby Firth was present in Tommy Diver.

Ruby told him to come in. She introduced Jury, picked up her workbasket, and left the room. Tommy's face, which had looked indecisive and antique, the face of an old person who was unsure of his welcome and made fragile with the knowledge of it, took on a momentary liveliness; it was, despite everything, a handsome face. And it could reflect even now that youthful excitement Jury had seen before in kids that they were being taken notice of by Scotland Yard. Maybe their mums and dads wouldn't spare them a tuppence worth of time, but Scotland Yard could actually sit and talk.

When Jury rose and shook his hand, Tommy seemed to search about for a response more sophisticated than the *hello* he came up with before he stumbled a bit, moving backwards to one of the sleekly modern chairs.

"That must not have been fun this morning," said Jury.

His answer to this was oblique and defensive. "Look, I'd know my own sister, wouldn't I? You don't forget your own sister." He pulled the harmonica from his pocket, started fooling with it, apparently embarrassed by this answer to an unasked question. "The police said Aunt Glad and Uncle John are coming up from Gravesend. I expect I'll catch it, now."

"Aunts aren't much for listening. I had one, too."
It was true; she'd never been one for listening to
troubles, either, which was what Tommy Diver
meant. "I can always come back; we can always talk
later. Do you play that?" Jury nodded at the harmonica.

Tommy's eyes grew brighter. They no longer had
the dull look of the tea packets, but the patina of
antique brass. "Too much, Ruby said. Want me to
play something?"

Jury felt again that queer sense of déjà vu. He'd
seen the boy somewhere before. "Of course. I
haven't heard one in years."

He ran up and down the instrument, an old one
and without much nuance, and then played "Waltzing Matilda" like a dirge. It was beautiful.

Not only could he talk about his sister, he could
talk at great length: he'd been waiting for someone
to talk *to* since Marsh and Ballinger had picked him
up that morning. Ruby? Oh, Ruby was all right, but
it wasn't the same thing, was it?

Inwardly, Jury smiled, since he wasn't exactly
sure how he himself fit into the category of "same
things." But he was more than willing to sit there
for over a half an hour and listen to Tommy talk
about Sadie. They'd been very close, the boy had
said. That's what surprised Jury about the last five
years. "You haven't seen her, Tommy. Why?"

For a while, he was silent, watching the painted
coals in the hearth lick upward through the imitation logs. He sighed. "It's Uncle John. Mullholland's

their name. He never did much like Sadie, thought she was a bad lot, and when she just packed up and left, you'd've thought she'd made a pact with the devil, or something. She went to London. They didn't even like me getting her phone calls." Nodding toward the packet of cigarettes, he said, "Mind?"

Jury took one for himself and put the packet on the table by Tommy's chair. "Did you ever try and talk to them about her?"

"No. He wouldn't've, anyway." Tommy looked at Jury bleakly. "When you're eleven, you don't ask a lot of questions. Not if there's no place else to go."

"I know," said Jury.

Tommy Diver looked at him with just the ghost of a smile. "Sounds like maybe you had an uncle, too."

"But not a sister. . . ." He wished he hadn't said that when the smile disappeared. Quickly, Jury asked, "How was it, then, they let you come to London?"

"They didn't. Said I was just going to spend a couple of nights with my friend, Sid. He works one of the tugs. He's great, Sid is. Sadie sent me some money. Told me I was to buy a fine suit of clothes to wear to Sunday mass, or wherever. Well, I hadn't much use for Sunday clothes; I bought this." He pulled a leather jacket from the back of the chair, handling it as if it were made of beaten gold. "Always wanted one."

"I'm glad you got one. Your sister must have been doing pretty well to send you that."

"Not until a couple of months ago. It was then she

came into some money. Won the pools, she said."
He cleared his throat, bent his head over his jacket,
which he smoothed as a woman might have an er-
mine coat.

And he didn't believe his sister had won the
pools, either. "Go on."

"The idea was, I was to come to London someday.
Leave Gravesend and see what I could do for myself here in London. I said, 'Why not now?' and she
said no, I was to come after she'd found a larger
place. Said things were looking very good—" He
stopped and ran his hand over the jacket, as if in its
feel and scent there were something of Sadie.

But things hadn't looked good at all for Sadie
Diver. "So you came anyway?"

He nodded. "But this was just for the two days.
And it took some talking to get her to agree." The
flickering smile appeared again. "I could always talk
Sadie round. Even if she was too clever by half."

"And she said she'd meet you at her flat."

"That's right." He sat back with a lurch, as if the
cold fingers of death had pushed him.

Jury got out of his chair, left the cigarettes on the
table by Tommy, and said, "We can talk again." He
disliked bringing it up, but he had to: "A person can
change a lot in five years, Tommy."

There was a long pause. Tommy shifted uncomfortably, frowned, shrugged, shook his head a little,
as if in these sudden and jittery little movements he
could find what he was looking for. "Sadie was a
flashy dresser, she wouldn't have been caught dead
in that old coat—"

He lowered his head over the new jacket; he shoved it from him in the way of the guilty man who's made someone pay very dear for him to have it.

"Don't even think it," said Jury, his tone as hard as he could make it.

21

────────🔔 WAPPING Old Stairs was a double set of steps, the ancient part now little more than a downward slope of lichen-green, mossy stone, through which one could just make out the outlines of steps going down. The other set was newer and usable. The slipway lay in the cavernous declivity formed by the two high walls, one of them the high side of a waterfront pub called the Town of Ramsgate. The manager of the pub wasn't terribly enthusiastic about the street's being cordoned off by police; yet, he might have been enthusiastic about the murder, since there wouldn't be standing room inside once the curious were permitted to shoulder up to the bar and ask questions.

Unfortunately, few questions could be answered, since the pub had closed at eleven and no one had seen or heard anything that was very helpful to the

Thames police, over a dozen of whom were now fanning out up and down Wapping High Street. Several hours previously, there had been several dozen.

From his vantage point on Wapping Old Stairs, Wiggins was looking over at the water-markings left on the side of the pub. He asked Roy Marsh a question about the tides. Jury was standing beside Marsh, both of them trying to keep their purchase on the slanting slipway between the steps and the tall side of the Town of Ramsgate. There wasn't much room here, barely enough for the dinghy in which the corpse had been found.

"If it hadn't been moored, the tide would have dragged it out."

Wiggins turned an anxious face in the direction of the water nearly close enough to seep into his shoes. He took three steps back and up the stairs.

"Where'd the boat come from?"

"Don't know. It's in bad shape; someone could simply have left it here just to get rid of it. It's moored at the launch at headquarters. We're checking, but I have an idea we won't be getting far on that one. She was under a tarp. She died from the stab wounds."

Jury was hunched down looking at the chalked outline of the boat, the chalk itself partially washed away, the pinioned string loosened slightly from the wet.

Roy Marsh looked up the narrow conduit of stair-steps to the street. "In dead dark, and with the pub closed, it would be a secluded place, wouldn't it? If she'd been walking along up there"—he nodded toward the street—"anyone could have dragged her down these steps."

"Do you really think it was a stranger?" Jury was looking out across the Thames, watching a speed-boat zip by, leaving smaller, quieter craft bobbing in its wake, people out after the rain, enjoying the mild weather. Small pleasure-craft dotted the wa-ter. Again he thought of what it must have been once—the black hulls of ships, the russet sails nearly blocking out the sight of Southwark. Now, on the other side of the river, the dark horizon of the Sur-rey docks rose against an orange-streaked sky.

"Why wouldn't it be a stranger? Seems obvious."

Jury could hear the belligerence, could feel the sergeant's eyes boring into him. His answer was oblique: "The way the body was left. Why leave it in a secured boat? Why not let it slide into the water?"

When Marsh opened his mouth, probably to re-ject the theory that Sadie Diver was killed by some-one who knew her, Jury went on: "Perhaps some-one wanted her to come here, a half-hour walk from Limehouse—"

"Twenty minutes. You think they wanted to get her away from her own neighborhood because it would be harder to connect her up with that flat in Limehouse?"

Wiggins spoke from his stand on the stairs. "With identification on her?" He'd apparently been listen-ing rather than simply inspecting the steps for slime. Now he said to Jury, "Can't have it both ways, can you, sir?"

* * *

In the sanitized glare of the white-tiled room, the mortuary attendant pulled back the sheet from the corpse.

Jury stood, looking down at the face as still as garden statuary, for a long enough time that Wiggins frowned and said, "Something wrong, sir?"

He looked at Wiggins, then at the attendant, feeling he had to fix both of their faces in his mind. He felt as he had when he was a boy, when the carousel starts going fast and then faster and faces and forms stream together so that one has to watch closely to sort them out. Finally, the whole circle of faces might as well be one.

There was dead silence for one whole minute, in which the attendant wasn't quite sure what to do, and in which Wiggins took the small photo Jury handed him and looked at it for a moment. "This is Simon Lean, right?"

Jury nodded.

Wiggins looked at it again, frowned, looked back at the dead face of the woman on the mortuary table. "And her?" He frowned. "Sadie Diver?"

"Hannah Lean. His wife. But she seems to be back in Northants, Wiggins, very much alive." Jury nodded to the attendant to cover up the body.

"I don't understand, sir."

"Neither do I." He looked down at the snapshot, one of the two he'd taken from Watermeadows. "I wondered why Tommy Diver looked so familiar."

* * *

He needed a place to think.

A church, he supposed, was as good a place as any for that, as he turned off the Commercial Road into Three Colt Street where the Five Bells was shut up tight in that blind way pubs have of looking in the few hours between the afternoon closing and the evening opening hours. He parked the car at the side of St. Anne's and got out.

Both street and churchyard were deserted. He walked round to the western side, up the several flights of fanlike steps, across the vestibule, into the entryway. The body was a rectangle, the vestibules at the other end were rectangles within this larger one. The Ionic columns, the galleries surrounding the large hall were remarkable in their simplicity. He thought of the architect who had not been considered "correct" in the mind of the day. Simplicity where one would have expected the ornate. Jury knew nothing about church architecture. He knew only that he could use a little simplicity.

The moment the door closed behind him with a thud, the hollowness enveloped him. Not St. Anne's, but his own. It was the reason he avoided churches.

He sat down in one of the pews at the rear, took a missal from the rack, opened it and closed it, put it back. He was unable to think of anything but the young woman at Watermeadows. Only now the face was superimposed over the one lying in the mortuary.

He looked down the nave toward the altar with a

sense akin to fear, though it wasn't that exactly, rising like bile in his throat. The wave of anxiety he felt seemed less related to the possible danger at Watermeadows than it did to the fact that such a deception could be practiced, and done so well, so convincingly. He looked down the nave into the deep pool of shadow that surrounded the altar.

For him to take it so personally was unprofessional, but he couldn't seem to help it. He had been gulled, and perhaps he felt some special acrimony because to dupe a Scotland Yard superintendent might be considered as some sort of acid test. Yet there had been no reason, none whatever, for the suspicions he had right now to have entered his mind at Watermeadows yesterday.

The double, the doppelganger, except in this case it was not the ghostly presence of the dead haunting the living. He was afraid it was, in some strange sense, the other way round.

22

———— ⚠ HE made a note of the estate agent's name beneath the "For Sale, Freehold" sign. The house was probably advertised as an extremely desirable waterfront property; Sadie Diver's flat, however, was nothing more than a glorified bed-sitting-room, its glory emanating largely from its having an actual kitchen. In this case, the kitchen was little more than an alcove with a heavy curtain on rungs in lieu of a door. A narrow window looked out on cracked earth and building lots. At a considerable distance and with no way to get to it was the Thames. The advert, Jury imagined, would contain the usual hyperbole—"enchanting view of the Thames," "recently renovated," and so forth.

A fridge, a cooker, a white enamel sink and drainboard constituted the fixtures. Above the sink was a hanging dishrack that held three plates of varying sizes, two cups, three glasses, and some cutlery. Even though forensics had given the place a complete turnout, Jury still took the precaution of touching no more than he had to. He opened the cupboard door by wedging his penknife under the chrome knob and pulling. What was on the shelves was sparse: more plates, cups, glasses. In one corner were several plates that matched, all with a fine gold band. The good stuff, presumably, for entertaining.

Jury walked through the sitting room, where the only thing that was out of place was the pulled-out sofa bed and crumpled covers, and into the bathroom. It was small but quite modern, with yellow and white tiles, their monotony broken by the occasional one with a painted bird. Yellow fittings, low w.c., stall shower. There was even a small airing cupboard. Again with his knife he pried open the medicine cabinet above the sink to find the few bottles there very neatly arranged on a single glass shelf. He looked at the drain in the sink, then in the shower. The one in the shower was covered with a removable aluminum trap to catch hair. With the tip of thumb and forefinger he carefully removed it, looked at it closely, returned it. He shook his head.

He stood now in the center of the sitting room and looked around slowly: the rumpled bedclothes, the pillows on the floor beside Tommy's small suitcase. A set of bookshelves stood against the wall across from the sofa. The few books were thrillers and picture books of London. Magazines were neatly stacked on another shelf. The two issues of

Country Life were months old, gathering dust in this otherwise spotless room.

A glass-fronted curio cabinet stood against the opposite wall. In it were a blue crystal bird, a brass box that looked Indian, a white-robed Bedouin warrior on a horse that reared on its hind legs. Brandishing a rifle with a bayonet, he was a perfect metal miniature. Jury opened the glass door, reached in, and then drew his hand back. Remembering the Safe-T-Loc bags he'd seen in the kitchen, he went to get one, came back, and picked up the horse by hooking his knife beneath the legs. He dropped it into the plastic bag, pinched it together, put it in his pocket. He peeled off another from the container and carefully dropped in the crystal bird.

Jury rang Wapping headquarters and got their print expert. Yes, they'd lifted the victim's prints from the crockery, a few from the woodwork. There were elimination prints—

"Whose?"

"Delivery boy's, neighbor down the street, brother's." There were others they hadn't matched up, quite a few. Latents, partials—

"Did you dust the stuff in the cabinet? An Arab soldier on a horse and a couple editions of *Country Life*?"

The print man was alternately whistling between his teeth and repeating "Arab, Arab," and then said, "Two partials, not the victim's. Magazines . . . several. Not the victim's."

There was a silence, and Jury said: "Just how many prints of the victim *did* you find?"

"Take a little research. But, as I remember, damned few. To tell the truth, the place might almost have been unlived in."

"That's what I thought. Did you lift any from the bottles in the medicine cabinet? Also, there was a small stack of gold-rimmed plates in the kitchen cupboard. Were the partials good enough to get a make?"

"Yes and no."

"Meaning?" Jury could almost visualize the man's grin, having his little joke.

"Nothing. Isn't it always yes and no?"

Jury hung up, but not before telling the print expert that forensics needed to go over the place again.

He sat down on the edge of the bed for a moment, opened his notebook, closed it. Sadie Diver seemed to be passing before Jury's line of vision much like a figure at the end of a long passageway between buildings, someone who had suddenly appeared from nowhere and gone back to it. The notion, he tried to tell himself, was absurd. She had a history: a brother, an aunt and uncle, a flat, a job. He checked his notebook again. Place called Streaks in Tottenham Court Road.

He took the package from his pocket, held it up to the light and looked at the robed figure, the flashing legs of the horse. Hannah Lean's favorite.

Lady Summerston had said something like that.

23

—————⚠ "I thought you worked in pairs," said Ruby Firth, as she opened the door to him for the second time that day. "Proper police procedure isn't being observed," she added wryly, taking up her same position on the sofa, where she must have been working under the dim light of the table lamp. The loft was even more shadowy now at dusk. The planet-ringed top of the torchieres gave off their unearthly, green glow. Beside the basket of material samples, bindings, and braid, lay her outsized horn-rimmed glasses.

Given the velvet gown, the three-inch heels, it was hard to believe that the "citified Laura Ashley" had really been plying her needle when he knocked. "Are you used to police, then?"

Ruby had picked up a small silk shade that she was in the process of mending. Her expression

232

didn't change as she regarded him over the tops of
the horn-rims. At the moment she looked like an
inquisitive teacher. "I have a feeling that question is
double-edged." With her teeth, she snapped a
thread, then picked up a bit of apricot braid. "I've
had police for breakfast, lunch, and now apparently
for the evening meal. Sorry, but I've a gallery opening to go to. Champagne and nibbles. I don't know
about the quality of the paintings, but I do know the
quality of the decor. I did it."

"Sorry. It's necessary. Where's Tom?"

"Gone over to Pennyfields to eat Chinese. I
thought perhaps getting out would cheer him up; to
tell the truth, if I'd had to listen to that harmonica
much longer I'd've screamed. Does he have to play
such doleful music?"

"Just having his sister murdered, I expect he'd
feel doleful."

She said nothing to that except, "Well, at least
'Waltzing Matilda' has stopped for a while. I was
getting pretty tired of it." Her look was the usual
uncompromising stare. "Tired of police, too. I've
told everything I know twice over."

Jury shrugged. "You may think so, but things
sometimes go missing. It's hard to remember every
detail first time around. I want to talk with Tommy,
too."

"Then you can just catch him up. I gave him some
money to go to the Ruby Dragon. At least it's
brighter than most." Her eyes were still on the
shade, as she drew up a bit of the braid to make a
kind of pleat.

Jury couldn't put his finger on it, what he didn't like about Ruby Firth. She had held out a hand to Tommy Diver, true, but he wondered how long it would be before the hand would drop away and close on something she fancied more at the moment, the way it reached for the gin and tonic now. Was it a mask of irony she wore, or would the mask drop away like the hand to reveal beneath it another mask? Something cold touched him, the spread of the shadow he had felt in the church, perhaps.

He wondered if Ruby Firth were capable of commitment. He wondered about her casual response to the death of Simon Lean. Almost impossible to tell if it was real or faked. Roy Marsh, on the other hand, couldn't conceal his feelings about her. Now, as she held the shade at arm's length, considering her handiwork, he might as well not have been in the room.

Her look at him, when he mentioned Roy Marsh's name, was defensive. Impatiently, she said, "I've known him for years. What on earth does that have to do with the case?"

It was as if knowing him for years dismissed Marsh from notice as a man. "Did he know Sadie Diver?"

"He could have done." She shrugged. "Ask him."

"I'm asking you. I think you know."

She had taken an oblong of puce satin from the box. Jury doubted this needlework had to be done then and there. Ruby Firth would have to be a cold woman indeed if a bit of satin and braid could take her mind off murder, especially a murder in which two men with whom she'd been intimate were involved. "I expect he could have seen her. After all, Narrow Street's only just down from here a bit. And we did go into the Five Bells."

"Men apparently liked her, at least that's the impression I got in the pub."

Her eyes came up to meet his, looking mildly amused. "If you're suggesting he threw me over, well, men don't usually do that, Superintendent." This was punctuated by the sound of satin ripping. Yet he heard in that defiant statement some other emotion, something edgy, nerves frayed like the length of cloth she'd just torn and now folded into the workbasket.

"I must get to the opening." She shoved the basket aside and rose. In that sculptured black-and-green gown she looked slim as the torchiere before which she stood.

Surely, she wasn't so naïve as to think she could dismiss him as she had his questions about Roy Marsh. But Jury let it go, and let her go, too. "Sorry to have kept you. You will, of course, make yourself available. Wapping police will want to talk further with you." He rose to go. "Where's that restaurant, then?"

"In Pennyfields. Turn right and it's just at the bottom. . . . Superintendent?"

Jury had his hand on the doorknob. "Yes?"

"Will he be going back to Gravesend tonight? Or tomorrow?"

"Tommy? I expect his aunt and uncle will collect

him quite soon. I'm not sure precisely when. Can't you—" Jury then felt in her an unease, a posture, much like the one she'd taken before the thin floor-lamp, that threatened to crumble. The rest of his reply—*stand it for one more night?* —stuck in his throat, as his anger started to crumble, too. He managed a smile that he didn't feel. *"On the Beach,"* he said. She looked puzzled. " 'Waltzing Matilda' was the theme song. That might be why you think it's so unhappy." She didn't understand, apparently. "But I expect you're too young to remember that. Thirty years ago, that must be. Ava Gardner was in it." Jury didn't know why he was standing in this doorway, rattling on about an antique film, except that he sensed that she needed support. Almost as if she had met his thought, taking it literally, she swayed slightly, clumsily, as if the high heel of her shoe had caught on an invisible rug.

He went on, for he knew she was leaning on the sound of his voice. "It was just that the nuclear cloud hadn't reached Australia yet. It was the last safe place on earth—for a while." He could sense the conflict. If he had pressed his question about Roy Marsh, he might have discharged the tension and gotten an answer. Or it might have worked the other way; he might have tossed away any chance he had of gaining her confidence. He felt, though both of them stood on the firm polished planks of the floor, that they were like voyagers on a pitching vessel.

"I always thought it was a hell of a sad song, too,

since they all had to die in the end. Good-night, Ruby."

When he glanced back through the door he was closing behind him, she had not moved an inch. She still stood as elegantly stiff and dark as the dim lamp that cast its faint green shadow across her hair.

* * *

Jury found him behind a mountain of chicken fried rice.

Pennyfields was strung with Chinese restaurants, as was much of Limehouse, most of them very good, none of them fancy. The Ruby Dragon was the most ornate of the lot. A few gold-and-red-trimmed paper palaces and pagodas hung from the ceiling, turning gently in the small breeze stirred by the door's opening; a mural depicting a slant-eyed and strangely bearded dragon was painted a gummy red that reminded Jury of dried blood; there were rice-paper partitions and black lacquered screens. Still, he could judge from the clientele that the Ruby Dragon was a family restaurant, catering for the locals just like the others in Limehouse. The menu dependable, the service unsmiling, the food good.

Tommy had, apparently, already eaten his way through a phalanx of appetizers; there were the remains of spring rolls, wonton soup, and shrimp balls. Jury asked for tea.

"Here, eat some of this," said Tommy, shoving the dish toward him.

"Thanks, no." Jury smiled as Tommy looked round him at this banquet rather guiltily. "There's no Chinese places near where we live. Not even a take-away." Unhappily, he shoved his rice about. "I guess you came to take me back."

" 'Back'? You sound like an escapee. No, I just wanted to talk with you some more. Ruby told me you were here."

"She gave me the money. It was nice of her; I guess she got tired of me hanging round." Apologetically, he touched the harmonica sticking out of his shirt pocket. "I don't know that many songs. My favorite's 'Waltzing Matilda' and one I wrote myself. It gets on people's nerves." He sighed. Then he smiled. "It sure gets on Sid's nerves. He's always on about me playing it down in the engine room." His head leaning against his fisted hand and turning the fork over and over in the other, he seemed to forget about the rare treat of Chinese food. "But they— Aunt Glad and Uncle John—say I got to take at least two 'O' levels. What good's that stuff if you just want to work on boats? They keep telling me how Sadie got this real good education at the Little Sisters of Charity; what good's that ever done her—?"

He looked across at Jury in fright. Suddenly, he must have remembered that his sister's education would never be thrown up to him again.

* * *

He hadn't seen her since the convent days, Tommy told him, as they stood at the gate of St. Anne's. "It was really a lark, seeing Sadie with her head all wrapped up in that black scarf. They shaved it off. Her hair, I mean. They're bald, nuns are. Terrible, I think." The look he shot Jury was just a tiny bit defiant, as if he were willing to argue the point.

"I don't think they are, though. Bald, I mean. And if your sister was a novitiate, well, they'd have let her hair alone. Cut it just a bit perhaps." Roy Marsh had given him what information the Thames police had collected. That the girl had entered a convent struck Jury as out of character. The picture he had of her was of a rather brassy, even pushy, and not unselfish person.

"Seems wrong to me, anyway. There's a lot about the church seems wrong." He glanced at Jury to see how he was taking these increasingly heretical judgments. When Jury didn't rise to the bait, he seemed relieved and immediately lost interest in the right and the wrong of it.

The unsmiling waiter set down a high-piled metal dish of sweet-and-sour pork in its glaze of bright orange sauce as Tommy told Jury stories about his childhood—long past, he seemed to think—when Sadie had been his best, sometimes his only, companion. There were Wendy-houses, picnics in secret, dark caves, playing truant from school . . . indeed all of the things that one reads of in the idyllic descriptions of books or sees on the telly— the sort of childhood no one ever really had, or if one had, would not remember clearly through a haze of eternal summer.

Jury thought he understood why Tommy had been so quick to say that the victim wasn't his sister: he had never really had the relationship with her he was now inventing. The difference in age would have been only one factor, really. It would have been possible, he supposed, for a certain kind of seventeen-year-old girl to indulge a small brother in the way Tommy imagined, but he doubted Sadie Diver was that sort of sister. That she had gone for months, years, without trying to communicate (except to send him the snapshots) and then had only done so (and probably regretted it) in her new economic circumstances as a way, probably, to get the message to the Mulhollands that she was better off than they would ever be.

"So Sadie wasn't exactly nun-like, right, Tommy? Not the quiet and contemplative life for her, hmm?"

He was already halfway through his mountain of rice, spooning the pork and pineapple on it for good measure. "Her? Don't make me laugh. Sadie quiet and . . . whatever . . ."

"What gave her that religious turn, all of a sudden?"

"Aunt Glad and Uncle John gave it. They thought she was, you know . . . kind of wild. It was just for a year."

"You have to be fairly smart to enter one. There are exams you have to pass. It's not for tearaways."

Tommy smiled over his teacup. "Sadie could be anything. It's my thinking she did it just to get them out of her hair. Or what was left of her hair," he added darkly.

That patina of breeding, of reserve, of nun-like calm was something Sadie Diver could have acquired. It sounded as if she were sharp and resilient.

From the report Roy Marsh had given him, the Mulhollands were pretty resilient themselves. *Hard as hard cheese,* had been his impression. He'd said the lad hadn't seemed too happy after he'd talked to them, either.

Tommy was going on with a tale of Sadie playing nurse to the four dogs and three cats, as a bit of a plan evolved in Jury's mind. Since Tommy too would have to "keep himself available" as he'd told Ruby Firth . . . why not? The boy had come up to London with such candlelit hopes, all of them sputtered out now because this girl round whom he had spun a lot of dreams had been murdered. Why, on top of this, should he have to go back so soon to a house where tea and sympathy would be absent? At least, at the Ruby Dragon, you could get the tea. He looked at the harmonica sticking up from the pocket of the jacket that hung across the lad's thin shoulders like an old life he couldn't slough off.

Jury checked his watch and took out some bills. "Come on, if you're through, and I'll take you along to the pub. I've got to meet my sergeant there."

"Me, sir? But they won't let me in, I don't think. Under age."

"We'll manage it."

The way the pale face lit up reminded Jury of the rice-paper screens. Light came and went behind them, transforming imprints almost magically. He nodded.

Jury added: "Since you've got to keep yourself available for police, I was thinking it might be better for you to stay in London at least tonight. Also, I may need you to go to Northamptonshire."

Northants or China, it made no odds to Tommy Diver. Just as long as it wasn't Gravesend. "Yes, *sir.* Stay at Ruby's, you mean?"

"No, I was thinking of somewhere else you might like better. Friend of mine has a flat."

"Is it a policeman, then?"

"I'm sure she thinks she is."

24

━━━━━━━━🔺 MOLLOY was polishing a glass and looking dubiously at Tommy Diver.

"He's older than he looks, Molloy," said Jury, who was looking round the scene for Wiggins.

Tommy folded a stick of gum into his mouth and ordered a lemon squash, giving Molloy back his stare.

Jack Krael was in his usual place at the bar, staring at his fixed point in space; Wiggins was in the alcove lined with tea packets. He walked over to the bar, looked from Tommy to Jury, as if someone must have forgotten the licensing laws.

"I don't think Marsh was too happy about you wanting the autopsy shoved forward. They were dragging their feet even about the photos. Sergeant Marsh said he'd bring them himself. I don't think he likes me; could hardly get a cuppa out of him. That wind that blows off the river. I swear I can't imagine why anyone'd volunteer for Thames Division. Have to be an expert swimmer." Wiggins shivered. His hand went up to his neck and he announced he was getting a bad throat from that stop on Wapping Old Stairs. He took the cup Molloy sat before him and got out his packet of black biscuits.

Tommy watched him break one up into the water and said, "You could do the same with burnt toast." He made sucking noises with his straw.

The cup halted in midair as Wiggins looked down at Tommy. "What?"

"Wouldn't cost you eighty p, either, like that lot." Tommy poked at the cellophane-wrapped packet. "Just toss the bread in the fire and let it char. Same thing. What do you do for your sore throat, anyhow?"

As Wiggins put down some money for another lemon squash, he said, "Camphorated oil. A nice hot compress."

Tommy shrugged. "Try an old sock. Just make sure it's full of sweat—real dirty. The sock'll do it every time. Thanks." He took his bottle of squash.

Wiggins finding in the boy an unexpected resource, drew him aside, apparently amazed that a germ-ridden sock might hold curative powers.

Jury took the opportunity to disrupt Jack Krael's meditations. "Have a look at this, will you?" Jury showed him the photo of Simon and Hannah Lean.

"Same chappie as was in that other picture." He shrugged.

"What about the woman?"

Jack Krael looked harder this time, took it in his own twisted fingers and frowned. "Looks like Sadie Diver. Except when I saw her she was always got up like a dog's dinner. What's she doin' with him?"

"Like this, you mean." Jury put the snap of Sadie side-by-side with the other. "More like this, you mean." Full color, flash and dazzle. Enough rouge and blue eyeshadow to streak an evening sky. Hair like dark, high-piled clouds.

Jack Krael reflected. "That's her; that's Sadie. Funny what a change of hairstyle can do, and all that muck they stick on their faces. This one here looks thinner." He flicked his thumbnail at the shot of Hannah. Then he looked at Tommy. "That's her brother, is it? I wondered he looked familiar. Hard on the kid, inhn't?"

"Pretty hard, yes. He'll be going home soon."

Jack Krael caught Tommy's eye. "You ain't from round here, then, lad?"

"No. Gravesend."

Krael's face broke into a rare smile. "Gravesend, is it? Used to run a tug there. Know anything about boats?"

Tommy managed a swagger, hard when you're drinking lemon squash through a straw. "You could say so."

"Well, set yourself up here—" and Krael hit the stool beside him.

Jury handed Wiggins the photo of the Leans and the snap of Sadie Diver, and told him to show them around to the regulars.

Wiggins glanced at it, frowning. "But she's in Northants, I thought you said."

"*Somebody's* in Northants. But it's not necessarily Hannah Lean."

People were drifting in, getting their drinks at the bar, settling themselves in for a recap of the twenty-four or so hours since they'd seen one another. At least, that was the way Jury sometimes thought of it, as he watched an emaciated customer slug coins into the jukebox and squint at the menu of songs. At the Angel sometimes Jury looked over the same faces he had seen so many times before and got the queer feeling that between bouts at the pub, time simply stopped. They'd disappear, come back, disappear again.

Roy Marsh came in carrying a manila envelope under his arm and looking like the whole lot of them could disappear and the world be none the worse for it.

"What's going on, Jury? What's the kid doing here?" He nodded toward the back of the room. His soft voice had such a cutting edge it could even penetrate the blare of "Mack the Knife," coming from the jukebox.

"He's all right," said Jury, mildly.

"I didn't *ask* if he was all right. I went round to Ruby's and no one was home. He's my responsibility, Jury. His people are waiting to take him back to Gravesend."

Molloy came down the bar with Jury's pint,

looked inquiringly at Roy Marsh, got a blistered glance in return, and scurried away.

"Let them wait. This for me?" Jury opened the envelope, took out the police photographer's pictures.

Roy moved an inch, leaned into Jury. The low voice had as much weight as the cement bag going down in Bobby's song. "Your sergeant said you wanted to be present at the autopsy. Not only that, you wanted it done tonight. You wanted antemortem dental records, you wanted this, you wanted *that*. This isn't your case, Jury; this is Thames Division's. A clear-cut case of homicide, and I think we're equipped to handle it."

Jury was studying one of the shots of the body. "I would have thought it was up for grabs, Roy; you and Ballinger couldn't seem to decide whether to throw it to the river police, 'H' Division, or the Port of London Authority. And it's far from being clear-cut." Jury nodded toward the jukebox. "Take that cement bag going down."

Marsh frowned. "What the hell are you talking about?"

Jury returned the pictures to the envelope and pinched the clasp tight. "Look, Roy. Killers don't ordinarily leave bodies on slipways where they're certain to be found—that one's right by a pub, remember?—when they could just toss them in the river, let the tide take them away—"

"Bodies rise."

"Weight it down. Or even if the murderer's in too much of a damned hurry to get *out*, he's gained nothing by leaving the body on the slipway." Jury looked at Marsh. "So I'd say the killer wanted it found. Letting it wash into the river, he couldn't have been certain, or what condition it'd be in."

"Why?"

"To make sure it was known that the woman was dead. Especially if the woman was rich. The disposition of a fortune in the future, for example."

"That example tells me sod-all, Jury."

"Sorry. I'd explain it, but I'm not sure if what I think happened, did." But he didn't add that he wouldn't explain it because he wasn't sure about Marsh himself.

"You're making something out of—get the hell out of here, Kath."

Kath had muscled her way between them. "It's yer kind that's goin' to get axed when I'm on council."

"One of these days, Kath, I'm running you in for disturbing the peace."

"Ha! Listen to 'im, listen to 'im. You run me in. Shut yer gob, with what I know about you—Mol-*LOY.*" She took the drink he sloshed toward her, winked at Jury, and said, "Ast 'im what 'e's doin' over to Limehouse Causeway sittin' in 'is car. 'Ere, sonny, don't fergit t' vote." She shoved several pamphlets at Roy, who let them fall to the floor.

Jury studied him, scanned the room for a table. "Let's sit down for a minute."

"I've got work to do."

"A minute."

They walked back to a table in the corner near

the jukebox. The place wasn't half-full, so there was relative quiet.

"It was never much of a secret about you and Ruby, was it?" When Roy refused to say anything, managed to sit as if he were still standing, Jury said, "I wouldn't suppose you'd take very kindly to him, would you?" Jury showed him the photo of Hannah and Simon Lean.

It was hard to believe that such a low voice could have such a cutting edge to it. "Leave her out of this." It came out between a hiss and a whisper.

"I wish I could."

"I'd never have guessed. If you want to yank me in for questioning, I'm always available to police." He pulled the snapshot around with his finger, looking at it again. "How did he know Sadie Diver, then?"

"That's the point, Roy. The woman isn't Sadie Diver. It's his wife, Hannah." Jury returned the picture to his pocket, took a drink from his pint, and watched the expression on Roy's face turn from anger to disbelief to that stony look Roy used to mask all expression.

Roy got up, made no further comment, except to say, "The autopsy's set up for ten tonight."

Jury sat there for a moment in the relative silence of the corner, the music of the jukebox only a blur. The warmth of Linda Ronstadt's voice had replaced one of those interchangeable, metallic groups.

He looked through the haze of smoke toward the alcove where Tommy was now standing at the table with the cardplayers, and wondered if the boy really believed that his sister was dead. Half of his mind might have accepted it, half not. Listening to Tommy in the Ruby Dragon, Jury had felt a certainty that Tommy wouldn't have recognized his sister, not so much because he hadn't seen her in these past years, but because he hadn't really known her. He wondered if that was what his sister and Simon Lean were counting on, in the event that questions were ever asked. . . .

That was what bothered Jury. That Simon Lean might have been extraordinarily thorough, that he had taken into consideration that someone might suspect the switch. Lean must have allowed for the possibility that the murder of Sadie Diver could mean he'd be questioned by police. . . .

But, of course, the woman at Watermeadows would have provided him with an alibi. Hannah Lean. He was lighting a cigarette and in a sudden wash of anger let the match burn down to his fingertips. He tossed it in the tin ashtray, switched his attention to the music, mercifully soulful now with the singer's doleful recollection of the fishing boats at the bayou.

Through the screen of smoke, he looked for Tommy. It was seven o'clock and they'd have to get going. Still he sat there with his hell of a headache, wondering if Wiggins had aspirin.

"*. . . savin' nickels, sa-a-vin' dimes . . .*"

Jury pressed the heels of his palms against his head, thinking that Sadie Diver no longer had to worry about saving.

He looked up to see Alf stalking toward the door, Wiggins on his heels, grabbing his coat-sleeve, saying politely. "If you'd just hang about, sir, thank you."

Frenzied eyes looked from Wiggins to Jury to the door through which Roy Marsh had passed. "He tol' ya, dihn't 'e? 'Twas that cop, weren't it? Been on about the rumors. I been watchin' you both, talkin' about it. I'd nothin' t' do with it, it's all behind me. All the way from Australia I come an' the rumors follows—"

Tommy Diver had come up behind him. "You from Australia? Listen, I'll bet you like this, then." Whereupon he whipped his harmonica from the pocket, ran up and down the scales, and overrode the mournful voice of Linda Ronstadt with his even-more-mournful "Waltzing Matilda."

25

——————— A JURY would have known they were near the Floral Hall when Wiggins started sneezing, even if he hadn't already known the area. Wiggins had interrupted his talk about Jack Krael to envelop his nose in a handkerchief. Fortunately, Jury himself was negotiating the turn or one of the Covent Garden porters would have been separated from his handtruck.

Wiggins continued his sad litany of loss. "I know how he feels, sir; it's all going; might as well say good-bye to the lot. Just imagine what this place was like back when dockland was a hive of activity."

He spoke of that time as if it had been centuries ago, not decades. "I remember," said Jury.

"You're not *that* old, sir. Now it's just all those trendy little shops." Wiggins replaced his small aspirator—he'd sworn he was working his way into asthma—and continued repining the loss of the past. "Apricots from South Africa, figs from Italy . . ." He sighed. "The pea-shuckers, incredible, they were."

Jury smiled at Wiggins's extolling a past that one day of living in would have had him flat on his back. No matter how colorful, there was filth and squalor, and no mass-produced charcoal biscuits. "You're allergic to figs, Wiggins," he said as he pulled the car up to a double yellow line.

"Am I, sir?" Wiggins stowed the handkerchief and frowned.

Jury had no idea. "And Racer'd be the first to tell you a pea-shucker's life is full of grief." He smiled: parking illegally was one of the perks of the job, and he took a child-like delight in looking through the windscreen at the puzzled, mildly surprised faces of pedestrians watching him dump his plainclothes car on the double line and casually get out. Jury had to nudge Wiggins out of his fig-ruminations by leaning in through the window and saying, "Are you coming along?"

Wiggins popped out of the car immediately. The Starrdust was one of his favorite places, and he was definitely going along.

The Starrdust was as far from a trendy little boutique as hitting another galaxy could be. Jury had been here a few times, and still never got used to the dark. What light there was inside came delicately streaming from a sort of mock-planetarium ceiling where a goldish glow behind the cut-out stars and planets mixed with the silver blue behind a quarter-moon. And because the lights behind them winked on and off, as if Mars and then Venus were coming on and sinking back, the whole gave the effect of slowly turning. The lights caught counter, customers, fixtures together in a sort of Hephaestean golden net.

Always playing on Andrew Starr's old phonograph were scratchy recordings that fit this mood. Hoagy, Dinah, Glenn Miller. Today it was Dinah singing the song Jury had heard in the background over the phone. Stars were falling on Alabama and Covent Garden. For when they had entered, one of Andrew's shop assistants was up on a high ladder, rigging up what looked like a silver pail attached by a string to the molding of the door. A spill of tiny gold and silver stars showered on Jury's shoulder and Wiggins's hair.

She gave a mouse-like squeak and scrambled down the ladder.

And when she saw who it was, she said it again, clapping her hand over her mouth as if the little squeal might get out of control. It brought her counterpart—not twin, but counterpart—from the cubicle of office to see what was going on. One of them was Meg; he thought the other's name was Joy. They had similar spun-gold hair held back by combs decorated with rhinestone stars. Their eyes had that same starry luster, but perhaps it was the darkness. They were dressed in silvery blouses and black cord jeans with gold suspenders so that side-by-side and with the shiny pail between them they looked like extraterrestrial milk-maids.

"Sorry. Sorry." They said in unison as Dinah wound down on the phonograph.

"We had the clock on the door for lunchtime—"

"But you mustn't have seen it," Joy put in quickly, as if Meg might have been suggesting Jury and Wiggins were great nits who couldn't read.

"Not to worry," said Wiggins, "a shower of stars is better than a bucket of water." He picked a star from his eyebrow and smiled contentedly, for he seemed to feel at home in the Starrdust. Its other-worldly imperviousness to earthly diseases and sloughs of despond appeared to comfort him.

Starr himself was fairly well known in the astrology trade (if that's what one could call it), and the shop had a mix of books on the subject, some very rare, some newer. Andrew's custom had a remarkable range, from the penny-farthing kiddies to the titled and wealthy, who took his horoscopes as some do the *Times*— as gospel. The thing about Andrew Starr was that he believed also they were gospel-true. How else could he have concocted this little sanctuary in the middle of the babble of Covent Garden?

Wiggins, whose sneezing attack had stopped the minute he'd walked in, was showing Tommy the little hut that Starr had assembled for the kiddies who came in. *Horror-Scope* was written in cursive neon-blue above the door, and its walls were studded with half-moons and stars. There was scarcely room to walk between that and the latest addition to the shop, which stood directly across from it: a gauzy tent, like a large bed-canopy, that floated its wispy, silver pleats from a central core out and over a round support of wire. This was Madame Zostra's domain.

It was probably that voice that had been singing along with Dinah, far off in the kitchenette. It was a very narrow, but very long shop, and people had a way of appearing out of the dark. As Heaven had replaced Alabama on the record-player, one of the twins looked round and said, "I expect you're wanting to see Carole-anne. She's just wetting the tea and Andrew's gone to get some super food. He always does that when we haven't time for a proper lunch. It being May, the tourist trade's just plain hell."

"Hell's not the half," said Meg with a quick bob of her platinum head.

The word startled Jury, it seemed so out-of-place here. And the black-gowned form floating out of the dark forking up a piece of gâteau gave it no credence, either. "Super!" Mouth full, she added, "Took you long enough, dihn't it?" To the twins she said, "Andrew's back and he brought some of that Black Forest you like."

The twins left with Wiggins and Tommy in tow, for they had just emerged, bending way down to clear the sign, laughing.

"Who's that, then?" Carole-anne whirled around to watch the newcomer disappearing down the narrow passageway.

"Friend of mine."

She looked suspicious. "*I* never met him," she said, thereby canceling out the acquaintance, since she hadn't as yet approved it.

"You will. As to what took me so long: I've only been gone for a day—"

"Day-and-a-half. Had your tea?"

Jury shook his head. "Thought you were slimming."

"Knowing you're going to die makes you crave sugar."

Jury winced. "Carole-anne, I've got what looks like a double murder on my hands. That kind of makes me want to husband my time, love."

"Makes you *what?* Cor, don't we ever talk fancy after we've been one day with an earl. Have some gâteau

" She held a laden fork toward his mouth.

"No thanks, I'm slimming. What were those hysterical calls about?"

She nodded toward the tent. All important business—that meant any business of Carole-anne's—was to be conducted within its massed shadows. It was a little like entering a smaller cave after leaving the anteroom of a larger. There was a round table covered with the familiar star-and-planet pattern on dark blue felt and a chair either side. In the middle was a crystal on black velvet, between two golden balls that cast a yellowish glow upward, as in the child's game of holding a buttercup under a chin. In front of this was a deck of cards. Tarot.

Carole-anne had put by her cake and donned her hat. One of them, for Carole-anne had many hats.

This one was an elaborate turban-like thing of silver lamé, looped round with pearls and swagged in thin gold chains (probably from its wearer's large supply of costume jewelry). She sat like a swami, legs crossed, hands folded, staring into the crystal ball.

Jury sighed. What she was really doing was quickly trying to construct a believable tale of the Madame Zostra Murders. After two minutes on this cushion, Jury knew his back would kill him. "If something doesn't take shape in there in ten seconds, I'm leaving, love." He wouldn't have come in the first place, if it hadn't been for Tommy.

Beringed fingers quickly went to cover her eyes. Lapis lazuli eyes, which accounted for a good bit of the Starrdust's fresh clientele. Andrew Starr had spent a great deal of money on Madame Zostra's various appurtenances. He was a dreamer but no dummy; he could probably hear the cashbox clang when he first saw her. Though Jury was quite sure it was Carole-anne who'd convinced him to organize the whole show.

"The aura is all wrong. You're disturbing it with your doubts." Apparently, even she thought that sounded pretty unconvincing, for she immediately dropped her hands and picked up the Tarot pack. She started shuffling it.

Jury stared. "The Tarot. Carole-anne, people don't *shuffle* those cards."

She shrugged and started up-turning them and slapping them down. What was this—murder, his fortune, or blackjack? Naturally, when the Hanged Man appeared, she shoved it toward him, saying,

"It's appeared—" (she was trying to remember the number of murders) "—twice." *Zip* went the splayed line of cards back together.

"Now we've sorted that out, I want you to take care of Tommy. When the shop closes, take him back to the flat."

"Is that him, then?" She had made her lightning-move, good as any contender for the Gold, up and yanking back the smoke of gauze. After all, she might be getting control over a totally new person.

They were coming down the passageway, amid laughter and giggles. The evening break was over, and Jury could see outside a little clutch of customers getting impatient.

Jury said hello to Andrew Starr, a good-looking, pleasant young man who'd turned his particular métier of horoscopes into a lucrative business. Before he could finish his introduction of Tommy—who stood there slack-mouthed, just looking at Carole-anne—she said, "You're going to *love* it here." He was whisked inside the tent of gauze.

Andrew Starr went ahead to unlock the door, let them out, and let the customers in.

Jury crossed the street to the car, Wiggins following reluctantly, looking back over his shoulder, feeling perhaps that his future was in there, held hostage in the *Horror-Scope* play-house, until someone with more wisdom that Scotland Yard had ever had could free it.

Wiggins sneezed.

26

──────── △ GOD'S will had had as little to do with the death of Tommy's sister as it did with the running of the Mulholland household. That, Jury imagined, was left squarely to the iron will of John Mulholland and the iron hand this short and sturdy man kept fisting round the cap he held. The wife was thinner and taller—tall sitting down—with a blank face that looked as if the bandages had just been removed, so unblinkingly expressionless was it.

Or perhaps it was just Jury himself, having moved so quickly from the dark environs of Andrew's shop into an interrogation room at Wapping that struck him as a glare of white light by comparison.

Mulholland would not sit down, nor would he answer the superintendent's mild and friendly greeting with a like one. Down to business, with no garnishments of sadness or remorse, no platitudes even to cover up the apparent lack of feeling. He had answered the questions of Wapping police; he had seen the niece's body; he wanted merely to collect his nephew—with whom he was obviously furious for having tricked the family—and return to Gravesend.

"I'm sorry for the inconvenience, but I'm keeping Tommy in London for another day or two. He'll be well looked after."

" 'Keeping' him? We mean to take him *back*, and that's that."

"Well, no, it isn't, exactly. We need him for our inquiries."

Mulholland's square face suffused with blood; his mouth was tight, lips tinged slightly blue by his anger. "He don't know nothing we can't tell you."

"He might. He got here just after Sarah was murdered. And he knew her well. Look, Mr. Mulholland, the boy's not being tossed into a flaming pit. Let's not argue. I'd win." Jury smiled. "Sit down, won't you?"

If Mulholland refused to take a seat (which he did), Jury was happy to disconcert the man by pulling round a chair for himself. So did Wiggins, taking out his notebook and a fresh handkerchief, as if they had all the time in the world.

"I'm sorry about your niece," Jury said, looking from one to the other. The uncle glared. The aunt looked away. At least she, perhaps influenced by the sergeant's producing his own handkerchief, fetched a small one from her purse. It was almost as if someone else had come along to give her leave to release emotion that she must have been used to suppressing when her husband was her only company.

Jury felt sorry for Gladys Mulholland as she quickly removed the handkerchief from her mouth when her husband looked darkly at her. But he felt even sorrier for Tommy Diver. He was glad he was tucked away in the Starrdust. It wasn't a sixth sense that had told Jury what a return to Gravesend would be like, it was the clear memory of himself at that age. He'd been luckier, though, with his own relations, who had been kind enough before the death of his own uncle and the dwindling resources of his aunt had forced her to put him in Good Hope.

John Mulholland was not the man to equivocate, even if equivocation was warranted. The worst possible kind of witness, thought Jury. The kind whose own ego or pride would get in the way of any identification. The sort of witness, indeed, who might send the wrong man into the dock.

It was Gladys Mulholland who leaned forward, puzzled. "Is there a chance it's not our Sarah?"

At that *our Sarah*, Mulholland snorted.

Jury answered her question with his own. "What was she like, Mrs. Mulholland?"

That he would ask a question so innocent and seem himself to be at all interested in her niece and her opinion of that niece, both puzzled and pleased her. The tension eased. Arms as taut as wires relaxed; legs pressed tightly together moved slightly apart. She reminded Jury of a wooden puppet with controlling strings slackening.

Her husband had had to drop them. He now faced the window overlooking the Thames, resolutely. A question not directed to him was not a question worth answering, anyway. That was Jury's objective, to get him out of it temporarily. Mrs. Mulholland's recitation would otherwise have been interrupted again and again.

As she talked about the nice child Sarah Diver had been, Jury moved from his chair and nodded to Wiggins, who continued the questioning. Jury himself went to stand near the husband; he lit a cigarette and offered Mulholland the cigar he'd taken from Racer's humidor. The man looked at it with suspicion, but the desire for a smoke being stronger than the desire to fend off police, he took it with grudging thanks. Difficult to remain hostile and inflexible when you're standing round having a friendly smoke with a chap. Having the sergeant take over the interrogation also suggested that the investigation into the death of his niece was now on a lower key. Superintendents tended to intimidate witnesses, Jury had found only too often.

Mrs. Mulholland was talking about the days before Sadie "went to the bad."

"How do you mean, ma'am?" asked Wiggins.

"Wild, too clever by half, just like her mother. That'd be Bessie Mulholland. *My* maiden name was Case." She tapped Wiggins's notebook, and inclined her head toward her husband. *"His* sister," making sure the sergeant understood the Cases were quite another kettle of fish.

Mulholland had turned from the window to challenge this: "She weren't like the rest of us. A black sheep, was Bessie. And what about that brother of yours—?"

Wiggins interrupted by saying smoothly, "I know what you mean. I've a sister myself." He went on: "But exactly how 'bad' was 'bad' in the case of your Sadie?"

"Sarah," said the aunt. "Named after her in the Bible—"

"Was it drugs, then? Men?"

Mulholland apparently felt he had kept out of it long enough. "She was getting up to all sorts of things, even when she wasn't as old as Tom. I think she had all the conscience of a cat. And I've never known anyone who could put it over on you like Sarah could. Stand there and lie through her teeth and look innocent as anything—"

"She must have done. Looked innocent, I mean. After all, she got into the Little Sisters of Charity. A Mother Superior is usually nobody's fool."

There was an extended, embarrassed silence. The Mullhollands did not look at one another—he turned back to the window; she studied her interlaced fingers.

"It's odd, your niece's choosing the convent, especially given the sort of young girl she was."

Mulholland turned his big square face on Jury. "That was the agreement, that she'd stay for a year at least. It was either that or she needn't come home."

His wife twisted in her chair. "Sorts of things we Cases never got up to."

"A course not," said her husband. "Who the hell ever fancied the Case women enough to drag their knickers—"

Thereupon came a weepy cry from Gladys, who dropped her head in her hands and sobbed her small hankie into a tiny ball. Wiggins offered her his handkerchief.

"What you're saying is that Sadie—pardon, Sarah —was given the choice of sorting herself out with the Little Sisters or sorting herself out on the road," said Jury.

"Damned right. And what's wrong with that?" A bull pawing dust couldn't have looked more belligerent.

Jury felt sorry for him, in a way. Having the care of a sister's child and having the child turn out to be a bad lot. It must have been hard for him to take, a reflection on his own abilities to raise children properly.

"Nothing at all. I don't blame you. Probably do the same myself in your position." Jury ignored Wiggins's stare.

Neither of them responded; both of them seemed relieved he'd have done the same.

* * *

He was definitely one of Hamlet's gravediggers, thought Jury. Willie Cooper always struck Jury as a doctor who could barely suppress his glee at the sight of a corpse, particularly when Scotland Yard was in on the cutting-up, even more especially when it was Jury. Or "R.J.," as Cooper chose to call him. Jury had been watching as Cooper made his careful measurements, described every bruise, scratch, mark, the chief of which were the abrasions on the victim's back. There were two superficial knife wounds; the one that killed her was the penetration of the lung in the upper apex. Blood, a good two pints of it, had seeped into the chest cavity.

"Single-edged," said Cooper.

To Jury it sounded all too familiar.

Cooper continued talking: "She could have slipped on the wet stairs, slipped or been pushed, to make those marks on the back. The clothes were torn."

"Meaning someone made a grab for her?"

Cooper looked up at him. Cheerful as he was in other ways, the eyes had a dead look as if they mirrored the eyes of all of the dead he'd seen. "I was talking." He folded two sticks of gum in his mouth, then collected a hair specimen, which he bagged. He was in clinical white, a rubber cap imprisoning his hair, surgical gloves on his hands. He stood with his arms akimbo, hands against his waist. "Not bad, R.J. In pretty good repair, considering the cadaver spent some thirty hours in combat with the cruel sea, as it were."

"River. And the cadaver was washed over by the tide, that's all. So is that your best guess, thirty hours?"

Willie Cooper selected a saw from the tray, shook his head, put it back. He was chewing gum furiously, smiling all the while. "When did you ever know me to guess, R.J.?" He paused, angling his head like a carpenter taking measurements. "I don't feel like the skull-work right now. Let's just slit her for openers." When Jury didn't smile, Cooper said, "Not a bad pun; so what's with you tonight? Have dinner with a sword-swallower, or something? Would you get the fucking tape over here, you bloody idiot? This one's run out."

The request was not directed at Jury but at a Pakistani attendant. Despite the words, the tone was perfectly good-natured. The attendant was at the table in two steps with a fresh tape.

Cooper took an instrument from his tray and drew a smart line from sternum to pubis. He then lay back the folds of flesh and looked over the organs with all the enthusiasm of a shopper who can't make up his mind given so much on the sale table. He removed them one by one—liver, pancreas, kidneys—telling the tape about the condition of each. "Heavy smoker. Lung looks emphysematous, just the bare beginnings. Liver: slightly jaundiced, no scars." Each of the organs was bagged separately and carefully labeled by the attendant. That was one reason Jury liked Cooper's work; he didn't send a slop-bucket of organs to headquarters. Some doctors did just that.

The further he got into his work, the more momentum the gum-chewing picked up. "Get me that report, Ivor." That's what he called all of his assistants. The Pakistani was off and back again with a sheet of paper. "Okay, an elliptical puncture wound half an inch long. You said the victim in Northants was killed with a sword stick?"

"Dagger-cane."

Willie Cooper was dumping entrails and what he liked to call "trash organs" back into the corpse. "Well, these wounds weren't made by one. Though it's possible more than one knife was involved." He pointed to an elliptical wound. "Could even be double-edged, that one. This other's cleaner, slightly narrower." He stopped, lit a cigarette. "Flick-knife, I'd say. Maybe a knife-fight." He smoked as intensely as he chewed, in quick little jabs. "Amazing, isn't it. This is supposed to be such an exact science. The things we can't tell for sure. Like rigor. Everything depends on knowing the conditions. In her case"—he looked down at the corpse—"we pretty much know them, that's why I said thirty hours, give an hour, take an hour."

Jury smiled. "Pathologists do guess."

"Just like you, R.J." He had put out his cigarette and picked up a small saw. "It's the sound I don't like. No matter how many I've sawed, I just can't seem to get used to the grating." To the mortuary attendant he said, "Sew her up in a few minutes. I need a rest."

Willie Cooper hoisted himself up onto the table beside the corpse, half-sitting, half-standing. Jury marveled at the little scene. Smoothing her hand, Cooper might have been the abstracted lover, lost in a brown study that the girl on the bed asleep couldn't share. "See this?" He spread the fingers. "The slashes on the index finger and thumb tell you she was fending off an attack. So what about this Northants stiff?"

"He was murdered, according to the medical ex-

aminer there, between nine and midnight. What
I'm wondering is this: could it be give an hour, take
an hour either way?"

"That depends *entirely* on conditions, Jury, as
you effing well know. Give me the details."

Jury told him about the *secrétaire,* the delivery to
the antiques shop, the discovery.

Willie Cooper looked down at the body on the
table, laughed slightly, shook his head, as if they
shared a joke to which the superintendent was not
privy. "What you're getting at is could the same
person have stiffed the Northants chap and my girl
here? Sure."

"You don't get what I mean: could she have been
killed *before* him?"

He looked doubtfully at the frozen face on the
table, turned his head this way and that, as if adjusting the light for a camera angle, and said, "That
would put Sadie's death earlier, your chap's later.
Hm. You're working against the evidence, R.J., for
what it's worth. The flow of air in that desk-thing
would have speeded up the rigor; the cold river
water would have slowed hers down." He nodded
toward the body. "But that makes no odds, since we
can allow for that." His eyes had a sheen to them
like glassy splinters when he squinted up at Jury.
Willie Cooper didn't balk at going against the evidence, since he often found evidence inconclusive.
"It's as much an art as a science, isn't it?" He held up
the saw. "This is still all we have to get to the brain.
What theory are you playing round with, R.J.? Do

you think someone killed Sadie here and *then* killed him?"

"Let's say it's a possibility."

"But why?"

"Because she might not be Sadie."

* * *

Across the little park in Islington where he was locking up the car, Jury looked at the house converted into flats. The other houses in the terrace were dark, except for the flickering bluish light of tellies here and there, casting shadows on walls like Plato's cave.

But not his house; no, it was carnival time, apparently, there. Everyone's flat was lit (including his own, even though he was out here). And the everyone included only three people. However, since Carole-anne was one of them, Jury added on another dozen. Which would have accounted for the music, the singing, the stomping.

It was when he let himself into his own flat—no key necessary; Carole-anne had already been there and collected his stereo—that he realized the Hippodrome was right above him, in the empty flat.

One of the neighbors must have been watching for his return, for the phone rang before he could toss his keys on the desk. Yes, it was Mrs. Burgess from the house next door. Since he was a policeman, he was the neighborhood ear. When it came down to noises in his own house, his ear got a truly good workout. He merely listened and murmured while he fixed himself a sturdy drink of whiskey, put down the receiver and shut his eyes, while the distant cricket-chirp of Mrs. Burgess's voice went on. Occasionally, he plucked the receiver from the sofa cushion and sympathized. After fifteen minutes of the Burgess voice threading through the blast upstairs, Jury told her (for the dozenth time) how difficult it was for her, but the place was swarming with cops, which accounted for the noise. They were making a drug bust, only they'd got the wrong house and it was as well she'd be up because they'd be over—*Click* went the receiver on her end. He shoved his own telephone under the couch as if it were a bad dog, and stretched out on the sofa, mercifully long. Was there a piano up there? Someone was certainly playing hell-for-leather. It was a rugless hardwood floor, and he could hear voices raised in a surge of patriotism seldom heard. If it was up to that bunch, England would definitely be saved.

Mrs. Wassermann, Carole-anne, and Tommy. Three people sounding like three dozen.

He lay there perfectly relaxed, his drink balanced on his stomach, and, unlike his neighbor, enjoying every minute of it. Sleep, by comparison, seemed drab, almost unwholesome. He kept trying to get up, to go upstairs and join them, but his mind was too weighted down with thoughts of Watermeadows.

The death of Hannah Lean would take Sadie Diver straight out of this poor Limehouse world and into a garden paradise, where the only thing that stood between her and enough money to buy half the county was Lady Summerston.

When he felt himself tighten up again, he took a large slug of his drink and tried to empty his mind.

It was helped by the slacking of ragtime upstairs. There was a silence, and into that silence poured the mournful harmonica. Feet scraped across the floor, slow dancing to the tune of "Waltzing Matilda."

Jury slept.

27

STREAKS was a hairdressing salon just off the Tottenham Court Road, a glass door with a big chrome handle located under a mock-chrome awning with the name trailing wisps of silver behind it, making Jury wonder if it was absolutely de rigueur that one leave the emporium with a multicolored hairdo.

" 'Ello, love," said the young woman behind the kidney-shaped chrome counter. Her hennaed hair licked upward, bluey strands interspersing the brassy orange, in a caricature of hell-fire. Looking Jury up and down, she said they might be able to fit him in before their next customer, who was due in at ten but was always late. Indeed, she could do him herself.

Jury smiled, said he hadn't come to be "done," and showed her his identification. "I'd like some

273

information about one of your employees. Her name's Sarah, or Sadie, Diver."

"Oh, well, I don't know her, do I?" She smiled as if that settled the point, her heart-shaped face cupped in her two hands. "You'd look absolutely smashing with just a bit of Firebrand, just a rinse, you know."

"That what you've got on yours?"

"This? Oh, this is old; must have done this two weeks ago. No, Firebrand's more browny."

"My hair's already brown."

"Highlights, love, highlights." She was certainly making a feast of running her eyes over Jury's head.

"I'll make a note of it. In the meantime, where's the manager?"

"That'd be Carlos," she answered, pouting. She indicated a youngish man sitting at one of the stations in a plum-colored chair. "Jeannine's just giving him a trim."

"Give him my card."

Sighing, she slipped from her chrome stool and made her way to the rear of the shop. The decor ran to chrome, plum upholstery, and mirrors—not the necessary ones above the long rows of stations, but mirrors that served no purpose. In the middle of the room was a round, mirrored floor, sunken and surrounded by big, glossy plants. Jury walked past space-age domes under two of which sat middle-aged women sprouting green and pink hair-rollers. Their eyes were riveted to fashion magazines.

Jeannine was an angel-faced blonde who turned upon Jury sky-blue eyes of cosmic emptiness and a

quaintly 'forties hairdo: blond curls bunched over
her forehead, the longer hair pulled back by two
combs. She wore a white leotard and a short,
pleated, plum-colored skirt.

Carlos was also dressed in white, with a plum tank
top under a loose *Miami Vice*–type coat. They
looked more like skaters than hairdressers; at any
moment they could have swung themselves onto
the mirror-pool for a competition. He nodded in
friendly fashion at Jury. "Just be a tick. You've got
wonderful hair; I haven't seen just that shade of
chestnut in simply *years.*"

Jeannine was snipping away and going on about
her "lady." "I mean, you just have to come out and
tell them, don't you, when they want a 'do' that'd
only look good on someone my age?" Here she
turned again to Jury, empty-eyed, smiling a smile
that looked left over from some time she'd forgotten. He had never heard a voice so lacking in inflec-
tion. She talked as if she were reading cue cards. "So
I said she'd be better off copying Maggie's hair than
Fergie's." A frown stitched her creamy forehead.

Carlos laughed, turning his bronzed face this way
and that, as if he couldn't get too much of his reflection. "That'll do. And don't forget Mrs. Durbin gets
a hot-oil treatment. Her hair stands up like she'd got
her finger in a socket. Sorry, Superintendent.
Donna said you were asking about a Betty Someone."

"Sadie. Sadie Diver."

"Oh, yes. Donna wasn't here then; she wouldn't
have known her. Sadie left about two months ago."

"For what reason?"

Carlos shrugged. "Didn't give one except to say it was personal."

Jury showed him the snap of Sadie Diver, the other of Hannah and Simon Lean. "This her?"

Carlos studied the two. "This is." He held up the picture of Sadie. "Dreadful cut. Looks like a pile of mushrooms." He paused over the picture of Hannah. "Hmm." He covered the hair as well as he could with his hand. "Must say I'm not sure . . . just a tick." He spun round on the ball of his foot and walked halfway round the glossy island.

In a moment he was back with a thick album. "I keep these so that my ladies can see what miracles I can work with just a decent haircut." He pulled a snapshot out and, with a small pair of scissors from his jacket pocket, deftly cut round the face in it. Then he positioned the shoulder-length, razor-cut hair—a geometric and angular cut with a bang slashed from the forehead at a guillotine-angle. "That's her." He showed Jury the change in Hannah Lean's appearance. "A kohl liner and some blush would help, of course." Then he frowned. "Why're you asking?"

"Routine."

Carlos raised his eyebrows; Jury smiled. "Where was she apprenticed, then? You'd have papers, her application, and so forth."

"Hell's bells." It came out with a sigh. Carlos dropped his voice a register. "I'll just tell you flat out and hope I won't have my license taken away. I was in a dreadful bind during the holidays, so when

Sadie walked in off the street, demonstrated an amazing expertise, I just hired her spot on." His look at Jury was anxious.

"Not to worry. Have you got the canceled checks?"

"Checks? I pay the girls cash whenever I can."

Jury pocketed his notebook. "Tell me, did you get the impression Sadie Diver was smart? Intelligent?"

He paused. "More like a sponge. She hardly talked about herself, never got into the sort of tête-à-tête Jeannine there does with her customers. She was popular, see; a great listener."

"Could you give me a list of her customers?"

"Donna can work one up. She had eight or nine regulars. But I doubt they know anything. What *has* happened?"

"Just say an accident."

There was a long pause. "Hell's bells."

"Yes," said Jury.

Carlos kept staring at him, and finally asked, "Who cuts your hair?"

PART THREE

*When will you pay
me?
Say the bells of Old
Bailey.*

28

———————🔔 "THEY'VE gone and set a date for that trial," said Dick Scroggs, his eyes glued to the *Bald Eagle*.

"What?" Melrose surfaced from Polly's thriller, which sat propped against the latest Booker Prize winner that he had just purchased at the Wrenn's Nest. He had thought at first that Theo Wrenn Browne, who had stood staring at him, white-faced and tight-lipped, would refuse even to sell the book to him. But Theo was not one to stand on principle where money was concerned. He accepted the ten-pound note, but not the small change of Melrose's conversation. He refused to speak, thereby letting Melrose know how traitors were treated in the Wrenn's Nest.

"The pig, m'lord. Your aunt and that *poor* Jurvis across the way." Where Scrogg's sentiments lay was perfectly clear. "Betty Ball's smart to stay straight out of it. If she can, I mean. Probably be suborned for a witness."

"Subpoenaed?" Scroggs, thought Melrose, would make a fine addition to Polly's new book. If Dorothy L. Sayers had known as little about bell-ringing as Polly did about the legal system, the belfry would have been an acoustical horror. Polly's courtroom certainly was. The barristers did nothing but yell, "M'lud! My learned friend, here . . ." and then blather out some nonsense that wouldn't have hung a horsethief.

Scroggs was still reading and airing his views. He snapped his paper smartly, and went on. "But of course there's some that can afford sharpish solicitors to get them off."

"It's only a small claims matter, Dick."

Scroggs rattled the *Bald Eagle,* turning it toward Melrose. "Well, it says here that Major Eustace-Hobson's to hand down the decision."

"That idiot?" Major Eustace-Hobson would have been right at home in *The Nine Barristers.*

"Only an idiot'd have this case, if you take my meaning."

"It's clear, yes."

"Not to worry, m'lord. Every family's got one." Melrose held his book up in front of his face.

"Just thank the Lord the superintendent's back."

Melrose lowered the book. "He is? Where'd you see him?"

"Over to Pluck's place." The villagers always referred to the police station that way. It sounded like a pet shop or a disco. Pluck did run it like a halfway house. People dropping in for a cuppa, asking his advice, taking him biscuits and cakes and so forth. If it weren't for the blue-and-white sign sticking out from the door, Melrose would have thought it was a tea-room. "At the station, he is. There's his Rover I saw queued up there with that Superintendent Pratt's and half the county police." Scroggs had left the bar for the window that faced the High Street.

"Let me know when he comes out, will you?"

Since the eyes and ears of Long Piddleton was "on the mend" with a sprained ankle, someone else had to keep track of things. Scroggs seemed perfectly happy to fill Agatha's shoes in this way. He leaned against the frame and stared out at a green-and-gold May morning, stained like the glass that spelled out "Hardy's Crown."

* * *

Superintendent Charles Pratt was staring at Richard Jury in astonishment. The arms he had raised in protest now dropped wearily to either side of Constable Pluck's swivel chair as he sat back and planted his feet on the desk. He shook his head.

It was his detective inspector, John MacAllister, who gave voice to that protest. If a sneering sort of laugh could be called that. Pratt shot him a warning look.

Jury himself was sitting, half-leaning on the windowsill. The silence that followed his comments remained unbroken until MacAllister said, "It's crazy."

"John!" Pratt swung his legs from the table.

John MacAllister merely shrugged, kept flipping through a thick wad of papers in a manila folder.

Arrogance was a dangerous flaw in a policeman's character, unless it was wedded to genius, as it was in the case of Jury's friend Macalvie (who'd be the first to agree).

"Let's say," said Pratt, placing his chin on his laced fingers, "it sounds highly improbable. If I can be frank—"

Jury smiled. "It sounds impossible."

As Jury had just echoed MacAllister's opinion, the inspector said, "You're damned right."

Pratt, like Jury, an affable man, had his limits. Insulting a Scotland Yard C.I.D. man was one that MacAllister kept pushing. "John, take Pluck or Greene and see if you can get anything else out of Mr. Browne. Chop, chop, John."

With a savage look at Jury, John MacAllister left.

"What has he said so far? Theo Browne, I mean."

"Nothing. Claims the book is his; Trueblood claims Browne nicked it from Watermeadows. I asked Trueblood why he hadn't taken the book with him, it being so 'priceless, priceless,' as he keeps wailing about it—"

Jury smiled. "And what did he say?"

"That Lady Summerston insisted she'd keep it until he'd paid for the lot. Said she'd make sure it was under lock and key, and it was, except Crick put it in that writing-desk or *secrétaire* with the other books."

"Lady Summerston's the sort who wants to appear to drive hard bargains, likes to do deals, thinking that's what her husband would do. I expect she thought if that book had been sitting round in plain sight for years, it would be safe enough to lock it up in that *secrétaire*," said Jury.

"And she can't say for certain if that's *her* book, not since Browne rebound it. Though I believe Mr. Plant: the chances of two of those turning up in one village are pretty slim."

"Slim as my theory?" Jury smiled.

Pratt looked at the photos again. "I will certainly allow the similarity is striking." He shook his head. "How could she get away with it—"

"They."

"Yes. Well, he's dead, isn't he? And I thought I'd enough on my platter with *that*."

Jury handed Pratt a paper from the file. "Copies of the cards in Sadie Diver's handbag."

Pratt looked at the double line of impressions. "NatWest Bankcard, Barclaycard—what are these?"

"Library book tickets. If you want to take out a book, you hand one over, collect it when you get your book."

"Surprisingly enough, I *do* read, Richard. Even been inside a library in my time." He held up the four small cards. "But she mustn't be much of a reader, if she has the tickets and not the books."

"I doubt that's the reason she had them. It could be just another way of establishing the murdered woman's identity. Like the credit card. Sadie wasn't a one to use credit, either, according to her brother,

Tommy. All of these within the last two months, Charles."

Pratt looked at the specimen page that showed the backs of the plastic cards. "Unsigned. Still, there'd be signature cards if we needed exemplar writing."

"Maybe. I think the credit card business is pretty lax. You sign something, send it back. Anyone could have signed."

"Well, then, the signature wouldn't be that of *either* Sadie Diver or Hannah Lean."

Jury left the window to sit in the cozy chair Pluck reserved for his visitors. "Documents experts can pick up similarities and differences. That means a subjective judgment. I know one especially brilliant. And sometimes he can't tell." Jury thought of Willie Cooper's comment about art and science.

Pratt sighed. "Okay, we seldom hope for an exact match, not in prints, writing, tire treads, whatever. We just hope for *enough*. Like seven out of a dozen points of similarity in a fingerprint." He slapped the folder shut, as if he were angry with its contents. "And who's this policeman found the body?"

"Roy Marsh, a friend of the woman I mentioned —Ruby Firth."

Pratt looked at him, smiled bleakly. "Does that connection bother you? What's it to do with the Diver woman?"

"Proximity. Also, he might be protecting Miss Firth."

"Between London and Long Pidd I'm getting one rotten headache." He said this from under the tent of his hand. "Like watching a couple of cats play with string."

"Sorry about the headache." Jury sat back, feeling extremely tired himself. At least he hadn't as far to go to doss down as Pratt. "If we pull it tight enough, it might make a cat's cradle."

Pratt looked up, smiled slightly. "Yes, I can see now it *is* possible. Proof of identity . . . But forensics will surely turn up enough, even if witnesses— even family, friends—are undecided. Good God, can one live in this world for more than twenty-four hours the way it is without proof of identity?"

"If someone wanted to take it away from you, it could be done. A wipe-out of a life."

Pratt's laugh was brief and bewildered. "Look, if the woman at the Watermeadows estate is indeed this Diver woman, and the dead woman is actually Hannah Lean, then *her* fingerprints are going to turn up at Watermeadows, correct?"

"And all you have to do is move in there with a print expert and dust the lamps, is that what you think? I don't. Look: if Simon Lean went to the trouble of planting things belonging to his wife in Sadie's flat, then he sure as hell would have done what he could to *remove* her prints from at least the most obvious places. And Sadie herself could certainly have wiped down the stuff in Hannah's bedroom, just to name one room. So after your lab men hit the most obvious places and can't make a match with those of the corpse, what then? Go over the *entire* Watermeadows estate? Do you think your Chief Constable would agree to the money and manpower involved in *that* project? And for what reason? Has anyone at Watermeadows been charged with murder?"

Pratt put his head in his hands. "Dental records, handwriting—good Lord, that sort of evidence can't all have been switched about."

"Not 'switched about' necessarily. Taken care of, in one way or another. Sorry. Hannah Lean's your chief suspect, isn't she, Charles?"

Grumpily, Pratt started stuffing papers into his satchel. "Nine times out of ten I know and you know it's a family member. Jealous husband, greedy wife, et cetera. Or, in this case, it's the other way round. And she was there, wasn't she? Doesn't have the shred of an alibi, and I'd say plenty of motive—"

"Perhaps."

Pratt snorted. " 'Perhaps!' My God, he passed up no opportunity to humiliate her, I'd say. Anything in skirts, even Miss Lewes. Not the most fetching woman—"

"But good for ten bob now and again."

"Considerably more than ten bob." Pratt brought the chair thumping down on its legs as he leaned forward to get at some papers. "Several thousand. Here and there, now and then."

"And did she go to the summerhouse that evening?"

"We've got casts of at least four different bootprints. Naturally, she's not too willing to admit one of them is hers."

Jury shook out his last cigarette, crushed the empty packet, and watched Pratt as he jammed the last folder into the satchel. "You've pretty much decided Hannah Lean killed her husband, though. Then charge her. That way you'll get her prints."

Pratt's look was sardonic. "Thanks for the advice. And if you're right, I might as well collect my pension. Perhaps I oughtn't to say this, but you seem determined to defend a woman who, to your apparent way of thinking, you've never even met." He zipped the case shut.

Jury looked away from Pratt's cut-glass gaze. "If she's dead, and no one knows it, she should be defended, shouldn't she? I'll see you later, Charles."

* * *

"The place is absolutely bristling with business, Dick. You'll have to get out the folding chairs. My Lord, even old Jurvis is coming across, it looks like, for a pint."

Melrose turned from the window and waited while Dick knifed the foam from the top of Vivian's morning Guinness. Even Vivian was in, growing paler, he thought, as if each day drew her closer to a visit from the Italian contingent. "I don't believe I've ever seen Miss Demorney in here before; she seems to favor Sidbury."

"It's my Thunderbolt. Draws them like flies, it does."

Kills them dead like flies would be more to the point, thought Melrose. The chief consumer of the new product was Mrs. Withersby, who had put away her pail and bucket to come down the bar and bedevil Melrose, whom she seemed to hold responsible for all of the ills that beset the village, as if, as feudal overlord, he should be taking better care of his suffering subjects. "There's some people who stick by kith 'n' kin no matter what, and some as lets 'em down when t'first little bit a'trouble strikes. The Withersbys ain't niver been ones to be afeared t' admit when fambly's done wrong. A'course, that's *us.* Can't expect them that don't live by the sweat of their brow to hold with that! And you see the kind a' mess Long Pidd's in *now,* don't ya, m'lord?"

Melrose had become fairly good at decoding Mrs. Withersby's messages, generally phrased to cover all eventualities. As in this one, which could have applied equally to the recent murder or the pig-and-bicycle debacle. If to the latter, it also said that both Lady Ardry was in the right and the butcher Jurvis was in the right. Melrose, in any event, was in the wrong. It was all shrouded in such mystery and delivered in a tone of such menace that the purport was of course to get Melrose to buy her the drink she so richly deserved having suffered so long under his suzerainty and total lack of concern for his subjects.

"A Thunderbolt for Mrs. Withersby, Dick, if you please." Dick never seemed to mind if the help drank on duty as long as someone was paying for it, especially if it was his fabled brew. Having received her portion, she moved back down the bar to the snob screen.

Diane Demorney was sitting at a table with Theo Wrenn Browne, whose skin was drawn so tightly over the delicate bones of his face that he looked like a burn victim. Propping him up, Melrose imagined. Even Marshall Trueblood, not much used to staring down danger, could look it in the face much better than Browne.

Trueblood was not about to look Browne in the face (*"beastly little man"*), obviously, as he had removed himself to the other side of the table to sit with his back to the couple.

Joanna Lewes had come in twenty minutes before and ordered a double brandy, which she had taken to a corner table and gulped down in two swallows.

Melrose walked over. "May I join you for a moment?"

"Entrapment," she said, turning over manuscript pages, and going at them with her pencil. "Did you wish to hear the next installment of the Heather Quick story?"

Melrose opened his mouth to say something by way of apology, but she went on:

"Still, it was far more enjoyable than being grilled by the Northants police. Not that they found out anything your superintendent didn't already know. I can't complain, though; I've got a good third of a book out of it. I could call our little tête-à-tête two nights ago a first draft." She reshuffled the papers. "Not that I ordinarily do *second* drafts, but in this case I'm wondering how close Heather is going to come to the dock." She slapped down her pencil. "If Heather can make a fool of herself, I daresay her creator should enjoy the same privilege. And since Theo Wrenn Browne was at the summerhouse engaging in cheap theft, I am as near to enjoying anything as one could be, in the circumstances. Just look at him over there, crying on *her* shoulder. Cold comfort there. And what about *her,* I'd like to know?" Joanna sighed. "I only wish police would get this whole thing sorted out. I've got a deadline."

Melrose wondered if her impatience to be done with the investigation was prompted by its consuming her time, or by not knowing the outcome so that she could polish off the Heather Quick story.

Vivian told Trueblood that he should be glad that Theo Wrenn Browne had drawn attention to himself and away from Marshall. "Isn't that right, Melrose? Though I honestly can't imagine Theo Wrenn Browne—"

"Ha! Anyone who could nick a signed edition and rebind it would be capable of anything, murder or even adding color to *Casablanca.*" He was looking nearly his old self, clad in an exquisitely tailored loose jacket in burnt orange with a multicolored scarf draped about his neck. A bit overdone for May, perhaps, but not if you're celebrating. "Joanna the Mad's apparently had her go with Superintendent Pratt. She has my sympathy—but I can't honestly imagine her having much to do with Simon Lean, lounge lizard." He crossed a silky, lavender-clad ankle above a Gucci shoe over his knee. He must have been gearing up for Italy himself. "You know, here we all are, sitting about looking at our mustaches as if this were the drawing-room scenario where the detective confronts us and unravels everything. So *where* is our friend Superintendent Jury? The Revelation Scene is surely at hand."

* * *

Jury's walking through the door had the opposite effect. The Jack and Hammer emptied within two minutes, except for Melrose, Trueblood, and Vivian.

"I haven't seen a place clear like that since Gary Cooper walked down the street in *High Noon,*" said Melrose.

"Hullo, Vivian," said Jury, smiling. "Ready for the big day?"

She rearranged the silk scarf at her throat and smiled inanely. " 'Big day'?" she repeated, in a wondering tone. Said Marshall, "Don't strangle yourself, Viv-viv." To Jury he said, "And have you nailed Theo Wrenn Browne yet? What're you waiting for?"

"He's still in the running. You know there's no way of absolutely proving that's the Summerston book."

"You mean the Trueblood book." He sighed. "Come on, Viv, let's go have lunch at Jean-Michael's and let them get on with it. I've been famous for fifteen minutes; when Mummy and the sisters show up with Count D., it'll be your turn—"

"Franco!" she snapped. "And he's coming alone."

Jury heard her mumble as they started for the door, "He damned well better be."

Melrose sat looking at the pictures after hearing the story that Jury had told Pratt.

He shook his head. "Do you mean to tell me that

on top of a double murder the woman at Water-meadows *isn't* Hannah Lean?"

"Not exactly 'on top of.' That's why Simon Lean and Sadie Diver conspired to kill his wife."

"And something went wrong."

"Something sure as hell did. That flat was kept by a person who was either compulsively neat and clean, or who didn't want her fingerprints turning up."

Melrose thought for a moment. "You mean it's now a case of making an identification? And the eyewitnesses are contradicting one another."

"Tommy Diver says the woman in Wapping isn't his sister; the uncle says it is. No one else is sure." He nodded toward the pictures. "See for yourself. Incidentally, Wiggins is coming along this afternoon with Tommy. I want him to visit Watermeadows," Jury added, grimly . "Would you mind putting them up for the night?"

"Of course not," said Melrose, absently. Then he clapped his hand to his head. "I don't believe it."

"What?"

"We may have our *own* eyewitness. I think I'll gag. Agatha. Don't you remember? She said she 'almost had lunch' with Hannah Lean. Ran into Mrs. Lean in Northampton, she says. Oh, no."

Jury was smiling, handing Melrose the two snapshots of Hannah Lean and Sadie Diver. "She's *your* eyewitness. Chat her up. Also, chat up Diane Demorney. You might be able to get something out of her."

"How wonderful. Why would Hannah Lean have gone to London on that night?"

"Enticed there by her husband, perhaps, under some pretext." Jury thought for a moment. "Ruby Firth was at the Town of Ramsgate that night. One thing strikes me: the last person who drove that Jag was most likely a woman. Certainly, no one nearly as tall as Simon Lean."

"He was in no condition to drive it," said Melrose dryly.

29

———————⚠ Up the gravel and through a corridor of yew hedges Jury walked toward the summerhouse. He had left the car in the lay-by that anyone might easily have used if he wished to approach the property. It was an obvious and simple way to the summerhouse, if one didn't mind rush grass and standing pools, as the cottage was a good hundred yards from the road.

A constable from the Northants police had been sitting on a stone bench near the summerhouse, reading *Private Eye* and too deep in scandals and parodies of scandals to notice Jury. When Jury was nearly in front of him, he looked up suddenly, got to his feet, and said, with a great deal of authority, "Sorry, sir, but no one's permitted on these grounds. Let's have your name, then, if you don't mind." From his breast pocket he quickly drew a small spiral notebook.

Jury showed him his warrant card and, before the man's discomfiture led to a rush of apologies, said, "I just wanted a look at the summerhouse. Everything quiet?"

"As the grave, sir."

What, he wondered, did he expect to find?

Nothing had changed, except that a white cat strolled in from the small dock beyond the french doors. On the lake, the blue and green boats bobbed. The white cat moved proprietarily through the furnishings, ignoring Jury as if he were just another armchair, and sat in the center of the room washing itself.

In the rough sketch propped against the mantel, had he expected to see the lineaments of the woman he had talked to yesterday? Traces of the younger Hannah Lean? He sat down on the sofa and looked at it, watched it more than looked at it, as if in the watching the eye might move, the tiny muscle twitch just by the mouth. Something. From the manila envelope he carried he drew the photographs of the dead woman. Yet he knew there would be nothing there to help him. Like tentative portrait-sketches, the faces of the dead look unfinished.

Jury returned the photos to the envelope and got up. The white cat coiled itself about his legs, purring.

* * *

It followed him down the path and across the little bridge, perhaps interested in this alteration to its daily round.

After London, Jury felt the need of hedges, gardens, air with the fresh scent of rain in it, and this clear-running stream. He welcomed the walk to the main house.

Yet he found himself searching the gardens and criss-crossed paths carefully, furtively, almost, and was mildly shocked to find himself stopping suddenly at the crunch of footsteps on the wider garden walk. Not only stopping but moving into the narrow opening between yew hedges. A man passed, the old gardener, moving arthritically along with his shears.

The cat darted between his feet and pounced upon the copper-leaved ground cover, on the trail, perhaps, of something elusive to the cat, invisible to Jury.

It had shaken him, that impulse to turn from the path, to avoid coming face-to-face with her. He sat down on a rough-hewn bench, one of several placed along the length of the pergola. It might have been a secret garden, the way it was enclosed by a long yew hedge down one side, a screen of trees and shrubs on the other, wisteria and some other with lacy mauve flowers. There must have been a dozen species of pink, copper, violet flowers that Jury could put no name to. The pergola dripped roses like rain.

The white cat dived into a cloud of tiny white

flowers. A stone figure of a woman whose arms encircled a bowl or a basket was placed at the far end against the hedge. It was also doing service, in its hollowed-out center, as a birdbath. At the chirp of a finch, the cat slithered out of its camouflage toward the stone figure.

From his pocket he took out the Bedouin soldier, the crystal bird. How easy to transport a few objects from Watermeadows to Narrow Street to make sure the prints matched. How forward-looking of Simon Lean. Pratt could be right, of course; different killers, different motives. It was hard to imagine Diane Demorney in a jealous rage, or caring really enough about anyone to kill him. Theo Wrenn Browne? Nicking that book could have been just as much a camouflage for murder as the white flowers were for the cat. And the weapon was right there. But given what Willie Cooper had said, it was just possible that Sadie Diver had killed both of them. Now having taken on Mrs. Lean's identity, she could take on the fortune that went with it. Far more money and far less danger. Simon Lean had little compunction when it came to removing wives. Ironic, that would be: Lean works out the plan meticulously, and Sadie takes advantage of it.

But it would have been madness, wouldn't it, for Sadie Diver to kill Simon Lean that night in the summerhouse. Police would have been on her in a moment. Why not wait until later, until his death might appear an accident, or, better yet, say that he'd simply "gone off." With part of the Lean fortune, perhaps. No one would have been surprised to find that Simon was simply acting true to his character. Any number of reasons could have been supplied for his leaving, since Simon wouldn't have been round to deny them. . . .

He watched the white cat, waiting its chance at the bird, sitting stiff as the statue itself, wishing he could wait that patiently, see that clearly to the first flutter of movement that would point to a solution. So his theory that Sadie had killed Simon Lean was either totally off the mark, or something had gone terribly wrong.

The white cat tensed, jumped toward the stone bowl, missed. The bird flew away.

* * *

Crick opened the door for him, his thin hand going automatically to the back of his ear as soon as Jury asked him a question. No, he hadn't seen Miss Hannah at all today, nor much during the last few days. And when he had it'd been at a distance. Miss Hannah was one who did for herself.

These questions were answered, answered in Crick's oddly newsy way, as he preceded Jury up the high cliff of staircase.

Nothing had changed. It was the same thought he'd had in the summerhouse. His mind approached Watermeadows across a wide expanse of years as he himself had approached it across the wide lawns. Like something seen not two days ago, but two decades. And that in the twenty years of absence, he would expect to find a hostess grown gray, a girl grown up, a butler deaf. It was a realization that came to him in another small moment of

panic—that's all that he could call it—and it was
because the central figure at Watermeadows was a
fraud. He felt disoriented; time was a blur; it was as
if he had known them all before and would now
make comparisons. It was the real reason for that
chill down his spine in the garden: that so ingrained
in his memory was the woman of yesterday he
would have to keep reminding himself that he
might never have seen Hannah Lean.

The envelope grew damp in his hand. At the top
of the stairs, he paused to look at the portrait of
Hannah Lean. It could not have been removed
without making someone wonder, and that and the
sketch and some snaps in Eleanor Summerston's
album were all that remained here if one wished to
make comparisons.

Standing a little to his right and behind him,
Crick only added to Jury's feeling of anxiety by saying: "Doesn't much favor her, does it, sir? Oh, very
fine that artist is, but I always thought him a bit
modish. It's Mr. Sargent I've always liked. No, this
doesn't really quite catch Miss Hannah's look."

In the moving fingers of light, the oils rippled,
and Jury felt he was looking at a face in water.

* * *

Without looking round from her table on the balcony, she said, "You're back. Well, better you than
that dreadful man from Northampton. Some Scot-
tish sort of name. That will be all, Crick."

The ritual dismissal done, Crick bowed to Lady
Summerston's back and left. The formality, Jury
was sure, benefited both of them, made them think

that the passing years, age, death had not subverted the relationship into one of mutual decrepitude and neglect of form.

"MacAllister, I think you mean," said Jury, taking the same unyielding chair he had sat in before.

Her fist smacked a stamp into line and she closed the album. She had of course buried her spectacles inside the front of what appeared to be a sari of jewel-like turquoise over which she wore a quilted jacket and the same handsome shawl as before.

"London doesn't suit you, Superintendent. You look pale. Have you had your luncheon?" When Jury nodded she still ran the gamut of possible refreshments and they settled on tea. That pleased her, because it meant that Crick could once again ascend the stairs with the silver service. She blew into the old-fashioned mouthpiece, announced her wishes to the butler, and told him that, as long as he was making the trip, he might as well bring some bread and butter, very thin, and some of the citron cakes.

"So do you, Lady Summerston. Look pale, I mean."

"I happen to be extremely upset, although I hide it well—don't I—and it's that MacAllison of yours who's done it."

"Not *my* MacAllister, Lady Summerston." Jury smiled.

"Well, I shouldn't like to say you're both tarred with the same brush, but as far as I am concerned, police are police. I make no distinction. You can all" —she inclined her head and smiled a little too sweetly—"go to hell in a handbasket." Now she had taken the cards out of the ivory box and was shuffling them furiously.

"I'm sorry. What'd he say?"

"Say? He as much as demanded I produce an—alibi." The word was clearly distasteful. She took a drink of water as if to wash it out of her mouth.

"And did you?"

Her fingers arched around the two parts of the split deck, she looked at him with astonishment. *"Et tu, Brute?"*

Jury wanted to laugh. "I am, as you said, just another cop. Could you account for your time?"

With practiced thumbs, she riffled the pack, evened it, split it again. " 'Time'? Time means nothing to me. I leave Time to Crick. You know perfectly well I do not leave my rooms unless I absolutely *must.* There is the odd dinner party, but that happens no more than once or twice a year."

"When was the last one, Lady Summerston?"

"When? God, *I* don't know. Ask Crick."

"Who were your guests?"

Impatiently, she said, "Oh, the usual lot."

"I'm not sure what that lot is."

"The Burnett-Hills, the Chiddingtons, a few others. They were Gerry's friends; I cling to them, I suppose, like Gerry's medals."

"Crick would, of course, have the entire guest list."

She looked up from her game of solitaire. "Naturally. But what on earth is all *this* in aid of? You think they all gathered at the summerhouse and ran him through like that Orient Express business. I've always thought it a marvelous idea."

"Presumably, they knew Simon Lean. And Hannah."

"Certainly they did. Are you going to subpoena them all?"

"No. I don't think that'll be necessary."

She had swept up the rows of cards, shuffled them, and was now slapping them down again in much the same way she stuck stamps and snaps in an album—intractable things that needed teaching a lesson.

Jury picked up the photograph album, lying on top of a James novel, *The Golden Bowl.* A small photo of her husband was propped against a Herman Melville. He wondered if books largely did service as weights and props. "Do you like that?" He nodded toward *The Golden Bowl.*

"I? Heavens no. It's quite heavy, though. I can press things with it, stamps and so forth. Do *you* read?"

Jury hid a smile, opened the album. "Well, that one I did, twice."

"Like your punishment, don't you? It's Hannah's favorite. She was just looking it over yesterday."

"Was she, then?" He continued leafing through the album. "I read it twice because I couldn't understand it the first time. I still don't think I do."

"Ask Hannah, then."

"Oh, I shall." His head bent over the album, he said, "You've stalked Time here, Lady Summerston, year after year." He turned the pages, found himself looking at picture after picture of Hannah Lean as a child, as an adolescent, as a teenager. That he found in these younger faces traces of the one of the woman he'd met hardly surprised him. Two much larger portraits had been removed. He closed it, upended it on his knee, and rested his chin on the hands that overlapped across its top.

At the sound beyond the door, she said, "Thank heavens, here's our tea. You are in need of something, that's certain."

Crick had brought a cloth and cleared the table so that he could lay it and set out the silver teapot, the succulent sandwiches and cakes. "Excellent, Crick," she told him, munching a watercress round. "Mr. Jury here would like the guest list for the dinner party we had in—" The pleated silk of her frock waved as she motioned with her arm. "—last month. Or whenever."

"That'd be nearer six months ago, my lady. Time does fly."

"Not past me, I assure you. Who was here?"

Crick rattled off the names and Jury took them down. Addresses? Well, certainly he could provide them from his book in the bulter's pantry. "Now Mrs. Geeson, I recall, has moved to Henley-on-Thames—"

"Oh, who cares, Crick? They could all move to Mars and never be missed. I'd like junket for my dinner, please. Vanilla."

"Madam." Crick bowed and withdrew.

She looked over her shoulder to see he was gone, reached down into the voluminous bag at her feet, and drew out a pint bottle of rum. "This might get the tea up on its feet." She poured a tot into Jury's cup.

"Tell me: have you seen much of your grand-daughter in the last two days?"

She frowned. "I seldom see much of her. We had a game of gin yesterday and she brought up my Horlick's at night. Why?"

Jury looked at the brown envelope propped against the table leg, unopened. It was a natural question: "I wondered if you found her much changed, Lady Summerston."

"Changed? Well, of *course* she's changed! Considering her husband has just been stabbed to death—would one expect her to be chirpy and cheerful?"

He smiled slightly. "She was never really that, was she?"

"No." Perhaps the mention of stabbing had her plunging the tines of a fork into a citron cake and transporting it to her plate. "Hannah's been extremely quiet for the last several years. Ever since she married the man. Never one for talking much. Well, *you* know that. You interrogated her." The emphasis on interrogation was not lost on Jury.

And it had been so far from that. She had talked a great deal—more than his questions warranted, really. He frowned at that. "When was the last time you played cards with her before yesterday?" Jury picked up a small sandwich, put it down without appetite.

"When, when, when . . . How tiresome. A week ago, possibly two. Crick would know."

Crick was apparently the repository of the family memory, the archives of the house. With his indefatigable memory and meticulous attention to detail, Crick was in a class with Wiggins. Jury would like to see them together: who could talk, who could take notes the quicker? That reminded him that his sergeant should be turning up soon with Tommy Diver.

"Was it the usual game?"

Now she had shoved the tea things back so that she could continue with her cards. "Of course. No."

He looked at her looking down at the deck. "No?"

Eleanor Summerston shrugged. "She won. What I mean is, Hannah always loses. At first I thought it was to mollify these old bones. Then I saw she was just a rotten card player. You'd think she'd been taking lessons."

Lady Summerston frowned as Jury moved into the sitting room. "You *are* being a bore. I don't know how you manage to connive at confidences."

He stood, as he had done before, looking at the metal soldiers. "You said she was fond of these soldiers, especially the Bedouin."

There was a long sigh. "You people *do* jump about so. I have no idea what I said."

"One's missing. Come see."

"You expect me to move from my favorite spot . . . ? Oh, very well."

With many a grope and grumble, she was beside him, and with surprising agility. She squinted, finally had to resort to taking out her glasses. "So there is. Crick must have taken it. Perhaps it

needed mending. Are you suggesting it was nicked?
It wasn't worth anything."

"And did she collect glass figures?" He drew the
blue bird from his pocket. "Like this?"

"I've seen one like it, yes. Where did *you* get it?
Do you catch stuff that falls off the backs of vans,
too?" She turned toward the balcony.

Back at the table, Jury fingered the envelope. He
should have opened it, taken out the photographs.
He knew he wouldn't; and, after all, it would be
premature. Premature and dreadful, if he was
wrong.

"Pick a *card.*" She held out the spread cards.

Jury put aside the envelope, drew from the fan.
Queen of spades. He looked from the queen up to
her woebegone eyes, her ring-heavy fingers,
dragon-encrusted shawl. And he thought of Carole-
anne, Meg and Joy. "I didn't know you were a card-
sharp, Lady Summerston," he said, replacing the
card as directed. Meg and Joy: they weren't twins;
put them side by side and it was clear, if one were
searching their faces to find out the differences. But
people saw what they expected to see. He'd had
enough experience of witnesses to know that. No
one saw with a completely clear, objective eye.

Evidence of this was that not even he had seen
precisely what she was doing in her great fuss at
reshuffling the deck. A simple trick he'd probably
seen dozens of times before and still couldn't remember its solution.

She held up the queen of spades.

"Very good." He smiled. "How well do you really know your granddaughter, Lady Summerston?"

She glanced at the book propping up the picture of Gerald Summerston. "I believe I agree with Mr. Melville," she said, tapping the spine of *The Confidence Man*. "Nobody knows who anybody is. I believe that's the way he put it." She gave him a shrewd, ice-blue glance. "I'd think you, of all people, could appreciate that."

He looked at the deck of cards and saw instead the deck on the coffee table in Sadie Diver's room. "Life is full of parlor tricks, Lady Summerston."

30

————— ☙ "AFRAID I've come at a bad time," said Melrose, as Diane Demorney divested him of his coat. "You appear to be about to go out." A linen coat and a handbag were lying across the arm of the sofa.

"Only to Sidbury." She immediately went about getting them drinks, wheeling over a chrome-and-glass silent butler.

He supposed he couldn't say, "Bit early in the day for me," since she'd just seen him at the Jack and Hammer. "Thank you. Some of that Cockburn's sherry, please." Then he watched as it gurgled its way into a whiskey tumbler.

The room didn't help. There were times when he thought that the best way to furnish a room was simply to throw in chairs, sofas, tables and see where they landed. Diane Demorney's studied attempt to make a statement with her decor had set this fancy in motion. How white could clash on white, Melrose couldn't imagine, but here it did. The only touch of color in the room, except for Diane herself, was an arrangement of copper-colored tea roses that blazed against a white painting, just as Diane, wearing a frock of exactly the same shade, flared up like a flame against her wintry landscape. He was sitting in some sort of white leather thing like a hollowed-out igloo that seemed to have no manageable parts, such as simple arms one could clutch or a straight back one could feel securely behind one. For a moment he was afraid she would join him there, but she sat instead at that end of the sofa nearest him.

"Have you lunched, then? We could go to Jean-Michael's. It's the only place in the county that has *cuisine minuet.*"

"Another time, perhaps. I have an engagement." That sounded dreadfully stuffy, so he added, "With my aunt." He smiled and then said, "I understand Simon Lean liked to go there."

If he meant to catch her out, he could have saved his breath to cool his porridge. "Yes. More sherry?" She lifted the bottle, looked at his glass. "You've scarcely touched it." She sighed. "How disappointing. I can't get you drunk." Swinging her patent pump from the end of her toes, she said, "I wonder if any woman could." Cocking her head to one side, as if taking her measure, she shook her head and said, "What you really mean is, Did we go to Jean-Michael's together? Yes."

"You're very frank. But the murder of Simon Lean doesn't seem to stir up waves of emotion in you."

"Must we talk about that? It's all so dreary." Diane hooked her shoe back on her heel, recrossed her legs, and added another go of gin to the pitcher. "Are you going to be boringly acrimonious?"

Melrose smiled. "I'm just mildly surprised that you seem to care so little that everyone knows about your affair with Simon."

"Are they talking? How nice."

"Part of the *they* is the Northants constabulary."

"They've been here. Your friend Mr. Jury has also been here. Now *there's* a man one would be happy to pick up the bill for."

"Did you for Lean?"

She laughed. "Once or twice. Simon had money, but he also had a turf accountant. He was extraordinarily charming. Well, he had to be, hadn't he? Handsome and soigné and clever. He had nothing going for him in the way of character. He was decorative."

"But you said clever; how clever?"

"Quite. He was a schemer, a plotter. 'A nasty bit of work,' as they say. Why did she marry him in the first place? Well, I've just said, haven't I? His facile charm. I'm surprised it wasn't the other way round. That *he* didn't kill *her.*"

"Did he mention his wife?"

" 'Did he'—?" She nearly spilled her drink, laughing. "For God's sakes, what do you think married men *do* when they're with the 'other woman'?"

Bored, Diane had risen and was walking around the room, shoes off, auditioning for whatever role might be available up at the manor, talking about Simon Lean's hatred of Lady Summerston, of his situation at Watermeadows. In front of the glaze of ice that passed for a mirror above the mantel, she pressed her lips together, turned her head this way and that like an actress checking her makeup, her best side.

Melrose listened closely, studying her just as closely, and at the room that surrounded her like a stage set. For as long as he had known Diane Demorney he had assumed that all of this backdrop —the artistry of her carefully arranged self, of her mind, even, and its little pinpricks of knowledge— was all a means to an end: money, men, admiration. He thought now that the persona was an end in itself. Probably, it delighted her to watch others watching her, to see her reflection in others' eyes, as if she were walking down a corridor of mirrors.

"So he resented Lady Summerston's grip on the purse strings."

"Naturally. One of the reasons Hannah so annoyed him was that she isn't interested in money, and didn't even make an attempt to get her grandmother to divvy up before she died. Of course, he had an allowance, and a very generous one at that. Lady Summerston could hardly be called a pinchfist. But if the money isn't one's own . . ." She shrugged and accepted a light for another cigarette, exhaling a stream of smoke, flawless as a ribbon. "The last time I saw him—yes, at that summerhouse, before you ask—he seemed quite edgy. My guess is she meant to ask for a divorce. Or already had."

Melrose frowned. "When was that?"

"Oh, six weeks ago, perhaps." She had leaned forward, her elbow on her knee, chin cupped in her palm. The black hair, cut slightly longer in front, curved in a perfect frame round her chin. "I am *starved*, my dear; sure auntie can't wait?"

"Sorry." Diane seemed to assume that if she were dressed for an occasion, some man would come along to name it.

Diane sighed and rose. "Then I shall just have to go by myself." She held out her light coat to him. The silk lining whispered against her arms as she said, "You know, I think I'd be absolutely smashing in the dock of the Old Bailey. And, of course, no one could possibly prove I did it; any sharp solicitor could get me off. It *would* be an experience!"

How many times had he heard that judgment passed in the last three days? By Diane, by Dick Scroggs, by Marshall Trueblood: *A sharpish solicitor can get her off?*

* * *

Agatha couldn't agree more, although she thought it was Jurvis who would have the experience of the dock.

"You must be joking," said Melrose, knowing that she wasn't. "Sir Archibald is a *barrister*. You don't even need a solicitor. Anyway, isn't old Eustace-Hobson going to sit on your case?" He wished it were literally true.

"I don't care for your tone, Plant. And I should certainly think you wouldn't stand on such technicalities where family's involved."

He supposed he would have to humor her if he wanted her to cooperate. "Very well, I'll mention it to him." Like hell he would. Even his solicitors would laugh themselves sick, to say nothing of Sir Archibald.

At the moment he was inspecting a hunt cup engraved with the Caverness crest. It was sitting on the fat-legged table where she kept her supply of port. His supply, rather: it was the Amontillado from the Ardry End wine cellar. "Where'd you get this? It's Father's"

There was a pause. "In a manner of speaking, yes."

"In the manner that he owned it."

"You weren't aware of the terms of Viscount Nitherwold's will . . ."

"At the age of two, I was not sitting about reading wills." Melrose replaced the hunt cup. Good heavenly days, if she had to go rooting that far back for a legacy, there was no point in discussing it. He let her go rambling on as he thought of the Summerston money. Hannah Lean must at some time have made a will. Surely . . . He interrupted the reading of Viscount Nitherwold's will to say: "Agatha, what was that business you said about 'almost' having lunch with Mrs. Lean?" How could one "almost" have lunch? he wondered.

"It was my day in Northampton. I was looking in the window of Tibbet's, you know, where you got that rather nice little emerald-and-ruby bracelet for me, oh, *years* ago."

As if he'd spent not a penny on her since. "You were taking it to Tibbet's for an appraisal?"

"Don't be absurd. I was merely looking in the window at a lovely emerald brooch. It's the one in the corner. Lower left hand, between a square-cut diamond and a Russian amber—"

He held up his hands. "I get the picture. What about Hannah Lean?"

"She walked into the shop. Well, I didn't know it was *she* at the moment; I found that out later."

"You went in."

"To ask to see the brooch. The manager was waiting on her. She's a bit mousy-looking for a murderess, don't you think? He'd brought out a diamond necklace." When she leaned toward her nephew, she must have forgot about her painful injury, for her foot came off the stool quite smartly. "Would you believe how much it cost?"

"Yes. Go on."

"Sixteen thousand. *Sixteen*—"

"Did she buy it, then?" From the picture he'd been able to form in his own mind about Hannah Lean, interest in jewels didn't fit.

"Yes. And told him to deliver it to Watermeadows. That's when I knew, of course, who she—"

"Deliver it?"

"—was, and introduced myself. I thought we could have a spot of lunch, but she seemed in a hurry. Naturally, she said she'd *love* to, some other time."

"Naturally." Had she not wanted to carry about such a valuable piece of jewelry? Or had the woman no intention of purchasing it, but had wanted instead to fix a face and address in the mind of the manager of Tibbet's? Melrose took out the two snapshots and showed them to Agatha. "Is this the woman you saw?"

"Yes. Where'd you get them?"

"Found them. How are you so sure?"

"What do you mean, *found* them? Were they floating by in the gutter, or something?"

Melrose simply refused to mention Richard Jury or he'd be here until the sun went down. Actually, it was so dark in the house anyway, with the creepers grasping the lead of the mullioned windows, that the sun might never have risen. "In Simon Lean's pocket," he said quickly. "Which *one* of these women, Agatha?"

"Both."

Oh, hell. He should have guessed. "You mean they're the *same* person?"

She sighed with impatience and spoke slowly enough so that even her nitwit nephew could understand. "This looks a bit more like her. . . ." She tapped the picture Jury had taken from Watermeadows. "But in this one she's wearing the same necklace."

"What necklace?"

Agatha pointed to the pearls round the throat of the young woman with high-piled hair. "She was wearing it that day in Tibbet's. The pearls. They're very good ones, too. And if there's one thing I know, it's jewelry."

That was certainly true, thought Melrose, looking at his mother's silver brooch on her bosom.

31

──────────── ◬ SHE was standing on the other side of the dry pools, wearing the same oversized sweater, her hands behind her. If it hadn't been for the clothes—outsized sweater and overlong skirt—she could have been one of the ornamental statues.

She was watching him closely as he walked from the stone steps across the grass, making no secret of her interest in his approach. There was no pretense of being out here to inspect the concrete, to see if there were further signs of erosion; or of some intention to cut flowers for the table.

"You're back," she said, when he had circumvented the pool.

"That's what your grandmother said." He looked up at a sky of the pale blue transparency of whey. "I wonder if that's really what Penelope said to Odysseus. 'You're back.' "

She did not respond except to offer him a slightly puzzled smile. Why had he said it, anyway? To catch her out? To see if this was the educated, presumably well-read woman who had lived at Watermeadows all these years?

Then she said: "More questions, I suppose. Inspector MacAllister was here yesterday with Superintendent Pratt. It's perfectly clear they neither of them believe me. They think I killed Simon. Shall we walk?" When she turned, he did not, and she said, "Or are you going to stare the truth out of me?"

He smiled slightly. "I wish I could."

That brought her around again, hands shoved deep in the pockets of the sweater like weights that would drag her down. "You think I'm lying."

"Yes. I think you're lying."

Her fingers pushed back strands of hair that wind whipped in her face. She started to walk away, stopped, said: "About what?"

"Your feelings about your husband, for one thing."

She walked back to him, and even in her step there was a kind of fury. In her eyes, a tiny flare-up of gold like a struck match. "Are you saying you don't believe I was about to divorce him?"

"Something like that."

"Why on earth *not?* Was I to put up forever with his infidelity?"

"No. But why had you put up with it for years?"

"People have their breaking point."

"You didn't—don't—seem at all broken."

"Then I'd have small motive for killing my husband. I mean, if I weren't insanely jealous."

He looked at her for a while, feeling the envelope with the pictures sweat in his hand. "You've got it the wrong way round, haven't you? Insane jealousy often ends just that way—in a vengeful killing."

She had been turned from him, her profile hard against the background of a distant stone wall; now she turned back. "You think I killed him, too. It's obvious that's what Superintendent Pratt thinks."

"It's become a bit more complicated than that."

"What do you mean?"

There was no place to sit down here. Jury said, "You were right; I think we should walk and find someplace to sit down."

"The summerhouse—"

"No."

"I thought you might like tea—"

"Your grandmother was kind enough to give me that." As they circled the second of the drained pools, Jury suddenly remembered that tea of two days ago. It was he who had made it, brought it in. She did not drink hers. She did not, literally, touch it. Of course, that gloominess of mind of which she spoke would explain wanting to be catered for. She had asked him if he would fix it; she had asked him to make his own drink. Had she not wanted to leave her fingerprints on the cup?

"I found the woman your husband was seeing." He waited, but she said nothing. They were sitting on the same wooden bench in the secluded garden where he had been just over an hour before. "She lives in Limehouse. Well-off, a decorator. She's done up one of those warehouse lofts that cost a mint." Still, she said nothing. "Aren't you interested?"

She leaned back, looked up at a sky that had hardened and darkened to slate and said, "It just doesn't seem to make much difference anymore. Is she especially pretty?"

Jury smiled, looking at her flawless profile. "You're more beautiful."

Then she said to him, the thin crust of ice that had been informing her answers broken, "So I might be a killer, but at least a good-looking one." There was more hopelessness than rancor in her tone.

"There's something else; something more important. The other woman he was seeing—"

" *'Other'?* My God, he must have lost count. Diane Demorney would make a third. Who is this 'other'?"

From the envelope he drew the pictures, handed her first the one that was least contorted, a shot that had concentrated on the face and upper torso where no blood had seeped through. Even he, who had looked at it a dozen times before, still felt that shock of recognition. Carefully, he watched her face. Her look was at first merely puzzled, and then she registered astonishment. Shaking her head, closing her eyes as though she'd drive this vision of her own corpse away, she said, "What is this? *Who* is this?"

"You've never seen her before?"

The eyes hardened, flashed metallically. "May I see the others?"

She outreached the gloved hand and Jury put the worst of the lot in it. Not too bad, perhaps, compared with the corpses he'd seen so soaked in their own blood that their clothes melded to their bodies. But there was blood seeping through the blouse, spreading across the shoulders like the double-pattern of a Rorschach figure. She said nothing and returned it, looked at the two others, again and said nothing. Her sigh was shuddery, broken.

"Her name is Sarah Diver. Lived in Limehouse."

She put her head in her hands, elbows on her knees. "Did he kill her?"

"No, we don't think so."

Jury followed her movements as she rose and moved about the garden. Her face was screened from his eyes by the shadows cast by the greenery. "When did you mention the divorce? How long ago, I mean?"

"I don't remember. A few months ago, perhaps. Two or three."

"He may have met her about that time: two months ago." There was no answer. "You're not stupid; if you'd divorced him, he'd have been straight out in the cold. Men in that position often choose desperate remedies. Very desperate, in this case, considering what he'd lose. But also extremely well thought out." Still she said nothing. "You said he was mad enough to kill you."

"You can't be suggesting that—?"

"What?"

"This woman was to impersonate me? That's impossible."

"It's perfectly possible, if you stop to think about it. Who had she to convince, after all, but Lady Summerston, Crick, your part-time help. And there would be a scattering of friends, if it came down to it."

Absently, she had plucked a rose from one of the overhanging vines and turned it in her fingers. "No. Simon couldn't have thought up such a plan. He couldn't even keep bridge scores."

"When a fortune is at stake, ingenuity has a way of increasing by leaps and bounds. But it wasn't just greed; there'd also have been the motive of revenge. He was pretty much despised in this house."

"That's not true! He was treated perfectly kindly."

Jury could not help a laugh at this, contorted by anger. "Oh, 'kindly.' One could say the same thing about Charlotte Stant. Exiled, but with perfect kindness. Or, you could say like Prince Amerigo. Kept, with perfect kindness."

The remarkable thing about her was her control over responses. She had the actress's gift of feeling something through, of gauging what was appropriate and yet keeping her face as clear as water, devoid of expression. The eye did not falter, no small muscle tensed in the cheek.

"Exiled by and kept by Maggie Verver. Your favorite book, Mrs. Lean. Your grandmother and I were talking about it."

"The Golden Bowl, you mean." She looked off, and then said the perfect thing: "It's been too long since I've read it. Your interpretation threw me for

a moment." She half smiled and took another few moments to add to it. "My own feelings about Maggie Verver are perhaps not as cynical."

If Jury had regarded his cases as battles of wits, he would have taken some perverse delight in her ingenuity. Her response was admirable. He said: "Perhaps the Prince was the one who, in the end, wasn't dissembling."

"This is total nonsense." She started away down the path. "If you think Simon was somehow the one who wasn't dissembling—well . . ." She raised her hands in a gesture of hopelessness.

"I was more interested, I expect, in the collusion. She was the alleged victim, Maggie. Don't you think so?"

Forcefully, she retraced her steps along the path. "And so was I, is that what you mean? At least I agree there, if what you say is true, except I'm not sure I care for the 'alleged' part. The victim of my husband, the victim of police. You're standing here telling me that Simon Lean and his mistress—or *one* of them—" The comment was etched in acid. "— meant to murder me. Now that would take an enormous amount of planning; it would involve switching identities. Not an easy thing to do, if one thinks of all the paraphernalia, the baggage we carry about to establish it in the first place. There would be witnesses. There would be, for example, handwriting. Not to mention fingerprints. All that has to be done is to compare the prints of the dead woman—"

Quickly, she turned, absorbing herself in gazing

Martha Grimes

at a robin that had lit on the bowl of the statue. The fabric was crumbling; she had said too much. A normal reaction would have been confusion, almost stuttering confusion, a not knowing what to say, an inability to get beyond the blind horror of even the suggestion that one's husband and lady-friend had plotted one's cold-blooded murder. She would hardly have approached it as an exercise in policework.

So she attempted to curtail further discussion. "It's rubbish. It wouldn't have worked."

"You're fond of your grandfather's collection of antique metal soldiers, aren't you?"

She looked at him for a moment. "Yes, I am. What on earth's *that* to do with it?"

He drew the carefully wrapped soldier from his pocket. "Recognize this?"

She held it clumsily in the gardening glove. "It's part of the display in Eleanor's sitting room. Why've you got it?"

"A better question is: Why was it in Sadie Diver's rooms?"

On the outstretched glove, she handed it back, regarding it as one might an artifact from a dead past, something that ought to have been buried in the tomb with the deceased.

"Can't you make the connection? An object from Watermeadows taken to a flat in Limehouse. For what reason? Other than to have something there— together with a few other carefully chosen pieces— with Hannah Lean's fingerprints on it."

She looked at him queerly. "Stop talking about

326

me in the third person. As if I'm not here. I've had enough, Superintendent, in the last two days to do me a lifetime. And this new theory—" She shrugged it off in disdain. "I'll say what I said before: it wouldn't have worked."

"But it did, didn't it?"

He had surprised her into an expression that told him she took his meaning, immediately. Instead of total disbelief there was total comprehension.

* * *

In the cavernous kitchen, Crick was working over a copper double-boiler, tricked out in a white apron. He was, he said, making the junket for Lady Summerston's supper. On the counter were a container of milk and some Burgess's rennet essence.

"I've got the guest list right here for you, sir, the addresses, too." He wiped his hands down his apron and scrutinized the list. "Now this Mrs. Brill, she's moved to Clacton. Awful place, I think, but she wanted the sea air, she said." He looked at Jury. "Gouty, she is. I've never held with sea air if you've got a lung condition—"

Jury smiled. He did not honestly expect to get from these scattered friends of Lady Summerston any useful information; still, it had to be done. "Thank you, Crick." Jury pocketed the list. "Tell me, have you a set of dishes or dinnerware with gold edging?"

"The Royal Doulton? Or the Staffordshire? Then there's the Belleek."

"The set with gold edging."

Crick tried not to appear surprised. "They *all* have gold edging, sir."

Jury smiled. "Then could I just have a look?"

"Certainly. Most of it is in the dining room. Here are a few pieces of the Belleek. Her ladyship likes her luncheon on this."

It was the same pattern as the several plates in Sadie Diver's flat. "Thanks. Incidentally, Lady Summerston tells me she likes a hot drink before bedtime."

"That's right, sir. Likes her cup of cocoa or Horlick's. Or hot buttered rum." He turned a tiny, knowing smile on Jury, then went back to stirring his milk.

"Would you make sure you fix it and take it up yourself?"

This earned Jury only a slightly raised eyebrow, but no question. Crick believed in carrying out instructions to the letter. "Certainly, sir." He was testing the milk with his French tasting spoon, letting it run from the stirring end of the bowl to the smaller end. "A bit too hot, that is."

Jury put away notebook and pen and said, "I used to love that stuff as a boy. The milk's got to be just right."

Crick had turned the gas flame off beneath the pan. "Oh, yes, sir. Blood heat."

"Yes. Blood heat."

32

━━━━━━━ 🔔 TREVOR Sly parted the curtain and stood for a moment as if he'd been called for an encore. "Ah! Gentlemen, gentlemen. So pleased." He minced down the bar, worrying his long fingers, lacing and unlacing them. He squirmed up on his stool and coiled his legs round the legs.

"Before you get comfortable, he wants a lager and I'll have anything else."

"Cairo Flame?" Trevor Sly rubbed his hands like a moneylender.

"A cup of tea, I think."

Jury placed the snapshots on the bar. "Have you seen her before?"

Trevor Sly left the drink to drip beneath the pull, and looked at the photos. "It's Mrs. Lean. Come in with her husband a fortnight ago, like I said before."

"Can I count on your discretion, Trevor?"

"May the Lord strike me blind if you can't, Mr. Jury."

"Not before you look at this." He put the police photo of the dead woman on the counter. "Do you recognize her?"

Trevor Sly obviously thought he did. "God help us, it's Mrs. Lean. From up at Watermeadows."

"This woman?"

He looked at the picture of Sadie Diver, was about to say something, looked again. "Never saw 'er, but she does look like Mrs. Lean. I'm very good on faces, like I said. One reason I get so much custom."

"What if her hair was down? Not so heavy on the makeup?"

He shook his head. "Never seen that one, I'd remember 'er."

As Trevor Sly made his way back to fetch the tea, Jury slipped the photos back into the envelope, retied the string, and said, "He might be long on memory, but he's short on imagination. So Agatha's actually been some help to us."

"Good grief, you're not depending on *her*, I hope."

"It makes sense. I think Simon Lean had Sadie visit in Northampton for the purpose of making sure that, if the question ever *did* come up, there'd be two or three eyewitnesses."

"Trevor Sly can't tell the difference, though he thinks he can. It fits your theory; he'd probably be wonderful on the witness stand, he's so positive about things. Why're you looking morose?"

Jury sipped at the lager, played with a book of matches. A blue-and-green parrot perched against a backdrop of dunes and sun on the outside; the matches on the inside were cut in different lengths, the top designed to look more or less like a camel's profile. "I take back what I said about imagination." He struck a match and lit his cigarette. "I hope I'm trying to get at the truth, not just trying to prove my theory. Charles Pratt thinks I'm spending a hell of a lot of time defending a woman I've never met. I believe those were his words."

"What's wrong with that? What they attempted to do—what *she* might still be attempting—is diabolical. Especially, since the ultimate object is Lady Summerston."

"I told Crick to be sure he himself took up her nightcap. He prepares her food, anyway. I don't think she's in any immediate danger; it would be extremely unlikely that Sadie Diver would try anything now. And Hannah Lean . . . she wouldn't have any reason to kill her grandmother."

"You didn't meet her, remember?"

Jury rubbed his forehead. "I'm going on what Eleanor Summerston tells me, and there's no reason to doubt that. She said she sometimes felt that Simon actually wanted to—"

"—Kill her. That was it; the thing I've been trying to remember, only why would Sadie Diver make a statement like that?" The door to the Blue Parrot opened. "Sergeant Wiggins!"

Wiggins entered sneezing, gave Melrose Plant a hearty, if handkerchief-muffled greeting, and said to Jury, "Good God, sir, what *is* that stuff out there?" He nodded behind him, toward the alien outdoors, which, like the poor (he had once said), was always with us.

"It's hay, Wiggins. Probably a few cows here and there."

"Hay is hell, especially in all of that wet. . . ." But then he took a look round a pub that had never seen rain and forgot about his allergy. He unwound his spring-weight scarf (Wiggins called no season friend) and removed his anorak, gawking all the while. "Always wanted to go to the desert, I have. I always did think that a proper dry climate would straighten me out. Tommy Diver gave me a good recipe for crawfish broth. The best thing he knows for swollen legs."

Jury looked at him. "Your legs aren't swollen."

"No, sir. But it's always best to be prepared, I say." From the pocket of his coat he drew forth a small plastic bag with dark crumbs in it. "I hope you don't mind, Mr. Plant, but Ruthven was most obliging about charring me up some bread. . . . Could I have some of that hot water in a cup?" This he asked of Trevor Sly, who'd appeared through the curtain with cups, cutlery, and a pot covered with a cosy in the shape of a camel.

Jury smiled. "Go along with Racer the next time he goes to Antigua on official police business. In the meantime, is Tommy taken care of for now?"

"Oh, yes, sir. Lady Ardry's got him right under her wing." Wiggins had unfolded a small slip of paper. "Where's the publican?"

Melrose nearly burned his hand pouring the tea. "My *aunt?* How on earth did she nail him? You were to take him to Ardry End."

"I did, sir. Lady Ardry was there. Was just able to be up and about, she said." Wiggins took his cup of water and shook some of the charcoaled bread into it. "It was that that brought up the physic, actually. Tommy thought the swelling'd go down. But Mr. Ruthven said you'd no crawfish. The poor woman was attacked by a pig, or something, she was telling Tommy when I left."

"You shouldn't have left a helpless boy alone with her Sergeant Wiggins."

"Not to worry about *him,* Mr. Plant. He's a polite lad, even insisted on paying for our meal—we stopped at one of those Trusthouse Fortes. '

Jury was smoking and looking through one of the folders that Wiggins had handed him. "Don't upset yourself. I know Tommy; he'll be okay."

Wiggins had his head down, rooting through an inter-office envelope. "Here's the dental chart. But you're going to be disappointed. Her National Health record shows some work done, some fillings and bonding that didn't appear in the victim's teeth. The thing is, though, we found the work was never done. It was reported by a dentist with two dozen or more patients. It wasn't the only case, either. The chart may not even be Sadie Diver's."

"So all we've cleared up is a case of dental fraud." Jury slapped the folder shut, looked over at Dame Peggy Ashcroft and felt some of the misery of a traveler in a time warp, trying to reach a destination, only to find he'd been frozen in time.

"Not quite, sir. There's this from Dr. Cooper. He says the chart from Hannah Lean's dentist doesn't match up with the cast they took of the lady on the slipway, except for two or three points of similarity. The bad news is, one of them's an unusual bit of work—"

"I can guess: that turns up in both. And a further search will undoubtedly fail to produce the dentist who did the work."

"Don't they have to be identical?"

"No. It's the same with prints—the match doesn't have to be exact. Not only that, prints only prove a suspect was in a certain place. They can't tell you *when* the suspect was there."

Melrose sat back. "But, good Lord, you mean nothing's conclusive?"

Wiggins said, "It's more a matter of having this lot add up that's conclusive." Wiggins took a mouthful of his drink and went on. "There's the solicitors, Horndean, Horndean and Thwaite. Very reputable firm. Three weeks ago, Simon and Hannah Lean turned up in their offices."

"And did Mr. Horndean—?"

"Thwaite, sir."

"Did Mr. Thwaite identify the woman as Hannah Lean?"

Wiggins paused, morosely. "He was most hesitant to say definitely. Though he didn't see how the young lady in the photo with the piled-up hair and flashy makeup could be her. It just wasn't her style at all, he said."

"Well, then, what *is* Mrs. Lean's style?"

"From the little he'd seen of her, 'subdued' was his word. Mr. Thwaite hadn't heard from her in years until she contacted him about a bit of land somewhere in Somerset. That was what they were there about. It was a minor matter, but you might be interested in this." Wiggins drew out several pages, stapled. "They both signed, sir. It was related to the sale of this property." He took out several more pages. "Here's the report from the documents expert, comparing the two signatures—the one she signed then and the signature on a will—on Hannah Lean's will—that had been drawn up several years ago. Unfortunately, his conclusions were indefinite, partly because he had only the one signature as a standard. Also, Mrs. Lean—or the woman with Mr. Lean—was a bit ill with flu, and a bit shaky."

"How convenient." Jury lit a cigarette and studied the report from the handwriting expert. " 'The questioned Hannah Lean signature shows both significant similarities and significant differences with exemplar signature, and very possibly is an imitation, although I am disinclined in the absence of other standards to draw a conclusion,' et cetera." Jury shook his head. "Swell. He said there's some awkwardness in the downward strokes, a little patching and some tremor." He sighed and returned the papers to Wiggins. "Simon Lean had Sadie practice copying Hannah's signature and, rather boldly, I must admit, took him with her to the firm of solicitors."

"Mr. Thwaite said she rang about a week later to ask about progress on the will."

Jury looked at Wiggins, frowning. "And how did he know it was Mrs. Lean calling?"

"Well, there was no reason to assume it wasn't, I expect."

"Have you checked that call?"

"Not yet, sir."

"Just one exemplar signature, one clear set of prints turning up in the wrong place. That's what we need. Hell."

"Superintendent Pratt seems almost convinced you're right." Wiggins was unscrewing a small brown vial. "I think he's ready to charge Sadie Diver with the murder of Hannah and Simon Lean."

Trevor Sly, setting down the fresh tea, bobbed and bowed. "Anything else you gentlemen will be requiring? How is your cordial, Mr. Wiggins? My own dear gran had a receipt: corn whiskey and a lot of ginger."

"Sounds like the Cairo Flame to me," said Melrose, watching Wiggins's tea change color when the sergeant tapped in a tiny pill. "Aren't you afraid of overmedicating yourself, Sergeant?"

"It's always been my theory, Mr. Plant, that if a pinch is good, a pound is better."

"I hope you never get hold of arsenic, Sergeant."

The rain had stopped; a pale wash of sun came through the window, painting the wall where the posters hung the color of sand. Jury shook his head. He might have been talking about Peter O'Toole and Peggy Ashcroft when he said, "They thought of everything."

Melrose had picked up his cane, was sighting along it at the cardboard camel. "No, they didn't, old sweatshirt, to paraphrase Trueblood."

Jury looked over at him.

"They didn't think that something would go wrong, did they?"

33

♠ TOMMY Diver stopped dead.

They had just passed the summerhouse, when Jury saw the figure in the distance standing at the lake's edge, looking out over the water. She had turned as if they had called to her and then started toward them, across the lawn and between banks of japonica. She stopped quite suddenly, perhaps a dozen feet away.

Even though Jury knew the element of surprise was important, he had sat with Tommy, the car pulled into the lay-by, uncertain. Important, yes, but Jury couldn't do it—have Tommy run into her completely unprepared. Bad enough he'd had to identify the body in Wapping. To find his sister resurrected here at Watermeadows would undo whatever good had been done in the last twenty-four hours. Tommy had actually looked pleased with himself in the Five Bells, even more so in the Starrdust. He had begun, Jury thought, to turn his sister back into a memory, which was really all he'd had in the first place.

Thus, Jury had told him that here at Watermeadows was a woman who looked very like his sister.

Tommy had taken in Jury's meaning instantly, the expression on his face one of mingled hope and despair.

"Whatever'd Sadie be doing in a place like this?" He had half-risen from the car seat, looked out the window at the wide lawns, gardens, and pools, and shaken his head. "That's daft." Tommy was having none of it.

"Probably. But have a close look, anyway, okay? Then we'll go have a visit with Lady Summerston." Jury tried to make it sound as if that were the object of the trip. "I think you'll like Lady Summerston. She owns all of this, incidentally."

After a long silence, Tommy asked: "How old's that Carole-anne, anyway?"

The studied indifference of his tone was almost painful to hear. Jury had just glanced at him, and seeing Tommy's face looked hot as a burning coal, tried to laugh it off: "That's a secret between Carole-anne, the registry office, and God. My best guess is twenty-two or -three. She changes it like her costumes. Whatever fits the occasion she wears."

Tommy's yawn was as false as his world-weary tone when he said, "Lots older than me, I guess."

As if he hadn't known it all along. Jury could feel

the surreptitious look Tommy was giving him, and he kept his eyes on the windscreen. "Mmm. Funny thing about age. In ten years you won't really notice the difference."

That had been a stupid thing to say. Ten *days* at Tommy's age already seemed like ten years. So Jury was talking about their meeting out there in infinity somewhere.

"She really likes you." The barest hint of emphasis on that *you*, the Competition.

"I'm old enough to be her father, easily."

Despondently, Tommy said, "But like you said, ten years from now it won't make any difference. Time just expands all over the place, or whatever."

Angry with himself, Jury addressed himself in his thoughts: *You great nit, why don't you just stop trying to console him?* But no, nitdom won out. "Oh, no. To narrow *that* gap, why that'd be twenty years, twenty at least. Can you imagine Carole-anne waiting around for twenty years?" He smiled.

Tommy pushed the door open on his side. He said, quite soberly and sensibly, "No, and I can't see her waiting around for ten, neither."

Nit. Jury sighed.

Tommy looked at the woman now, his eyes narrow and squinting, like someone surfacing after the twilight sleep of an operation, trying to place the fuzzed image of the face before him. "Sadie?"

It was the look on *her* face that struck Jury, that spasm of recognition, instantly recalled, and another fitted into place. She had passed her hand across her eyes in the way that Carole-anne had done yesterday in the Starrdust. Jury felt his stomach tighten with anxiety. Not a fear of being lost in space, but that it was, like the Starrdust's ceiling, a fake one of jazz and glitter; a throwaway, dispensable universe.

"Superintendent," she said. It had looked like an effort to drag her eyes from Tommy Diver.

"This is Tommy Diver." He did not complete the introduction.

"I'm Hannah Lean." She put out her hand, her face now vacant.

Tommy barely touched the fingers before his arm fell away like lead. "You look just like my sister." His voice was bitter, his face parched with anger.

He walked away down the path.

Jury let him go, knowing Tommy would stop when he was out of her line of vision.

For a moment they merely studied each other; then she said, "I suppose that was clever of you, but it means nothing."

"No? You recognized him."

Pushing up the sleeve of the old sweater, that nervous mannerism Jury was quite sure had been one of Hannah Lean's, she turned her face and looked across the sheet of water. Gray in a gray afternoon. Then she turned back. "The boy looks very much like my grandfather at that age. It startled me."

He said nothing, just turned to go.

"Give it up, Superintendent."

He turned back. "You're Sadie Diver, aren't you?"

Her face was perfectly still. After a moment she said, "That's ridiculous. I'm Hannah Lean."

Jury's stomach tightened again. "This is a hell of a thing to do to that kid. He's only sixteen." Now he did walk off.

And she called after him, "Ah, but who's doing it, Superintendent?"

He heard the harmonica, its sound soft and diffident coming from the garden in which he sat earlier that day, while the white cat stalked through the groundcover.

The white cat was there again, or still there, curled by the statue of the nymph with the water-filled basket. Tommy was sitting on the opposite side, his knees drawn up, playing. When he saw Jury, he stopped, slapped the harmonica several times against his hand, and pocketed it.

He did not get up, just sat there with his arms wrapped round his knees, and said, "I expect that's why you brought me to Northants, isn't it?"

"Not entirely, no."

"Well, she didn't recognize me, did she?"

Jury said only, "What about you? Did you recognize her?"

With a great deal of agitation, Tommy pulled up a clump of grass, which grew long in this garden, and let the blades flutter off. The white cat opened an eye, yawned, continued its doze. "She wouldn't pretend not to *know* me. That's not like Sadie."

There was no real conviction in his voice. Jury was afraid the dream-world, like the blades of grass, was being borne away. "No. I expect it's not," was the only weak answer he could give to this.

As they walked on toward the house, her words kept running through his mind: *But who's doing it, Superintendent?*

* * *

Crick led Jury and Tommy in their long climb up the staircase, down the hall, through the door of Lady Summerston's room. He announced them formally, and she turned in her seat on the balcony, peering into the somber shades of her sitting room.

"Superintendent! You've cleared things up by now, I hope." On the chair beside her were the usual albums—the stamps, the photos—and the usual game of solitaire was in progress. "I refuse to have some dark column of a police constable standing outside my doorway, nor do I see any need of it. It's all very mysterious, and I hope you've come to explain yourself. Who's this?"

When Tommy Diver stepped from the shadowy room onto the balcony, she blinked, narrowed her eyes in much the same way as he had done himself. She put on her glasses. But all she said was, "You know, you remind me of someone."

The picture of the someone sat there on the table before her and even Jury could see the resemblance between Tommy and Gerald Summerston. Fortunately (he thought), she did not make the connection. Jury had always wondered if the old really do remember their youth much more clearly than the young remember yesterday. Perhaps so, but Eleanor Summerston's memories were shored up by the albums and, like the pictures there, turning sepia-brown with age.

Tommy's smile was the first genuine one Jury had seen since they'd left Ardry End. "Did you like them, then? Whoever I remind you of?"

The glasses now dangling from the narrow grosgrain ribbon, she said, "Oh, I'm sure I did. Do you like cards?" When he pulled out a chair and sat right down, she seemed to grow festive. "Let's have tea. Or beer. Young people like it; I never have."

Jury was standing, looking out over the dried pools toward the lake. She stood there in the same spot, gazing across the water. The sun came out briefly, fuzzed her outline, veined the lake like shattered glass. It was May, but it was winter light.

Tommy was saying that he'd like some tea; Lady Summerston decided that cakes would be nice. He scooped up the cards she shoved toward him, riffled the two halves of the deck, and slotted them together. Handling the cards lent him an air of authority.

"I'll just have Crick bring up the tray." She blew into the old intercom and placed the order. "Now! What shall we play? You don't happen to know poker, do you?"

It was the right question. Jury saw the glint in Tommy's eye. "Learnt it when I was a kid."

He slapped the deck down for her cut.

Jury walked back into the sitting room.

* * *

In the dark corner atop the bureau the antique soldiers stood, bayonets and rifles ready, prepared for action. He wondered what Hannah Lean's childhood had been like. Could it really have been happy, with the parents both dead? The face looking out from the portrait at the top of the stairs looked studious. Had she been so as a child? Enjoyed her lessons? Read books . . . ?

That made him think of the bookshop, the little girl with the Sendak book and the baby made of ice. The strange little figures in hooded cloaks scrambling through the window, leaving the changeling, taking the real baby.

And it was then that he realized where he'd gone wrong: it was all symbolic, all psychological, that story about the girl and her baby sister. There never had been an ice-baby, after all. Deep in her mind the older child had made it up. The baby was there all along.

Crick had come with the tea tray and gone again, his coming and going barely noticed by Jury, like the laughter on the balcony which seemed so far away. "Raise you ten," Jury heard Tommy say. Ten pence or ten pounds? The money Sadie had sent him.

Another puzzle-piece fell into place. Sadie might have been too careful to send a check, and it appeared to have been a largish sum. Jury walked out to the balcony.

"Tommy, how did your sister send you that money?"

Tommy looked up from his cards, surprised. "Recorded delivery. I expect she didn't want the money getting lost. Why?"

Jury left in search of a phone.

Wiggins had his mouth full of one of the cakes donated to keep up Constable Pluck's strength. Immediately, he started talking about Long Piddleton's being just the sort of place he wouldn't mind transferring to. If he could just get his sinuses used to the country air.

Jury interrupted and told him about the letter. "At least we *know* it'd be Sadie Diver's signature. Probably, she didn't even think about it or if she did, she certainly wouldn't have told Simon Lean that her brother was coming up to visit her."

"It's half-five, sir. I'll get onto it straightaway, but the post offices will be closed."

"I'm not asking you to post a letter, Wiggins."

"Sir!" said Wiggins, as smartly as he could, given the cake in his mouth.

34

————————🔔 "HANNAH?"

From the bench in the secluded garden, the one where he and Tommy had sat and talked, she turned her head to look at Jury. This time she was not able to draw the veil over her expression, which was simply shock, and so she quickly turned to look down at the wicker basket on her lap. It contained several cuttings of japonica.

"Mind if I sit down?"

Her reply to that was, "So you're giving me back my name. Thank you."

Jury sat beside her, watching her. "Oh, I don't believe you really want to thank me. Not just before you might have been charged for your own murder. Charged as Sadie Diver. Wouldn't that have made the Northants constabulary look bloody silly? Imagine the publicity when the last of an old and distinguished family is found to be an imposter who's murdered the real granddaughter *and* her own lover. They'd have a right meal of that, the media."

Her hands worked in her lap. The voice that answered was flat. "I don't know what you're talking about. God knows, I have no desire for publicity."

Jury offered her a cigarette. She shook her head. "Not ordinarily. But in this case I think it would have helped the whole charade along. When the case came to trial—which was what you wanted—publicity would have helped."

She sat, holding the basket of cuttings, as still as the statue at the end of the garden. Jury thought she must have wished she could turn to stone at that moment. "Probably you don't want to hear my scenario, but I'll tell you anyway: Simon left the house that night, but not to go to London. He was to meet Diane Demorney at the summerhouse later—"

"He took the *car!*"

"No, he didn't. You did. Since you'd told Crick and your grandmother he was going to London, naturally that's what they assumed when they heard it leave. The last time Crick saw you, you were sitting at the dining table, drinking coffee." When she again retreated into stillness, he went on. "You killed him. Not before you found out about the meeting at the Town of Ramsgate, though. I'd imagine it was a typical little argument between husband and betrayed wife and that Simon wasn't too upset about it. He was sitting down, facing you; the thrust of the wound suggests that. Then you did three things: managed to get his body into that *secrétaire* in case someone, Diane, perhaps? came along. You then got in the car and drove to Wapping to that prearranged meeting at the Town of Ramsgate."

She shook and shook her head, as if in utter disbelief, and smiled slightly. "Three things. What was the third?"

"You wrote that note."

She looked at him with pure astonishment. "From the Firth woman? Good God, why wouldn't I have said it was from this other person—Diver? is that her name?—why go the long way round?"

"For the same reason you burnt it, Hannah. Anything left out in the open, anything pointing *directly* to Sadie Diver, might have eventually made us wonder if, indeed, the signs weren't rather conveniently clear. On the other hand, the murder of a little hairdresser from Limehouse might have gone unnoticed. You wanted the two murders connected; otherwise, Hannah Lean would be the chief suspect for the murder of her husband. You have a more subtle mind than Simon had; and he wasn't exactly stupid. But if he'd meant to burn that letter, he wouldn't have waited months to do it, surely. That was a mistake on your part, to say that. Still, the joy of the whole thing was that he'd done all of the work for you."

"You call it joy." She looked away. "And how would I have known about Ruby Firth, then?"

"Your husband didn't seem to keep his affairs a secret."

Jury waited for a moment, hoping that Hannah

349

Lean was the sort who took enough pride in her own cleverness in confusing police that she'd talk. Only he knew she wasn't and that she wouldn't.

"My husband didn't confide in me," she said dryly. "So it's very unlikely he'd tell me all about this rather elaborate scheme he and his mistress had worked out in order to murder me." Now she did turn her face to look at him, the smile uncertain, like someone who had just remembered how to smile.

Jury went on: "The necklace that was delivered to the house. Simon probably meant to collect it himself, but knew it wouldn't make that much difference if you'd intercepted it. He could simply say it was a gift."

She turned her profile to him again, looking toward the japonica, thinking. And then she said, "I have no idea what 'necklace' you're talking about. Anyway, Simon wouldn't have done that: he knew I don't care for jewelry."

"Then he *wanted* you to suspect this affair. A means of getting you to London for a confrontation with his lady-love." Admitting nothing, she still had to defend her own plan, thought Jury. "That's just why you were determined to find out, especially since he didn't give it to you. On your usual trip to Northampton, you stopped in at the goldsmith's. He recognized you. And then you knew. Or at least enough that you suspected they might, or she might, have also gone to your solicitor. You could have called him under any pretext at all, and he would certainly have said something like, 'It was so nice to see you, Mrs. Lean.' Any number of things could have confirmed a suspicion that someone was playing your understudy."

She set the basket of cuttings aside, got up and walked over to the statue. A robin fluttered away from the stone basket. She stood there, back to him, her hand on the rim of the bowl. Without turning, she said, "And you brought the boy Tommy here, hoping he'd recognize his sister."

Did he? Jury knew she wanted to add. He sat leaning forward, hands clasped, looking down at a patch of dead nettle. Of course, he couldn't answer that unspoken question. He did say, "Your surprise wasn't an act. Tommy looks like your grandfather at that age."

"I must have been a real disappointment to him —my grandfather."

Jury looked up, frowning. "Why would you say that?"

She shrugged. Her back was still to him. "Awkward, shy, plain—" Again she shrugged. "A rather frivolous thing to be thinking of, in the circumstances."

Could she really have seen that portrait of herself every time she climbed the stairs and thought that? "You really loved your grandfather, didn't you?"

Her head made a deep nod. "And Eleanor. I'm glad Simon's dead. I'm glad we're—both out of danger." With her hands stuffed in the pockets of the tweed skirt, she turned and resolutely faced him. "Eleanor would have been next, Superintendent. Have you thought of that?"

Martha Grimes

Of course, she didn't believe she was out of danger. "Many times, many times."

For a while she said nothing, just stood there. "Then I'll be charged, I take it, with murder. Hannah Lean would have made an ideal suspect: no alibi, but opportunity, and enough motive for ten suspects."

"You *are* Hannah Lean."

She came to the bench, lifted the wicker basket, and said, "Are you quite sure, Superintendent?"

35

🔔 "AND are you?" asked Melrose Plant.

They were sitting before the drawing room fireplace, Jury on the sofa, Melrose in his comfortable brown wing chair. The leather was so old it had lost its resilience and much of its patina.

But Jury wasn't smiling. He wished he felt as comfortable as the aging dog Mindy looked. She seemed to do little but make rugs of herself at appointed places through the house. Now she was slumbering before the fire.

"It's rather unsettling," Melrose went on, when Jury didn't answer. "To think that one could go about impersonating someone else impersonating one's self. It's like dealing off the top and bottom of the deck at the same time. It makes you wonder, doesn't it, if you know who anybody really is."

Jury did smile at that. "Eleanor Summerston's very words."

Ruthven moved solemnly into the room, carrying a silver coffee service and a telephone. "Your sergeant wishes you to call him, Superintendent." He handed Jury a slip of paper as he set down the tray. He went about plugging in the telephone and asking Melrose, "What time will you be requiring dinner, m'lord?"

"Oh, eightish, I think. All right?" he asked Jury.

Jury nodded and Ruthven cleared his throat, tapped his gloved fist against his mouth, preparatory to giving one of his Parliamentarian uppercuts. "Your aunt has informed Martha she will be joining you." His tone was like a death knell. At the end of the room, the long-case clock bonged out the hour of six in sympathy.

"It would be nice if she would tell *me*, the merry host. What's Martha cooking?"

"A very nice suckling pig, sir."

"Jurvis's?"

"Certainly, sir. Mr. Jurvis has the finest selection of meats for miles around. And reasonably priced, if I might add."

Melrose reflected. "Well, we could take the apple out of its mouth and put a sign in front of it saying, 'Special, seventy-nine p.' On the other hand, a better idea would be to call my aunt and tell her she *won't* be joining us." He watched Jury watching the fire. "Tell her we're both contagious, or something. You know how to handle it, Ruthven; you lie superbly."

Ruthven bowed slightly. "Thank you, sir. I'll just do that now, then." Gravely he exited, but suppressing what Melrose was sure was a fit of glee.

Wiggins said he'd tried to call Jury at Watermeadows, but he'd already left. There was no response yet on the recorded delivery letter. "Mr. Crick said that Master Tommy was with Lady Summerston, sir."

"Yes. We'll have to take him back to Gravesend tomorrow. She was enjoying his company so much she asked him to stay for dinner. The last I knew they were singing 'Waltzing Matilda' on her balcony."

"He was Australian, you know."

"Who was?"

"Why, Lord Summerston. We got to talking, Mr. Crick and myself, about the heat there. How dry it was, and quite pleasant. So naturally, her ladyship would be very fond of that song, if her husband was Australian."

"I expect you're right," said Jury, and hung up. In a way, it was merciful that Lady Summerston had retreated into the past. Or had she convinced herself that the gardens of Watermeadows over which she looked from her balcony were a grand scene in a play for which she had, in a sense, box seats. If she didn't care for the performance, she could put down the binoculars, take out her stamps and cards.

Melrose was eating pâté on toast triangles when Jury returned. There was a small plate of pâté and truffles sitting on the floor beside Mindy, who nosed it about and went back to sleep, snoring on. "Ungrateful wretch of a dog."

"How about dogfood? Ever try that?" Jury helped himself. "But if Hannah Lean had been arrested as Sadie Diver? It would all come out, her real identity."

"Double jeopardy. If not precisely double jeopardy, still, can you imagine what a circus a barrister would make of it in court? Coppers arresting a suspect under the *wrong* name? Do you really think the Crown would press for a second go at Hannah Lean? I doubt she'd ever have divorced him; I think she was wildly jealous and full of vengeance, and who could blame her? She knew she'd be the only real suspect. So she took over his plan. Ironic, isn't it? Poetic justice."

"I'd congratulate you, but you don't look happy," said Melrose. "You wouldn't have preferred it the other way round, though."

"No."

Melrose raised his cup. "Hell, Richard, it's spring. We can drink to that, at least."

Jury gazed down the length of the room into the dusk and a trellis covered with climbing roses.

"To friendship," said Jury, as he raised his coffee cup and watched the white petals drift down like snow.

36

———————— ⚲ THE moonlight was almost viscous, lying across the walk. And across that part of the lake that Jury could see from the walk past the summerhouse, it was so bright it seemed to have crystallized and cast a sheet of ice along the water.

Because he liked the walk between the summerhouse and the main house, he had left the car in the lay-by and was at that point now where he could see the tag end of the pier. He stopped to breathe in air that was lush with the mingled scents of flowers, like potpourri. From the hedge came a rustle, a dark shadow fluttered off; somewhere an owl cried; a nightjar cawed.

His gaze trailed off to the end of the pier, where he saw the flash of white. It was the white cat, sitting like a beacon against the sky's dark backdrop, stopped in its nocturnal rounds, apparently looking out over the lake.

One of the rowboats slapped against the pilings in a short stiff breeze that had come up. He didn't see the other one.

Not until the moon had woven in and out of wisps of cloud, bringing into sharp relief the middle of the lake. Out there, the other rowboat drifted aimlessly on the water, turning in slow circles.

Police training, unless you were volunteering for Thames Division, didn't concentrate on swimming. He was a lousy swimmer and it took twice as long as it would have done Roy Marsh to reach the boat.

She was lying facedown, her hand making a wake in the water like a girl out for a pleasant punt on the Cam. Her head was thrown over the side, her hair trailing dark ribbons.

The boat was small, and Jury had to maneuver carefully to hoist himself up and into it.

Carefully, he turned her over, saw the massive spread of blood. On the wrist that fell across her waist there were only tentative, almost searching, slashes; it was the wound on the wrist he drew from the water that had done the real damage. There was the smallest flutter of life beneath the fingers that felt for the pulse in her neck. Her skin was so translucent he thought he might have seen lake water through it.

She seemed to be making an effort to say something and Jury leaned closer.

"I'm not her." Her head lolled, fell back against his arm.

He put his arms around her, lay his head against her hair.

Ambiguous to the end.

37

◭ In the Five Bells and Bladebone, Jury sat listening to the jukebox and waiting for Tommy Diver to shake a few hands and say good-bye.

He pegged five ten-p pieces into the jukebox and went up to the bar with his empty pint. Molly must have been out sweeping the streets for business; it looked as if everyone in the Commercial Road had landed up here. He could barely see Tommy in the back, where they had, naturally, started a game of poker or gin. Jury wondered how much money the kid had left.

Kath emerged through the smoke into his line of vision and decided to be generous with advice if he'd be as generous in the drinks department. He stood them all a round. "Long as you vote, it don't make much of a damn who for. Excepting this one"

—she pointed to a picture of a porcine-faced gentleman—"that's standing for the same borough I am. He's a thief and a fornicator." Today she wore three hats, proceeds from her tenancy in the park: a sombrero, a trilby, and, topping those, a rugby cap.

"I'll remember," said Jury, stuffing the pamphlet in his pocket.

Jack Krael, eye fixed on a point in air before him, asked, "You getting anywheres with that Sadie Diver business?"

"Yes." Jury put down his money and motioned to Molloy to fill Jack's glass. "I think we've pretty much wound it up."

Jack looked around at Jury. "It weren't Ruby, were it? She, ah, knew the man, and there was talk going around . . ."

"No, definitely not. She's right out of it."

"Good." That point settled, he returned his gaze to the air. Jury stood, back against the bar, listening to Linda Ronstadt, still trying to get home to the bayou:

"Savin' nickles, sa-ha-vin' dimes . . ."

Then Jack said, "If it wasn't her, who was it then? Or can't you say? I expect you can't."

Jury was silent for a moment, listening to the description of the fishing boats. "No one you knew. A stranger." He stubbed out his cigarette in a tin ashtray.

"It's too bad about the lad, though." Jack was

rolling a cigarette, pinching in the end, patting his pockets for matches.

Jury gave him a light. "Yes, it's too bad." He tossed the dead match in the ashtray. "Well, we better be going."

Jack stuck out his hand. "Pleasure. Come round sometime."

". . . and be happy again."

"Thanks," said Jury.

PART FOUR

When I grow rich,
Say the bells of
Shoreditch.

38

ONE WEEK LATER

──────── ☖ MAJOR Eustace-Hobson, local magistrate, managed to open his eyes long enough to inform Lady Ardry yet once again that she must stop addressing him as *M'lud*, that it wasn't appropriate in this sort of case. He failed to add, however, that he wasn't a lord, and sank back into his chair, small hands folded over a hard little grapefruit-like paunch.

Agatha should count her blessings, thought Melrose, as he sat between Vivian and Jury in the old schoolroom made quite warm by the presence of some thirty observers. Major Eustace-Hobson was known for meting out a sleepy justice whenever he undertook a duty such as the present one. He was not a man who believed that Britain ever had been a nation of butchers, or that the welfare of the realm depended on its greengrocers.

He was, in other words, a dreadful snob, who kept sweeping away Mr. Jurvis's objections and allowing Agatha her long-winded perorations.

In the absence of Sir Archibald, Agatha had decided to act as her own counsel, and was doing whatever she could to impress upon the court the physical pain this was causing her because of her foot. Raymond Burr in a wheelchair was a symphony of motion compared to Agatha dragging her foot. For a good five minutes now she had been blathering on about the rights of pedestrians, a dangerous tack to take, thought Melrose, since she herself had been driving her car. But she maneuvered around this point adroitly by shifting attention to that bane of the pedestrian's life: the zebra crossing.

"You know and I know—well, we *all* know—" Here she swept her arm about the schoolroom. "—the disgraceful failure of motorists to allow us, the beleaguered pedestrians, to cross where it is our legal right to do so. I am merely pointing out that to put that pig on the pavement is as unlucky for the pedestrian as a speeding car at a zebra crossing. Now—"

Quickly, before Jurvis could get to his feet and question that analogy, she droned on. There was no question she had done her homework. She had cited and cited from behind a barricade of dusty books and papers, and was citing now:

"There was in nineteen-aught-fourteen the case

of a gentleman who sued the local pub because its old gallows sign had become unhinged—"

Jurvis jumped up. The poor man could stand it no longer. "If anything's unhinged round here, it's—"

Major Eustace-Hobson's eyelids snapped up and he told Mr. Jurvis in a very sharp tone that that would be enough.

"But there's no comparison, sir: 'twas the *sign* moved there. My pig, it didn't move a step."

As Jurvis was told once again to sit down, Richard Jury, seated between Plant and Marshall Trueblood, pulled the Northampton paper from his pocket and reread the account of Hannah Lean's death. A verdict of suicide had been reached, "whilst the balance of the mind." And the motive for this was, of course, the shock caused by the tragic death of her husband.

Rough justice, at least, thought Jury. Pratt had done a superior job of stonewalling reporters. He had agreed with Jury that despite what happened finally, it was certain that the two of them meant to do away with Hannah Lean: the recorded delivery; the stuff that had been taken from Watermeadows, the talks police had had with the manager of Tibbet's and even Trevor Sly—all pointed to that end.

And then Pratt had added sadly, "Any sharpish solicitor could have got her off for the murder of her husband. Didn't that occur to her?"

Jury folded the paper, the account he'd read by now half-a-dozen times, and put it back in his pocket. It was just in time to hear major Eustace-Hobson handing down a verdict.

Agatha won.

* * *

"And justice triumphs yet once again," said Marshall Trueblood, as he stood in Shoe Lane lighting a green cigarette. "I think dear Agatha must have sent out invitations." The four of them stood watching the onlookers swarm out of the old village school at the end of the lane. Like filmgoers, they came out chatting and laughing and having a jolly time going over the performance.

As they left Shoe Lane for the main street, Melrose heard Alice Broadstairs say to Lavinia Vine: "One pound thirty. You know that *is* a good price for mince." Lavinia nodded. *"Awfully* good. We shall have to stop going to that man in Sidbury."

"That's the most *unfair* decision I've ever heard!" said Vivian, her face made even more beautiful by the heightened color her fury lent it. "If anyone was the perpetrator, it was Agatha! Poor Mr. Jurvis."

"Jurvis! Don't be an idiot, Viv-viv," said Marshall Trueblood. "He'll do a smashing business after all of this."

"It's the principle," argued Vivian.

"It's the money," said Trueblood. He was holding the *Ulysses* under his arm. He tapped it. "It was only when Theo was told the book was relatively worthless because it'd been rebound that he decided to be awfully generous and return to me what was mine."

"How could it be worthless? Who told him that?"

"A quite well-respected collector, a friend of mine, called round at the Wrenn's Nest."

Melrose stopped. They were standing outside of

Pluck's place, where three villagers were trooping in with cake boxes and biscuit tins. "How much did you pay this respected collector?"

"I? I?"

"You, you." The four of them continued down the pavement.

Diane Demorney came up to them on the arm of Theo Wrenn Browne. "I must say I haven't enjoyed myself so much in days." Days, apparently, having been numbered since the investigation had taken the spotlight away.

"It was fixed," said Vivian, rather snappishly.

Diane raised an eyebrow. "Well, good God, darling, I certainly *hope* so." Her smile at Jury was blinding. "I'm having everyone round for cocktails, sixish. Do come."

"Just look at that," said Trueblood. "What'd I tell you? Won't be an ounce of beef mince or a chop to put your name to after that lot's through." A line snaked from the door of Jurvis's shop past Ada Crisp's and the Wrenn's Nest. Like strangers meeting in a bomb shelter, the people in the queue seemed to have developed a camaraderie.

"Come on, I'll buy you all a Yellow Lightning, or whatever Scroggs is calling the new one," said Trueblood, pulling at Vivian's arm. "It'll put blood in your veins, Viv-viv. You want to look spiffing for Count D. —"

"Oh, *shut* up!" And as they started away, she turned back. "Aren't you coming?"

"Oh, yes," said Melrose. "I just want to show Richard something."

"I'll be damned," said Jury. They were standing out in the road looking up at the shop. There was a large, old sign with fresh paint. At least that part that spelled out *Jurvis. Fine Meats.* was fresh. It had been lettered in gold like an arch over the faded sign of the Pig and Whistle. It hung from a wrought-iron standard over the door. The plaster pig, now having achieved celebrity, stood right at the sill of the door in all of its glory and flamboyant garlands.

"Remember, I told you Sly's place was once the Pig and Whistle. Naturally, he charged me a king's ransom. Jurvis loves it. I don't think Agatha's seen it yet." Melrose noticed the folded-up paper in Jury's pocket, and also noticed it had got a lot of wear. "That was a terrible business," he said, eyes still on the sign. "A dreadful irony. She should just have killed the bastard. Sentiment would have run completely in her favor."

"That's what Pratt said. Something like that."

There was a long silence, as Jury and Plant stood there in the middle of the High Street, eyes turned up toward the sign.

"So the pig was guilty," said Melrose.

"And the perp walked," said Jury.

They turned and crossed the street to the pub, where Jury took out the paper, looked at it once again, and dropped it in a dustbin beside the door.